Praise for Sue Ann Jaffarian's
Odelia Grey Mystery Series

"Jaffarian keeps getting better and better at blending
humor, suspense, and romance."
—*Publishers Weekly*

"Jaffarian plays the formula with finesse, keeping love
problems firmly in the background while giving her
heroine room to use her ample wit and grit."
—*Kirkus Reviews*

"An intriguing, well-plotted mystery that
will entertain and inspire."
—*The Strand Magazine*

"Odelia Grey is the perfect take-no-prisoners
heroine for today's woman."
—Camryn Manheim, Emmy award-winning
actress and author of *Wake Up, I'm Fat!*

Praise for Sue Ann Jaffarian's
Ghost of Granny Apples Mystery Series

"*Ghost à la Mode* is a charming tale,
as appealing as apple pie; I predict a long life
(and afterlife) for Sue Ann's latest series."
—Harley Jane Kozak,
Agatha, Anthony, and Macavity award-
winning author of *Dating Dead Men*

"A delectable first in a new paranormal
cozy series from Sue Ann Jaffarian."
—*Publishers Weekly*

"A fun new series. Ghostly puzzles are one of the trendy
new themes in cozy mysteries, and this is a good one."
—*Booklist*

"Emma handles her 'gift' of seeing the dead
with aplomb and class. I'll look forward to seeing
where the sequel will take Emma and Granny."
—*Deadly Pleasures*

About the Author

In addition to the Madison Rose Vampire Mystery series, Sue Ann Jaffarian is the author of two other best-selling mystery series: the Ghost of Granny Apples Mystery series and the Odelia Grey Mystery series. She is also nationally sought after as a motivational and humorous speaker. Sue Ann lives and works in Los Angeles, California.

Visit Sue Ann on the Internet:

www.sueannjaffarian.com

and

www.sueannjaffarian.blogspot.com

SUE ANN JAFFARIAN
BAITED
BLOOD

. A MADISON ROSE VAMPIRE MYSTERY

MIDNIGHT INK
WOODBURY, MINNESOTA

FIRST EDITION
First Printing, 2011

Book design by Rebecca Zins
Cover design by Ellen Lawson
Cover image ©iStockphoto.com/Ivan Bliznetsov

*Cover model used for illustrative purposes only
and may not endorse or represent the book's subject.*

Midnight Ink, an imprint of Llewellyn Worldwide Ltd.

This is a work of fiction. Names, characters, places, and incidents are either the product of the author's imagination or are used fictitiously, and any resemblance to actual persons (living or dead), business establishments, events, or locales is entirely coincidental.

Library of Congress Cataloging-in-Publication Data
Jaffarian, Sue Ann, 1952–
  Baited blood: a Madison Rose vampire mystery / Sue Ann Jaffarian.—1st ed.
    p. cm.—(Madison Rose vampire mystery; 2)
  ISBN 978-0-7387-2312-9
  1. Vampires—Fiction. 2. Los Angeles (Calif.)—Fiction. I. Title.
  PS3610.A359B35 2011
  813'.6—dc22

                           2011011039

Midnight Ink
Llewellyn Worldwide Ltd.
2143 Wooddale Drive
Woodbury, MN 55125-2989

www.midnightinkbooks.com

Printed in the United States of America

.ONE

The body floated facedown in the pool like an inflatable joke, something meant to scare people at Halloween or at parties. But to Madison Rose's eye, it didn't look like some plastic gag; it looked real. Dead real.

A short, strangled scream shot out of her as she dropped her coffee, the mug splitting like a ripe melon when it hit the terra-cotta patio tiles. Kicking off her shoes, Madison took a running leap into the water and made her way to the body to check for life. Once close, she noticed it had been impaled through the chest with a large stick, the end protruding from the man's back. Swallowing her horror, she checked his pulse. Finding none, she checked again. And again. It was no use. Madison made her way out of the pool. No matter who the man had once been, it was crystal clear to her that he was now a murder victim.

After crawling out of the Dedham pool, she paced along the edge as the late February air nipped at her wet body, sending sharp needles of chill up her spine. She pushed her discomfort aside to concentrate. Because the Dedhams were vampires, she couldn't call the local police. They would arrive and wonder why Doug and Dodie couldn't be roused. When sleeping, the Dedhams looked and passed for dead. They were dead. How would Madison ever explain that to the authorities? She decided to call Mike Notchey.

"Notchey." Madison spoke low into the cordless phone she'd retrieved from the kitchen wall. She clutched it in a trembling hand as water dripped from her clothing, forming a small puddle at her feet. "We have a problem at the Dedhams."

"What kind of problem?"

"Um, it's not something I want to discuss on the phone. Can you get here more sooner than later?"

"Hmmm." He paused, thinking about his schedule. "I could be there in about an hour to ninety minutes. That soon enough?"

"Not really." She looked out the window at the body, wishing it would swim away or vaporize. She wasn't picky. "But I guess it'll have to do."

"Sorry."

"I'll have fresh coffee waiting for you," she coaxed.

"Then I'll see you in an hour."

"And there's leftover pot roast," Madison added to sweeten the deal. Dodie Dedham made a kick-ass pot roast—one of Mike Notchey's favorite foods.

"Make that closer to forty-five minutes."

With only a minor twinge of guilt, Madison looked around the sunny and spotless Dedham kitchen—spotless except for the puddle she'd made. She'd lied about the pot roast. Coffee, yes. Pot roast, no. She'd done what she had to do, said what she had to say, to get Notchey to move faster without telling him the serious nature of the situation.

After mopping up the drips from the floor, Madison grabbed a large pool towel from the laundry room and went back out onto the patio. She stared at the body. It was still there, drifting gently on the tiny ripples made by a slight breeze. Lifting her gaze to the trees and foliage that covered the surrounding hillside, she shielded her eyes against the sun and scanned the area for any sign of someone watching. She saw nothing.

It was just after two in the afternoon on a Sunday. Madison had spent the night at Samuel's after working with him until almost four in the morning on council matters. Samuel La Croix was the head of the California Vampire Council. Madison was employed by the council to assist in its day-to-day business affairs—things that were often best handled by a live person during the day. Of course, to outsiders, it wasn't called the California Vampire Council but was known by a rather mundane company name. She also helped Samuel with some of his personal business matters.

It was a good job—a lot better than her last as a waitress at Auntie Em's, a diner in Culver City. The council job paid much better and was more interesting. The council even provided her with health and dental insurance, something that amused Madison, considering vampires never got sick or had a cavity, but the gesture had also touched her with the thoughtfulness behind it. She'd never had health insurance before, except as a kid, and that had been provided by the State of Idaho for foster kids.

The vampires even paid for Madison's tuition at a local junior college. She took several classes during the week with an eye to transferring to a university the following year. As long as she continued to work for the council, it would cover her education, and the vampires even encouraged it.

Madison usually did most of her work for the council mid-evening, either at the Dedhams' or at Samuel's, though sometimes she would have to make calls on its behalf during the day. It was a flexible job that was easy to juggle around her class schedule and homework, but once in a while she'd have to work through the night with Samuel or attend middle-of-the-night council meetings. At times, working for the vampires was lonely, and she missed being around the people at the diner. Being a loner for most of her twenty-three years, it was something Madison would never admit to anyone and barely admitted to herself. Nor could she tell anyone what she did for work—not truthfully. When the people at the diner had asked why she was leaving, she simply told them she had been hired as the personal assistant to the head of a foundation. At school, she was pleasant enough but didn't encourage the friendship of other students.

When she had returned home from Samuel's, Madison had grabbed the Sunday paper, a cup of coffee, and her iPod and headed out to the patio to read and relax before settling down to do some schoolwork. Doug and Dodie Dedham lived in a charming and spacious home tucked into a hillside of Topanga Canyon. She'd come to live with them last October when her own apartment had been destroyed. The Dedhams had adopted her as their granddaughter, and that was how she was introduced to outsiders. Like the job with the council, living with the Dedhams was much nicer but at times lonely because of the opposite hours the Dedhams kept to hers. Doug and Dodie were upstairs now, suspended in what passed for vampire sleep. Their bodies wouldn't revive until the sun started to set. It was the same with Samuel. She'd gone to sleep in one of his guest rooms while he was still awake, and she'd left his sprawling villa in the hills above

Los Angeles long after he'd gone to bed. Except for the couple of hours between sundown and her own natural bedtime, Madison and the vampires were often like ships passing in the night.

Leaning against one of the posts that supported the patio roof, Madison wrapped the towel around herself tighter and studied the body. It was of a naked black man, slim but very fit, with muscled shoulders, a trim waist, and strong legs. His black hair was cropped close to his skull. She guessed him to be on the young side, though she hadn't looked at his face while in the pool and wasn't about to do it now.

She shivered, this time more from fright than from cold. "Dammit, Mike," she cursed into the air. "Step on it, will ya?"

Michael Notchey was a detective with the Los Angeles Police Department. He knew about the vampires and was friends with many of them, especially the Dedhams. When he arrived, they would figure out something together.

Madison and Notchey had become close friends in the past couple of months. Sometimes she felt they were becoming more than friends. Two weeks ago, on Valentine's Day, Mike had come over to watch a movie with her and had brought pizza. He had claimed it was so she wouldn't be lonely while Doug and Dodie were out on the town celebrating with theater tickets and a late-night supper at Scarlet's, a vampire restaurant. After the movie, Mike had kissed her. It had been a long and passionate kiss, which he'd terminated abruptly. He'd left just as fast. Confused and frustrated, Madison had watched him bustle out the door. There'd been no moments like it since, and Notchey acted as if it had never happened.

Like Madison, Notchey was a beater. A beater was what the vampires called a living person—*beaters* because the living had heartbeats and vampires had none. Madison looked again at the body in the pool. Chalk up one less beater in the world.

Besides the Dedhams' housekeeper, Pauline Speakes, Mike Notchey was Madison's only regular human contact that she could talk to about the vampires. Since today was Sunday, Pauline was off work; otherwise, she might have been the one to find the body. She'd been with Doug Dedham for many years, even before he had met and married Dodie. Madison was sure Pauline's first call would also have been to Mike Notchey.

When it was no longer possible to ignore her chattering teeth, Madison decided to run upstairs to pull on some dry clothes. The dead man wasn't going anywhere. Again, she looked around the Dedhams' back property, wondering if whoever had dumped the body in the pool might be watching. As before, she saw nothing.

It took Madison only a couple of minutes to slip out of her wet clothing, scrub herself dry with a towel, and slip on a sweatshirt and yoga pants. She also pulled on wool socks and slippers. Drying her long brown hair would have to wait; so would the hot shower. Grabbing another towel and her brush, she started back downstairs to wait for Notchey. She was on the upstairs landing when she stopped in her tracks. Quickly, she reversed direction and covered the hallway to the master suite. She knocked. Receiving no answer, she opened the door a crack and peeked in.

The Dedhams were on the bed, cuddled together in the spoon position, with Doug's arm wrapped lovingly around Dodie's middle. The Dedhams appeared to be in their late sixties or early seventies. Doug had been a vampire for a few hundred years, but Dodie had been turned less than twenty.

"Guys?" Madison called to them. Since it was winter and daylight hours were shorter, the vampires slept less than they would during the spring and summer. But even in February, the sun wouldn't be going down for a couple more hours. Madison closed the door and ran back downstairs to wait for Notchey.

Walking through the house, Madison started towel-drying her hair. When she got out to the patio, she plopped herself down onto a chair and bent at the waist, letting her long dark hair fall forward while she ran it through the folds of the towel. When she came back up into a sitting position and tossed her damp hair back, she screamed.

It was a short shriek, as if someone had come from behind her and slapped a hand over her mouth, cutting it off. It was a scream of surprise that turned into silent horror.

The body in the pool was still in the pool, and it was still the only body in the pool. But it was no longer floating with its arms extended in a perfect textbook display of a dead man's float.

Dropping the towel, Madison jumped to her feet and stared at the pool in disbelief. Her feet were frozen, as if the tiles had become quicksand and swallowed her up to her ankles.

The body was at the far end of the pool, near the wide steps that led down into the shallow water. It was still facedown, but its arms were over the edge, its head resting on the apron, as if someone had tried to haul it out of the water and been scared off. Madison looked around the back yard's wooded property and again saw no sign of anyone else. When she'd left the body to go inside to change, it had been near the steps but definitely still in the water.

Finally loosening her feet, Madison took a few careful steps toward the body. Doing some quick calculations, she added up the time that had passed since she'd first seen the body, called Notchey, and went upstairs. The man couldn't be alive. No one could float facedown that long and not drown. And there had been no pulse. In spite of her initial shock, she hadn't been hasty in her determination; she'd checked thoroughly. She was sure of it.

Then his right arm moved.

Flying the few yards from the patio to the far end of the pool, Madison dashed to help the man she'd presumed dead.

Grabbing his arms, Madison tugged him forward, then remembered the stake in his chest. She didn't want to disturb it and injure him further. His arms were cold and rubbery, his body limp. He certainly seemed dead. Had she not seen his arm move, she never would have believed him to be alive.

At least his face was out of the water now. Madison knelt, gently placed her hands on either side of the young man's skull, and turned it to one side to assist his breathing. That done, she again felt for a pulse but found none.

Madison shifted to the side to get a good look at him. He was a young man with a smooth, handsome face the color of dark roast coffee. His eyes were open, staring at nothing. Seeing his face, she had no doubt that he was dead now. Obviously, he'd been alive the first time she had checked for a pulse, but she'd not been able to tell. He had finally died in his effort to save himself.

Madison felt horrible. If she had not made a mistake, he might have lived. Tears rolled down her cheeks as she berated herself for making the fatal mistake. As she wiped her eyes with the back of a hand, the dead man's hand shot out and grabbed her other arm like a crocodile snatching an unsuspecting meal. Then it released her and slumped to the ground.

"Holy shit!" Madison jumped up and backed away, wrapping her arms around herself like a protective coil.

With his eyes still wide with death, the man inched his arm forward, then let it drop again. He moaned, and his jaw went slack. With caution, Madison moved to get another good look at his face, confirming what she now suspected.

Fangs.

TWO

Madison danced from one foot to the other at the end of the Dedhams' bed.

"Doug!" she shouted at the comatose vampires. "Dodie! Wake up. I need you!"

She glanced at the clock on the bedside table. Mike Notchey would be here soon, but it wasn't Notchey she needed now. What she needed were the Dedhams, and not in a few hours when they would awaken naturally. She needed them *now*.

Madison played with the bracelet on her left wrist. It was the bracelet the vampire council had specially made for her. Samuel had explained that it was made with the hair of each member of the council woven together with the leather, and as long as she wore it, no other vampire could harm her. If that were true, it should keep her safe from the vampire downstairs, though Madison wasn't sure she wanted to put it to the test right then and there. Besides, even if the vampire in the pool did come around, what would she do with him? She needed the Dedhams or one of the other vampires.

It was then she remembered something Pauline had told her. Doug and Dodie could be roused under emergency circumstances. Madison dug through her brain to remember how.

Blood—that was it. Only the smell of blood could bring them out of their dormant state.

Madison dashed into the master bathroom looking for something sharp. She'd learned that the hair on a vampire's body still grew, as did their nails. She looked for a razor. She found a man's electric razor but not one with a blade. Then she spotted a nail file. It was made of metal with a sharp, pointed end.

Madison tried to slice into her index finger, but the file wasn't sharp enough. She tried again, but no luck. Any hole it would make would be large and painful. Madison left the Dedhams' bedroom and ran down the hall to the small extra bedroom Dodie used for sewing and other crafts. Rummaging around in Dodie's craft box for something sharp, she found what she needed—an X-Acto knife.

Back by the Dedhams' bed, Madison nicked her index finger with the sharp knife, making a small, clean cut. Squeezing the finger to make it bleed faster, she held it in front of Dodie's nose like smelling salts. She didn't have to wait long.

Dodie's eyes popped open, and her fangs unfurled. Afraid Dodie would mistake her for a fresh meal, Madison backed away, out of reach, until Dodie was fully awake.

Dodie sat up and shook her head. When she noticed Madison, she sheathed her fangs. "What on earth is going on?"

"Downstairs," Madison choked out. "A hurt vampire."

Wasting no time, Dodie directed Madison to Doug's side. "Poke your finger under his nose, then step back."

Madison did as Dodie asked, barely jumping out of the way before Doug bolted upright with his fangs ready for action.

"Dear," Dodie said to her husband as he shook off the sudden wakefulness. "We seem to have a problem."

"There's a vampire downstairs in the pool," Madison blurted. "He's hurt."

Doug Dedham bounded out of bed and dashed downstairs with the supernatural speed he was known for. Dodie grabbed her robe and followed almost as quickly, with Madison bringing up the rear.

When Madison got downstairs, Doug and Dodie were already lifting the young vampire out of the pool. Dodie, who had the vampire gift of extra strength, was hauling him up by his arms. Doug was in the pool, the water up to his waist, lifting the man's legs. The two elderly vampires moved the young vampire as if he were weightless. Madison joined them on the edge.

"Careful of the stake," Dodie told her husband. "We don't want to make things worse. Now turn him on his side so I can take a good look."

Doug, his pajamas soaking wet and his thick silver hair still in bed-head disarray, jumped up on the edge like a much younger man and did as instructed. Before becoming a vampire, Dodie had been a retired nurse. Now she dispensed first aid to vampires and their living friends, though mostly to the living when the play got too rough.

Madison leaned in and watched as Dodie checked out the position of the stake from the chest side. "I thought a stake through the heart killed vampires."

"Usually it would," Doug told her.

"This is bad," Dodie pronounced, "but not fatal. I think the stake only nicked his heart. Lucky for him. If it hadn't touched the heart, he could have pulled it out on his own and healed. If it nicked the heart, it would account for why he's so weak—that and being left in the sunlight."

Doug surveyed their property as Madison had. "But who would have put him here?"

"Is it someone you know?" Madison asked. "Maybe he was hurt and found his way here for help. If he was weak, he might have fallen into the pool."

"I've never seen him before," Dodie said. She looked up at her husband. "Have you, dear?"

Doug shook his head. "Not that I can recall."

"Very strange." Dodie carefully moved the stake to see how it would be best removed, drawn through the front or pushed through the back. "Another vampire would have brought him to us later in the day or just pulled out the stake to let the poor boy heal."

Although his eyes still stared vacantly, the man mumbled something.

"Did either of you understand that?" Dodie asked while she worked.

"I heard it," Doug answered, "but I didn't understand it. I don't think it's English." Madison simply shrugged.

"Hold him tight, Doug," Dodie instructed. "Don't let him move. I'm going to push it from front to back."

As the stake was removed from his body, the man grunted again in the unfamiliar language.

"Hey," they heard a familiar voice call as it came through the kitchen toward the patio. "Where's the pot roast?"

"That's Notchey," Madison told the Dedhams. "I called him when I thought this guy was a regular dead body."

Madison called to Notchey, "Out here."

Notchey came out the patio door. "I knocked on the back door. When no one answered, I tried it and found it unlocked. You guys know better than that."

"I unlocked it," Madison told him, "before we came out here."

Mike Notchey was surprised at first to see the Dedhams up so early and out in the daylight. Then he noticed the injured man on the ground by the edge of the pool. He rushed over to them.

"What's going on here?" asked Notchey, his voice taking on its usual cop tone. He glanced at Madison. "Is this why you called me?"

"Yes," she explained as Dodie slowly worked the stake through the man's chest and out his back. "But at the time, I didn't realize the guy was a vampire. As soon I did, I woke Doug and Dodie."

"Here, Mike," Doug said to Notchey, "hold him steady while I help Dodie ease the stake out."

Once Notchey had a firm grip on the vampire's shoulders, Doug took hold of the stake, moving it slowly through the man's back. He finished easing it out as Dodie's front portion disappeared into the man's body. As soon as the sturdy shaft of wood was out, the wounded vampire let loose with another jumble of words and released a heavy sigh of relief. A few seconds later, his eyes shut, then reopened. When they did, they were no longer vacant and staring, although they were far from focused. After another few seconds, they rolled back into his head.

"We need to get him out of the sunlight." Dodie's brow furrowed with concern for her patient. "He'll recover consciousness faster."

"We need to get all three of us out of the sunlight," Doug pointed out, "while we have strength left to get him into the house." He was referencing the fact that sunlight, while not fatal to vampires, did sap their personal enhanced powers, especially strength, rendering them weak and feeble as exposure continued.

Dodie looked the young man over. "He certainly is a strapping lad."

Madison had to agree. Now that he was out of the water, she studied the naked vampire. His body was as well developed on dry land as it had appeared in the pool. His face was slender, his cheekbones high and fine. She had to work hard to keep her eyes from wandering over his exposed genitals.

To her side, Madison heard a small chuckle. Turning, she saw Notchey watching her with amusement. Her face burned with embarrassment. "What?" she shot at Notchey as she quickly turned away.

Doug and Dodie tried to get the man to his feet. Notchey stepped in, taking Dodie's load. "Here, Dodie, let me do it."

"Thank you, Mike," Dodie said, stepping aside. "I'm afraid my strength is waning."

Notchey slipped one of the young man's arms over his shoulders and wrapped his own arm around the man's waist, letting the hurt vampire lean against him. Doug, even as his own strength diminished, took the other side.

"Get some sheets," Dodie instructed Madison, "and spread them over the sofa in the den. We'll put him there for now."

Madison ran ahead to get the sofa ready for occupancy while Dodie supervised the slow and careful moving of her patient.

When the men lowered the vampire onto the sofa, he let out another gush of words. Doug shot a look at Notchey. "Anything you recognize?"

Notchey shook his head. "Nothing I've heard before."

The vampire on the sofa closed his eyes and leaned his head back as Dodie covered his body with another clean sheet and patted him gently on the shoulder, conveying without words that he was safe now and in good hands. This time, he seemed to be resting, rather than slipping back into unconsciousness.

"Would someone get my first-aid kit for me?" asked Dodie, unwilling to leave her patient's side.

"I will," volunteered Madison.

She took off upstairs to retrieve the medical bag Dodie kept handy. When she returned, Doug was on the phone, leaving an urgent voice mail for Samuel to come by the house as soon as he could. The head vampire always checked his voice mail and e-mail upon rising.

As she handed the bag to Dodie, Madison noticed the vampire's chest wound. "Is it closing already?"

"Yes." Dodie removed antiseptic and a gauze pad from the bag. "The external wound should be completely gone by the day after tomorrow. We vampires don't heal in seconds like on TV, but we do heal quickly." She applied the antiseptic to the wound. The vampire flinched a bit but didn't open his eyes. With Notchey's help, they turned the young man on his side again so Dodie could swab the back wound.

"As with humans, cleaning it will speed up the healing," Dodie explained. "Even if we aren't in danger of infection, it removes foreign particles that could slow the process." She studied the young man on the sofa with a compassionate eye. "But if the stake nicked his heart, I'm afraid this young man will be down for about a week." Dodie put the antiseptic back into her bag. "The heart is the one organ that is slow to regenerate in a vampire," she explained. "If it was badly damaged, it might take him longer to heal. We may not know for a few days how bad the internal injury was. The only way we'll know is by how quickly he bounces back. It will also depend on how long he's been a vampire. The older the vampire, the quicker the healing process."

"Really?" Madison was surprised.

"Yes," Dodie answered, keeping her eyes on her patient. "Doug heals much faster than I do from physical injuries. On Samuel, this same chest wound would be almost unnoticeable by now."

Samuel La Croix was the oldest vampire Madison had met so far. He'd been sold into slavery as a young boy in Africa and had been turned into a vampire during the time the Romans ruled Egypt. By contrast, Dodie was the youngest vampire Madison knew. She'd willingly turned vampire to spend eternity with Doug.

When Doug returned to the den, he was dressed, and his hair was combed back away from his face. His strong jaw was set with concern for his wife. "Why don't you go back to bed, sweetheart," he told Dodie. "I'll keep an eye on him."

"I couldn't sleep a wink now." Dodie glanced at the clock on the mantle. "Besides, we'd be up soon anyway." She picked up her medical kit. "But I will scoot upstairs and get cleaned up."

"I can watch him," Madison offered after Dodie left, "if the two of you want to go back to bed."

"Thanks, Madison," said Doug. "But it's best a vampire stay with him, especially since he can't communicate with us. We'd have more control over him if he spooks or turns violent. Now that he's out of the sun, his strength will start returning. But if we're going to stay up, let's close the shutters so it's darker in here."

"Where do you think he came from?" asked Notchey.

Madison went to the two large windows in the den and closed the plantation shutters against the intruding sunlight. "You think that tattoo can tell us anything?"

Both men looked at her at the same time, but it was Notchey who spoke. "What tattoo?"

"The one at the small of his back," answered Madison. "I noticed it when you brought him in, right before you put him down on the sofa."

"You mean, when you were checking out his ass?" teased Notchey.

Madison flashed Notchey a sour face, but her blush told the truth.

With a jerk of his head, Doug enlisted Notchey's help. Together, they turned the vampire onto his side and checked out the area on his low back. The vampire groaned slightly but didn't open his eyes. Just above the divide of his buttocks was a small mark.

"Is that the Star of David?" asked Madison.

"No," Doug answered in a chopped, harsh voice.

Notchey leaned in for a closer look. "It looks sort of like the Star of David. It's definitely a six-point star, but it has something in the center—a circle or something. It's difficult to tell."

"It's a hexagram with an eye in the center," Doug announced as they shifted the man onto his back once again. "And it's not a tattoo. It's a brand." His face clouded over as he spoke. "I thought

I saw something there when Dodie was removing the stake, but I didn't want to believe it. Guess I was hoping it was just a birth-mark."

Madison looked at Doug with wide eyes. "You mean, he was a slave or a prisoner, something like that?"

"Of sorts." Doug nearly spit out the words.

Notchey asked, "You sure it's not a gang tat or some other organization?"

"It's definitely not a gang tattoo." Without saying another word, Doug turned and lifted the back of his shirt. Reaching back, he pulled down the waist of his jeans a couple of inches, showing Madison and Notchey the same brand in the same place on his body.

THREE

y the time Samuel La Croix got to the Dedhams', the wounded vampire was strong enough to sit up and eat. Since the
Dedhams did not keep human blood in the house, Dodie
had made him a concoction of various types of animal blood.
She was a whiz at mixing flavors to stem the monotony of drinking blood every day. She and Doug dined out when they wanted
human blood.

When the nameless vampire first tasted the thick red brew,
he'd grimaced and nearly spit it out, but one look at Dodie's
disapproving eye changed his mind. He swallowed, then let out
a string of words in his own language to let everyone know it
wasn't his flavor of choice. When he'd eyed the two humans with
a hungry eye, Madison fidgeted with the bracelet strapped to
her wrist. The young vampire noticed and studied her, his brow
scrunched in curiosity. Once he realized neither Madison nor
Notchey were on the menu, the vampire drank Dodie's blood
smoothie, draining the glass in three big gulps. Dodie refilled the
glass and he downed that, too, but less quickly.

While the vampire ate, Doug tried pantomiming to get some information. First, he pointed at himself and said *Doug*. Next, he pointed at Dodie and said *Dodie*. The young vampire parroted the words. Doug went through it again, giving both his and Dodie's names when he pointed. Next, he pointed at Madison and Notchey: "Madison. Mike." That was followed by pointing his finger at their guest and shrugging.

With a flash of understanding in his eyes, the young man pointed to himself. "Keleta."

"Colletta?" Doug asked, pointing at the young man's chest.

The young man shook his head. "Keleta," he repeated more slowly. He pointed again at himself. "Name. Keleta." His voice had a rich accent that no one seemed to recognize, but at least they now knew his name. Doug, Dodie, and Madison repeated it. Keleta rewarded them with a nod and a small smile. Notchey stayed in the background, observing. Keleta repeated all their names to make sure he'd understood them correctly. When Samuel showed up, they had gotten no further than the names, since it was apparent that Keleta spoke only a few words of English. Before Samuel could interview Keleta, Doug gave him a rundown of what had transpired, from Madison discovering the body in the pool to noticing the tattoo, including informing Samuel that he had the same tattoo.

Samuel asked to speak with Keleta alone. As everyone filed out of the den, Samuel asked Doug to remain. Dodie, Madison, and Notchey could only stare with blunt nosiness as Doug apologetically closed the door to the den, shutting them out.

"Do you think Samuel understands his language?" Madison asked.

They were in the kitchen. Disappointed by the pot roast ruse, Notchey eagerly accepted Madison's offer of turkey chili as compensation. Dodie took charge of heating it up for Notchey and Madison for their Sunday supper. Madison had protested, saying she was capable of taking care of feeding them, but Dodie insisted, replying that looking after them gave her something to do while they waited.

It wasn't lost on Madison that Dodie was agitated. Madison had known Dodie Dedham for about four months, but during that time the older woman had proven unflappable, a solid rock in times of trouble. Now she seemed worried and nervous. Madison watched the older woman as she took the chili out of the microwave, gave it a half-hearted stir, and put it back in for more heating time, leaving the metal spoon in the plastic dish. Before Dodie could press the start button and set off sparks, Madison jumped up and stopped her. Without a word, Madison opened the microwave and retrieved the spoon, then put the microwave back into action.

When she saw her error, Dodie's mouth turned downward. She raked a hand through her light auburn hair and looked about to cry. Madison took Dodie's cold vampire hands between her warm ones, led her to a seat at the kitchen table, and took the one next to her.

"You said Keleta's going to be fine in a few days."

"And he will be," Dodie answered, not looking at Madison. The old woman seemed a million miles away, which was so out of character.

Mike Notchey took a seat at the table across from Dodie, his astute investigator's mind honing in on Dodie's vibes. "This isn't about Keleta's well-being, is it, Dodie?" When Dodie still didn't look up, he continued probing. "Two things could be going on. One, you're worried someone knows you and Doug are vampires." No reaction. "Or, you know who dumped that kid in your pool."

When Dodie's eyes snapped up sharply to meet his, Notchey knew the last question had found its mark.

"Who was it, Dodie?" he asked. "Another vampire? Or a beater with a score to settle?"

"My gut," Madison interjected, "tells me this wasn't the work of a beater." She paused, then looked at Dodie. "And what about the brand on both Keleta and Doug?"

That question really snapped Dodie out of her daze. "Doug showed you that?"

Madison nodded. "While you were out of the room. Keleta has one just like it."

Dodie looked down again. "I thought it was the same mark. I noticed it when we were bringing him in here, but I hoped I'd been mistaken—that it was just a birthmark or something like that."

"Doug said he'd hoped it was just a birthmark, too." Madison squeezed Dodie's hand. "What has the two of you so worried?"

"What does the brand mean, Dodie?" asked Notchey.

The microwave beeped, signaling that the food was heated. No one got up from the table to get it.

"What does the mark mean?" Notchey asked again.

"It's not what," answered Dodie in a small, troubled voice. "It's who."

Notchey and Madison glanced at each other, then put their attention back on Dodie, waiting for an explanation.

Dodie started to say something, then stopped, clearly exhausted. Madison got up from the table. Retrieving a mug from the cupboard, she poured into it what remained of the smoothie Dodie had prepared for Keleta from the blender. After removing the chili from the microwave, she stuck the mug in for a few seconds to warm it up.

"Here," she said, handing the mug to Dodie. "This might help."

Dodie took the offered mug. "Thank you, dear." She took a few sips, then a deep breath, before continuing.

"I'm afraid she's back," Dodie told them in a voice barely above a whisper, as if that explained everything.

"Who's back?" asked Notchey.

"Annabelle." Dodie paused to take another comforting sip of warm blood. "Annabelle Fogle."

"And this Annabelle Fogle, she's a vampire?" Notchey shifted in his chair as he waited for confirmation of what he already surmised. He could deal with beaters, but murderous vampires were another story.

"Yes. She's the one who turned Doug." Dodie took another sip of blood. "And probably Keleta. From what Doug's told me, Annabelle purposefully hunts male bloodline holders, brands them, then turns them so they carry her mark for eternity."

Looking down at her own left palm, Madison studied it. Bloodlines were special lines in the palm of the hand, darker than the others, that appeared on the left palm of people predisposed to being vampires. Only people with bloodlines could be turned into vampires by other vampires. Much to her relief, her own palm showed no special lines. But it didn't keep her from checking.

Madison did some quick math in her head. "So if she turned Doug, this Annabelle has been a vampire for at least a couple hundred years."

"Much longer," answered Dodie. "Doug was turned in the early 1800s, and he told me that Annabelle was around during the Salem witch trials. Those were in the late 1600s. How much further she goes back, I'm not sure."

"She's a vampire witch?" The hair on Madison's arms stood like a drunk's three-day stubble.

"No, just a vampire. But I understand she stirred things up for a lot of those poor women in Salem. Doug told me Annabelle was one of the women spreading the lies about them. After, she turned a couple of the victims' husbands."

Madison was speechless. To her, the Salem trials were something from a history book, nothing more. "Are you kidding?"

"No, not at all." Dodie shifted her head from side to side in sadness.

"How ironic," commented Notchey, with a voice as dry as burnt toast. "They were hunting witches, real or not, and all the time they had embryo vampires in their midst."

Again, Madison and Notchey looked at each other; this time, it was more than a glance. They studied each other's face and saw the fascination and fear they shared.

Breaking his eyes away from Madison, Notchey turned back to Dodie. "Annabelle branded all the men she turned?"

Dodie shrugged her thin shoulders. "I'm not sure when she started the marking, but she was doing it when she met Doug. By giving them the brand before they were turned into vampires, they can never get rid of it."

Madison leaned in. "What does the mark mean, do you know?"

"I'm not sure what it means," Dodie told them, "if anything, beyond being her personal mark."

"It's like branding cattle," Madison said in disgust. "Or slaves."

Notchey got up and paced the kitchen. "So you think this Annabelle branded and turned Keleta, then dumped him in your pool? What would be her motive?"

"I'm not sure she needs one." They all turned at the sound of Doug's voice. They had been so wrapped up in what Dodie was saying, they hadn't heard him come in. Behind him came Samuel, talking on his cell phone as he walked.

"Keleta is resting," Samuel told everyone after ending his call. "That was Byron and Ricky on the phone. In a little while, I'll take Keleta to their home. They will take care of him and try to determine whether or not he's able to be rehabilitated."

"Oh, dear." Dodie looked at Samuel, her mouth a sad inverted crescent.

"Rehabilitated?" asked Madison. She was still learning about the vampire way of life and how the council governed to keep peace in their community. Dodie's reaction to Samuel's news put her on alert that rehabilitation was serious business.

"Keleta," Doug explained, "is young, only twenty-two years old, and it seems he hasn't been a vampire very long. He's a bit confused right now about the timeline. It's often difficult for young vampires to adjust to their new life, earn a living, and make their way without help. Byron and Ricky will spend time mentoring and teaching Keleta our ways."

"Usually," Dodie added, "the vampire who does the turning is responsible for the training, but in cases like this, it falls to others."

"Where's he from?" Notchey asked Samuel. "Could you understand him?"

Samuel stood in the doorway between the kitchen and dining room. He was dressed casually in jeans and an expensive cream-colored sweater. After depositing his phone in his pocket, he pushed up the sleeves of the sweater and leaned against the door frame, his hands in his pockets.

Samuel was a striking man, clean shaven, with a bald head and a scar that started behind one ear and ran down the side of his dark brown neck. Rather than taking anything away from Samuel's looks, the scar only added to his mystique and aura of power. When he smiled, he could light up a room. When he was displeased, even other vampires went on guard. He was wearing his usual sunglasses. Behind them, Samuel's eyes were milky from being blinded by the man who'd sold him into slavery as a young boy. But when Samuel had been turned into a vampire, his sight had returned unexpectedly, clearer than ever, even as his eyes still appeared to be blinded. Samuel La Croix looked as though he were in his mid to late thirties and spoke with a steady, commanding voice with a hint of an accent, not unlike Keleta's.

"The boy is from Eritrea," Samuel informed them. "His name is Keleta Kibreab. He's quite educated and speaks Tigrinya, which is an Eritrean language, as well as Arabic and Amharic, the language of Ethiopia. He does know some English, and it was coming back to him in bits and pieces as we spoke, but mostly I communicated with him in Amharic."

Madison put her elbows on the table and rested her chin in her cupped hands. "Could he tell you anything more?"

"As far as I could determine," Samuel continued, "he'd come to California with some friends for a holiday. A woman invited him back to her place. They had another drink when they got there, but it must have been drugged, because the next thing he remembers was the pain of being branded."

A collective shudder ran through everyone in the Dedhams' kitchen just thinking about being branded. Especially Doug, who had already been through the painful process.

"Reminds me of that Holloway girl in the news," said Madison. "She went on vacation and disappeared."

"Oh." Dodie's hand shot up to her mouth in dismay as Madison's comment flashed clarity on Keleta's situation. "His poor parents. They must be frantic."

"After that, he's blocked most everything out," continued Samuel. "He doesn't remember being turned but understands he's a vampire. He remembers nothing about the stake in his chest or about being brought here."

"And what about Annabelle Fogle?" asked Notchey. "Does he remember her?"

Samuel shook his head. "He claims he never heard the woman's name, just that the woman who turned him was older than him. She had long red hair and was very beautiful. The name Annabelle Fogle wasn't familiar to him either."

Doug shook his head. "Sure sounds like Annabelle."

"Any reason why she'd show up now and do something like this?" Samuel asked.

Doug ran a hand over his lined face in frustration. "Like I said, Samuel, she doesn't need a reason. She does what she wants as the mood strikes her. The last time I saw her was right before Dodie and I married. Annabelle tried to talk me out of it."

"Talk you out of it?" Dodie's voice became shrill—another unusual occurrence. "She tried to kill me!"

Everyone turned to Doug as if he were a witness fudging important testimony. He nodded, confirming Dodie's accusation. "That she did. That was sixteen years ago. We haven't heard a peep from or about her since."

"She wants you back, Doug." Dodie's face screwed up in anguish.

Doug went to his wife and took her in his arms to comfort her. "Now, now," he cooed to Dodie. "That's never going to happen, and you know it." Keeping his arms around Dodie, Doug turned to Samuel. "Could just be a little dramatic statement."

"Dramatic is right." Dodie looked up at her husband. "She tried to murder another vampire just to get attention."

"We don't know if she meant to kill Keleta, sweetheart."

"Why are you defending her?" Dodie pulled away from Doug, her usual spunk returned. "She drove a stake into his heart and left him in the daylight. If that's not attempted murder, then what is?"

Madison's eyes popped out of her head. She'd never heard the Dedhams have cross words, let alone fight, though she had to side with Dodie on this issue.

Samuel held up both his hands like a referee stopping a prize fight. "Everyone calm down. First off, we don't know if it was Annabelle Fogle who did this to Keleta, so let's not jump to conclusions. But as far as murder goes, I'm with Dodie. Whoever did this to Keleta meant for him to die and for you, or someone in this house, to find him." He lowered his hands. "Who knows, it could even have been a beater who knows about you and is making a point, setting you up for something. We need more information before jumping to conclusions."

"Tell you what," offered Notchey. "I'll check our missing persons file and see if Keleta's name shows up. If it does, it will give us a starting point."

Samuel nodded at the cop. "Thanks, Mike. That could be a big help. And I'll put out some feelers and see what I can find out about Annabelle Fogle. Isabella Claussen should be able to help with that." Isabella was another vampire on the council. She was tall, slender, and gorgeous, and she traveled the world as a type of ambassador to other vampire communities. She was Samuel's eyes and ears outside of California.

Samuel stood up straight. "Doug, do you have some clothes for Keleta? I can't take him to Byron and Ricky's naked."

"I'm much taller than the boy, but a pair of sweatpants and a sweatshirt should do the trick. That okay?"

"Anything. They will provide him with other clothes once he gets there."

Madison looked out the kitchen window at the pool. Even in the coolness of February it looked so calm and inviting. Just a few hours ago, she'd found a dead body floating in it. Now that dead body was in the den, sipping a glass of blood. Madison had seen her mother shot to death when she was five and had been in and out of abusive and unstable foster homes until she was eighteen. She'd hoped to build a stable and calm life for herself, and even though they were vampires, until now the Dedhams had seemed to live such a life. Madison couldn't help but wonder if it was she who brought the hard times and bad luck. Maybe she was a lightning rod for awful things.

Pushing the thought aside, she returned to her concern for Keleta. "Samuel," she started, not turning around, "what does it mean for Keleta to be rehabilitated?"

Samuel had the gift of reading people's personal history and their thoughts. He stepped up behind Madison and placed his strong hands on her upper arms. He turned her around to face him and took off his glasses to focus his cloudy eyes on her brown ones. He could see her self-doubt as clearly as if it had been written in the sky. Replacing his hands on her arms, he gave them a gentle squeeze and conveyed to her without words that this was not her fault and that she was not cursed.

She sensed his silent encouragement and wanted to believe him.

"Byron and Ricky will work with Keleta to assimilate him to our lifestyle," he told her, answering her spoken question. "You know that scholarship fund the council handles?"

She nodded but kept silent, not wanting to break the comforting sound of Samuel's voice with her own tongue. As terrifying as he could be when angered, he could also be as soothing as a glass of warm milk and a soft blanket.

"Byron and Ricky will make an appraisal of Keleta's value to the community. If the council finds him worthy, some of that money will be used to help him start his life as a vampire. We'll find him a place to live and secure him an occupation. We'll teach him how to live as one of us."

"And if he's not found worthy?"

"Occasionally, the council comes across a new vampire abandoned by his turner who is not able to be assimilated for one reason or another. Most often it's because they were turned too young to be left on their own. Other times it's their attitude—

usually intense anger at becoming a vampire against their will. People with that type of anger can put the rest of us in jeopardy."

Madison knew immediately what Samuel meant. For the most part, the vampires who lived in California enjoyed a peaceful life under the radar of the living. A big part of the council's job was to make sure the community remained undetected. Anyone—vampires or beaters—who put that peace at risk was dealt with quickly, with no second thoughts.

Madison raised her chin higher and bored her eyes into Samuel's. The others remained silent. "You didn't answer my question, Samuel. What if Keleta is not found worthy by the council?"

"You know the answer, Madison, so why ask?"

"Say it, Samuel."

Samuel sighed. Although still very young, there was something about Madison's intensity that touched him deeply. Although she often lacked self-confidence and had little to no tact, she was courageous and driven, and she faced the truth about life head-on like a truck being driven into a brick wall. She didn't stand for bullshit, and neither did he.

"If Keleta Kibreab is found by the council to be a threat to himself or to us, then he will be terminated."

Madison didn't need an explanation for that. She knew damn well what it meant.

FOUR

C ome on, slow poke," Madison called to Notchey.

The two of them had gone for a run in Topanga Canyon two mornings after Keleta had been found. Madison was done, back at the car waiting for Notchey to catch up. He'd kept up with her for most of the three-mile hilly jog, mostly out of sheer determination not to let a girl beat him, but in the last mile he'd fallen behind. He'd given up smoking a few months earlier when he'd been shot, but his lungs were still trying to get a handle on his smoke-free lifestyle.

While she waited for Notchey, Madison slipped into her warm-up jacket and breathed in the earthy scents around her. She nodded good morning to several people she recognized from other morning runs as they made their way from the trail to their own cars. There was a couple—the woman tall and lanky, the man shorter and built like a young bull—she'd been seeing a lot recently. They always wore matching Dodgers ball caps. They both gave her a small wave as they climbed into their black SUV. As one of the familiar male runners passed Madison, he gave her fit figure and flushed face an appreciative scan and smiled. She gave him a small smile back. An older couple were just starting up the trail. They always walked it, going a good pace, hand in hand. As they passed Madison, they nodded and smiled. They reminded her of Doug and Dodie.

At least three times a week, she ran these trails early in the morning, unless Samuel had kept her up most of the night with vampire business. Madison found it gave her day a kick-start, especially on the days she had classes.

Before coming to live with the Dedhams, she'd driven over from Culver City to hike the trails on occasion, but now they were practically in her back yard. Madison was naturally slim as a reed, but Dodie Dedham insisted on feeding her like a ranch hand. The running kept her in great condition. It also cleared her head, something she felt she needed more than keeping calories at bay. With the odd life she led, the physical exercise grounded her to the fact that she was the living walking amongst the dead. She'd invited Notchey, who usually ran on a treadmill in a gym, to come with her before. This morning was the third time he'd joined her. The hills were still kicking his ass, but he was getting better at it.

"Don't make me hurt you," Notchey wheezed out once he was beside her. He bent over and placed his hands on his knees, catching his breath. "I do carry a gun, you know."

Madison laughed. Opening her car door, she grabbed a bottle of water and handed it to him. He downed half of it. Then she tossed him a towel. "You have time to come back to the house for some eggs and coffee before work?"

He gave her a tired grin. "I was hoping you'd say that. I'll grab a shower at the Dedhams', too, if you don't mind."

"Of course not. You're family to them, same as me. You don't have to ask every time. Just plan on it."

"Besides, I have information on Keleta to give you to pass along to the council."

"Is it good or bad?"

Notchey leaned against the car and took another drink of water. He was of average height with a slim build. His hair was brown, which he kept too short to flatter his face and his eyes. His nose had once been broken and badly set. It put character in an otherwise plain face. He was only thirty-four, though he often looked older. Madison didn't know his personal history, but he wore the weight of his past like chain mail—heavy and impenetrable. In that, he was a lot like her.

"It's interesting, to say the least. Do you know if those guys he's been stashed with have gotten any information out of him?"

"Nothing that I know of." Madison took a drink from her own water bottle. "Mostly, I think Keleta's been resting and healing from his injury. And his English isn't that good, according to Samuel. What did you find out?" She poked Notchey playfully in his ribs. "Come on, tell me."

Mike wiped his sweaty brow with the towel. "I did find a missing persons report on a Keleta Kibreab. But here's the thing." He paused and took another couple of deep, normal breaths. "It's from about eighteen months ago."

Madison's jaw dropped like a runaway elevator. "A year and a half? I thought he was newly turned."

"He still could have been. Who knows—maybe he was held captive all this time, or maybe he's not talking out of fear? Remember, whoever tried to kill him is still out there. And that was probably the same person who kidnapped him."

Madison climbed into the driver's seat. "I'm going over to Samuel's this evening. Can't wait to hear his take on this."

As Notchey settled into the passenger's seat, Madison glanced over at him. "You should put on your jacket. You're sweaty, and it's chilly out."

"You've been hanging around Dodie too much. You're starting to sound motherly." In spite of his comment, he knew it was a good idea. Notchey turned to reach between his seat and Madison's to where his jacket lay on the back seat. It was just beyond his grasp. He twisted more until nearly half his body was wedged between his seat and hers.

"Having problems, old man?" she teased, turning in his direction.

"Got it." As Notchey turned back toward the front, pulling his jacket through the two seats, his head bumped Madison's.

"Ow."

"Sorry," he said, but he made no move to sit straight. "You okay?"

She laughed lightly. "If you haven't noticed, I have a thick skull." She looked at him, and their eyes met like in the movies, glued to each other with longing.

"Yeah," he said in a low voice, his breath glancing off her face. "I have noticed."

Before he could move away, Madison grazed her lips against his. His mouth welcomed the advance and responded, but, like before, after a bit he jerked back as if burned. Without giving any explanation, he settled back on his side of the front seat and slipped sloppily into his jacket. "Got any bacon to go with those eggs?"

"So what do you think?" Madison asked Samuel. "Do you think Keleta is a brand-new vampire? Or was he turned when he first disappeared?"

They were working in Samuel's home office. It was early in the evening. He'd already informed Madison that it would not be a long night for her because he was going out later with Kai, a gorgeous Chinese woman, a beater, who was his main companion. Madison had gotten to know Kai in the time she spent at Samuel's. A former model, Kai wasn't just beautiful, she was also sophisticated and intelligent. She was attending law school at UCLA with Samuel's financial assistance. Samuel kept a stable of three gorgeous women as his mistresses and assisted them all financially toward their future. Besides Kai's legal pursuits, one was studying architecture and another art, but Kai was Madison's favorite of the three. Samuel had an eye for picking winners.

They were kept women, something Madison had trouble accepting no matter how much she liked them individually. It wasn't that she was a prude; she wasn't by a long shot. She didn't hold it against Kai and the others. It was their choice, but it wouldn't be hers.

Samuel had made it clear to Madison that he would be more than willing to assist her in the same manner; she just had to say the word. But she had declined. These women traded their bodies and their warm blood for an easier lifestyle while furthering their careers; there'd be no waiting tables for these ladies. To Madison, it was the same as turning tricks on Hollywood Boulevard, just with nicer trappings. When she left foster care in Boise, Idaho, and was desperate for money, Madison had used her looks to entice drunks into the parking lots of bars with the promise of sex. She'd never delivered on the sex part, but she had rolled them—taken advantage of their drunken state to rob them. Usually, the men were too embarrassed to report it, until one did and she was arrested. Being so young and a first offender, she'd been let go with a harsh warning. It wasn't something she was proud of and she swore never to do anything like it again, and that included taking Samuel up on his generous offer, even though she did find him very sexy and appealing. Besides, Madison still wasn't sure what her goals were. Before she transferred to a four-year college, she'd have to figure out what she wanted to do with her life. Samuel was nudging her toward business management and eventually an MBA, saying she had a definite aptitude for it.

Samuel was slouched on the rich burgundy leather sofa reading Notchey's findings. He was wearing an Indian kurta, snow white with white embroidery, and matching loose lounge pants. Madison was at the desk in her usual jeans and sweater going over e-mails that had come into the council's general mailbox. E-mails to and from the council and vampires were written carefully so they would not disclose the nature of the sender or of the council in the event of a computer security breach. Even after nearly four months, it still took Madison a few moments to decipher some of the more cryptic messages.

"It's difficult to say what happened to Keleta," Samuel answered. "But at least now we know about when it began."

"Has Isabella had any luck finding Annabelle Fogle?"

"Not yet. According to some of Isabella's contacts, Annabelle was last seen in France about twenty years ago."

"Twenty years?" Madison threw a smart-ass glance at Samuel. "In vampire time, that's, like, what—last week?" Even though Samuel was her boss, she was comfortable with him.

"Cute." Samuel put down Notchey's report. "But she showed up right before Doug married Dodie. That's a four-year gap followed by a fifteen-year gap. She's either keeping low, died, or changed her name."

"But if she's dead, who branded Keleta?"

"Excellent question. I'm leaning toward the last option, that she's changed her identity. But unless one of her old friends recognizes her and tells us, we won't know that."

Madison stopped typing the e-mail response she was working on. "Do vampires change their identity often?"

"Some do. Before he was Douglas Dedham, Doug's last name was Hayes. He took the name of Dedham right before he married Dodie so they could start fresh together."

Madison liked that idea. A fresh start was what she'd wanted when she had moved to Los Angeles. "Is Samuel La Croix your real name?"

The head vampire shook his head with sadness. "I was so young when I was enslaved that I don't even remember my childhood name. I was simply called Blind Boy for a long time. When I got older, one of my owners gave me the name of Samuel. I heard the name La Croix when I was traveling many years ago and took a fancy to it."

Madison swiveled back and forth in the desk chair thinking about the vampires and their names, wondering how many of the others were using aliases.

"Colin was born Colin Wingate," Samuel informed her, reading her mind. "Reddy was his mother's last name."

Colin Reddy was a very handsome and sexy vampire on the council. He appeared to be on the edge of thirty years old. Half English, half Indian, in truth, he was several hundred years old.

"Speaking of Colin," Samuel continued, "as soon as he heard the name Annabelle Fogle, he disappeared."

"What?" Madison swiveled her chair 180 degrees until she was facing Samuel. "Does he know her?"

"She turned him."

"What?" Madison repeated with more surprise.

Samuel looked around the room. "Is there a parrot in here?"

Madison rolled her eyes. "Come on. You can't expect to drop a bomb like that and not have me be surprised." When Samuel just chuckled, Madison continued. "So this Annabelle Fogle turned both Doug and Colin into vampires. Did you know that?"

"I make it my business to know who turned every member of the council before they are appointed to the council. It's like reading a resume."

Madison pointed a finger at him. "Now that does not surprise me."

Another deep chuckle rumbled up from Samuel's chest. "Colin was turned after he happened upon Annabelle while traveling through India." He paused to clear his throat. "I had a conference call with the council, letting them know what had happened at the Dedhams' house and how it's possible this Annabelle was connected. Since then, Colin has been out of touch."

"Did he say anything to you about it?"

"Not a word." He looked directly at Madison. "Have you heard from him?"

She shook her head. As with Mike Notchey, Madison and Colin had become friends with a spark of attraction between them, becoming not friends with benefits, but friends with possibilities. Had Colin not been a vampire, she knew she would have encouraged his advances, but she wasn't ready yet to make that big a leap into the world of the undead and knew she might never be. Colin respected that.

Madison got her mind off of Colin. "This Annabelle has everyone upset, especially Dodie. I've never seen her like this. She's usually fearless."

"Dodie need not worry," Samuel replied, his voice comforting. "Doug is not about to go off with Annabelle or anyone else. He adores Dodie and chose her specifically as his eternal partner. He waited a long time for someone as special as Dodie to come along."

"But Annabelle tried to kill Dodie."

"True, but Dodie wasn't a vampire then. Dodie has a core of steel. Annabelle, if she's wise, would think twice about challenging her."

"Have you ever met her?"

"No, not personally, but I've met vampires over the years who have." Samuel smiled. "I've been told she's quite a handful: very headstrong and determined. She fits the description Keleta gave us."

In spite of Samuel's attempt to soothe her worries, a chill ran through Madison's veins like a slippery eel. "But why would Annabelle come back and bother the Dedhams after so many years?"

"We won't know that until we find her and talk to her. Personally, I'm more interested in why she tried to kill one of her own charges, then dumped him here in our back yard."

"It was the Dedhams' back yard," Madison corrected.

Samuel grinned. He liked the sharp banter he received from Madison. She was quick and gutsy. "You know what I mean. The council doesn't like the unexpected. If someone else had seen

Keleta instead of you, there's no telling what kind of uproar it might have caused."

A thought crossed Madison's mind. One of the things she enjoyed about working with Samuel was that he was always willing to answer her questions about vampires and their culture.

"Samuel, is it okay for a vampire to kill a vampire that they've turned? That seems an awful lot like a master-slave relationship, especially with the branding."

By the way Samuel leaned his head against the back of the sofa, Madison knew he was weighing his words. He'd always tell her the truth, but he didn't always tell her all the gruesome details. She wasn't sure if she liked the editing or not, but she trusted him enough to accept it.

"Yes," he finally answered in a blunt, short tone. "A maker does have dominion over the vampires he or she turns, but only to a point. It's rather complicated, but basically a vampire should mentor the newly turned vampire until he is able to fend for himself. Some go off on their own as soon as they are able. Others develop a special bond with their maker and choose to stay with them for many years, sometimes forever. We're usually very strict about the mentoring here in California, but if someone doesn't live up to their responsibilities, the baby vampire is sent to Ricky and Byron. They are quite good at working with the orphans. But in general, we consider vampires killing other vampires to be murder, just as humans killing humans is murder."

"But you'll exterminate Keleta if he doesn't make the grade. That's murder."

"Extermination of certain vampires," Samuel explained, leaning forward to give the topic the serious attention it required, "is sometimes necessary to protect the community. It weeds out bad apples or potential problems. And it is not done lightly. Keleta will be given a fair chance."

Madison still wasn't satisfied. "But it's playing God."

Samuel stood up and came to stand in front of Madison. He placed a hand under her chin and raised her face up to look at him. "Let me remind you, Madison, that vampires are already dead. We're just trying to manage those that God has already forsaken."

The two of them, vampire and living, remained in that position while Madison digested the words. She could feel the beat of her heart echoing in Samuel's fingertips.

"Is that why you chose a name that means 'the cross'?"

"As I told you, I just liked the name." Samuel gave her a gentle smile and removed his hand.

"Is it like this with vampires all over the world?" Madison asked. "You know, the managing, judging, and extermination thing?"

"I'm afraid not. There are some communities like ours that take it very seriously, but most do not. A new vampire either sinks or swims. Older vampires are allowed to do whatever they please. Our council is modeled after a very successful one in Switzerland."

"Leave it to the Swiss." Madison turned back to her work, breaking the intensity that had filled the room like heavy humidity.

Samuel continued to watch her long after she had resumed her work. "Are you quite comfortable with the computer and various programs?"

She glanced at him while her fingers worked the keyboard. "Pretty much, especially if I have a manual to check. I took a couple classes before I came down to LA, and I like working with computers. I've been teaching myself more stuff as I go."

"Good. I might add another duty to your job description."

Madison swiveled a quarter turn in her chair. "Director of Vampire IT?"

"Sort of." Samuel leaned against the desk. "There's a special vampire database I want you to learn. Currently, it's run by a vampire named Joni Langevoort up north. I may send you to her for training. I think it would be very advantageous for us to have you familiar with it."

Madison nodded her consent. "Always like to learn new things. Just let me know when."

"I think it will be soon." Samuel pushed off from the desk. "But for now I need to get ready for my date with Kai. We're going to the Disney Concert Hall tonight."

As he started for the door, Madison swiveled back around in her chair toward him. "One more question, Samuel."

He stopped in the doorway and waited.

"Don't your lady friends ever mind that you never take them to dinner? You know, like someplace elegant and fancy?"

A deep, rich laugh escaped his lips. "If they do, they manage to get over it. They know enough to eat before we go out." He winked at Madison and flashed his fangs. "I dine when we get home."

FIVE

ame scream, different day. Another mug shattered on the patio floor.

Madison couldn't believe her eyes. She closed them tight, held them shut, counted to ten, then opened them. But it was still there. Hopping over the spilled coffee and broken pieces of mug, she ran into the house and up the stairs.

This time, she went straight for the X-Acto knife, slicing a different finger. If this kept up, she was going to be slitting her wrists. As before, Madison woke Dodie first, then Doug. Although the two vampires had only been asleep for a few hours, they flew down the stairs and out to the patio.

The body was exactly where Madison had last seen it—in the middle of the pool, facedown, arms stretched out, naked. It hadn't made a desperate crawl to the side.

Doug jumped into the pool and pushed the body toward the steps at the shallow end, where Dodie and Madison waited to help. As with Keleta, a stake had been driven through the man's chest. They got him out of the water and turned him on his side to examine the stake.

Dodie's eyes moved from the stake to the man's face, then traveled up, seeking Doug's eyes. She shook her head very slowly. Madison first gave one Dedham, then the other, an anxious look, knowing instinctively what Dodie's look meant even before Doug released his hold on the dead vampire.

"Are you sure?" Madison asked.

"Look at his face, Madison." Doug pointed to the eyes of the man, who was now on his back.

Madison took a step closer and gasped in disgust. The man had a rugged face with a lantern jaw, a short beard, and longish, light hair, now plastered to his head like seaweed. His eye sockets were hollow, dark, empty orbs, shiny with residual pool water.

"Yuck." Madison backed away, a hand over her mouth to squelch a gag. "Why would someone do that? They'd already killed him. Is it some sort of sick message?"

"No, dear," said Dodie, standing up and going to Madison. She put an arm around the girl in comfort. "No one took his eyes. That's what happens when a vampire dies. The eyes sink into the skull almost immediately after death."

Madison stole a glance at the eyeless body again, summoning the courage to look longer. This was the true meaning of *lights out.* "Does he have the brand?"

Doug turned the body on its side and checked. He nodded toward the women and gently lowered the body back in place. "Yes, it's there. There's also this very nasty and old scar on his side. Looks like a sword or very large knife injury. Might help in identifying him."

"Now what?" asked Madison.

It was nearly ten in the morning. Madison had slept in, then gone downstairs for breakfast and coffee. She didn't have a class until two. Pauline had told them yesterday she would be in after running errands. She'd been spared once more from finding a body in the pool.

"Let's move the body into the house and out of sight," Doug suggested.

The man was larger than Keleta, and the vampires were slowly being sapped of their strength by both the sun and the lack of sleep. With Doug clutching the torso and Dodie and Madison on each leg, they carried the body into the house and deposited him on the kitchen floor just as Pauline came through the door leading to the driveway. She was carrying a couple of plastic grocery bags in one hand and dry cleaning in the other.

"Oh no, not in my kitchen," were Pauline's first words upon seeing the dead vampire on the gleaming kitchen floor.

Doug went to Pauline and took the grocery bags from her, placing them on the counter. "It's just until the knacker gets here. Dodie's calling him now."

Pauline, a short, thick African-American woman with long salt-and-pepper braids, dropped her large purse on the seat of a kitchen chair and draped the dry cleaning over the back of it. She stepped closer. "Anyone we know?"

Doug shook his head. "We don't recognize him. But he has the same brand as the last one."

"Lord, help us." Pauline shook her head and walked to the counter where Doug had deposited the groceries. Nearby, Dodie was talking to someone on the kitchen phone. Pauline looked over at Dodie. "Mrs. D, you tell that lazy-ass knacker man to pick this body up PDQ. You hear me?" She looked back down at the dead undead. "Gives me the willies, no matter how many times I've seen it before."

Dodie hung up the phone. "Not to worry, Pauline. Jesús said he'd be here before noon. He was coming here anyway with a delivery."

"What's a knacker?" Madison asked. "Some sort of vampire undertaker?"

Pauline and Dodie both glanced at Doug, the two women letting him know he could field the delicate question.

"It's an old English term," Doug explained. "A knacker picked up old animals, particularly farm animals, who were dead or too worn out to work, then rendered them or sold them to factories who processed them."

"Ewww." Madison looked down at the body. "Guess vampires aren't very sentimental about their dead."

Pauline started putting away the groceries. "Don't let Jesús hear you calling him a knacker. He'll box your ears. He prefers *handyman*." Pauline looked over at Madison. "Jesús is also the one who delivers the animal blood for the vampires who drink it. That's what he'll be delivering when he drops by."

Like a broken record, Madison's brain was still stuck on the knacker part and on Samuel's comment about God forsaking the undead. "So Jesus comes and takes away the dead vampires. Would that be considered ironic or fitting?"

"And don't you go letting Jesús hear you calling him Jesus, neither," Pauline shot over her shoulder. "He'll box your ears twice for that. It's always *Jesús*."

Doug chuckled. "Listen to Pauline, Madison, and save yourself some grief."

Dodie knelt down to look at the body again. "Well, if Jesús doesn't get here soon, there may be no reason for him to show."

The others directed their attention down at the body. There, before their eyes, it was already starting to shrivel like a balloon with a slow leak.

Doug knelt down next to Dodie. "He must have been a fairly old vampire."

"How can you tell?" Madison asked, not sure she wanted to get a closer look. "Do you count his rings like on a tree stump?"

Dodie shot Madison a frown for her flippancy. "No, but just as older vampires heal quicker, their bodies also decompose quicker upon death." She looked back down, her voice softer. "It's as if the earth is calling them home from too long a trip."

Doug left the room and returned with a sketchpad and pencil from his art supplies. Doug had a small office off the den where he also dabbled in painting and drawing. He moved a chair to a good vantage point near the feet of the dead vampire and began sketching the quickly shriveling face.

"Great idea, Doug." Dodie stood just behind her husband and watched his sketch develop.

"Can't you just take a photo?" asked Madison.

"You see any photos of vampires around here?" Pauline gave Madison a pointed look with the question. "There's a reason for that."

"While we can be photographed, we generally don't come out very well in photography," explained Dodie. "Sometimes not at all. It's another one of those odd mysteries. The sketch will allow us to capture details."

Madison shook her head, wishing the vampires had come with a printed manual. Learning on the job was exhausting.

"Okay, so from the way he's disappearing, can you tell how old a vampire he is?"

Dodie cocked her head to one side and considered the vampire on the ground. "He's definitely not as old as Samuel."

"That's for sure," added Doug. "I once saw a two-thousand-year-old vampire die. He was dust in a matter of minutes. I'd say this one is a few hundred years old."

Madison looked down at the body. The face was quickly resembling a dried apple doll. The torso and limbs were drying, the skin beginning to cling to the skeleton like plastic wrap covering leftovers. But still Madison was stumped. "Then why wasn't he decomposing in the pool? He looked normal when you pulled him out."

Doug continued perfecting his sketch. "Because water preserves our bodies. They don't even have to be submerged, just wet."

The information caused a chain reaction in Madison's brain. "That means whoever did this wanted to make sure the body was found, no matter how long it took."

"Most definitely," Doug said, not looking up from his drawing. "It was probably dumped right after we went to bed this morning, and it would have kept until we got up this evening."

"But what if it had been found by someone who didn't know about you?" Madison shuddered at the thought of an outsider calling the police to report a pool death. "If it is this Annabelle, she's determined to cause you trouble, isn't she?"

Dodie's jaw tightened. "Sure looks that way to me."

A knock at the back door made them all jump. Instinctively, Madison moved to block the body from the view of anyone coming through the door.

Pauline looked out through the sheer curtain at the door's window. "It's the knacker," announced the housekeeper, unlatching and opening the back door.

Everyone sighed in relief. The Dedhams seldom had random visitors, but until the body was gone, they would all be on edge.

A short, stout middle-aged man with bandy legs and light brown skin was let into the kitchen by Pauline. He was dressed in old jeans, a dirty knit work shirt, and heavy work boots. As he entered the house, he removed a beat-up ball cap to display thinning black hair peppered with gray and a broad face lined by the sun. He reminded Madison of a hobbit who'd become a day laborer.

"Jesús," Pauline said to the man, "this here's Madison. She lives with the Dedhams."

Jesús gave her a crooked smile of small, uneven teeth. "Ah, I hear much about the fair Madison already."

Madison wasn't sure if being known was a good thing or a bad thing. Either way, it made her uncomfortable. "You have?"

The small man nodded. "You did much to help Mr. Samuel and the others a few months ago. We're all very grateful." His voice had an upbeat, friendly tone to it.

When Madison looked puzzled, Jesús offered, "If the *vampiro* fall, we all fall. All our businesses."

"He's right about that," Pauline added with a jerk of her head.

Madison had learned that there was a very tight community of the living who served the vampires in various ways—as housekeepers, hairdressers, lawyers, drivers, and even some who provided fresh blood. Whatever services the vampires needed to continue their way of life but could not provide for themselves was outsourced to those amongst the living who vowed silence in return for extra-large paychecks. When Madison had agreed to work for the council, she had joined their ranks.

In an awkward gesture, Madison held out her right hand to Jesús, who took it between both of his work-worn hands and pumped it firmly. Done with the formalities, Jesús smiled at the Dedhams and walked over to study the body.

After crossing himself, Jesús pronounced, "Easy job." He turned back to the door. "Be right back."

When Jesús returned, he was carrying a large cooler. He placed it on the counter. "Here's your order."

Pulling a kitchen-size plastic garbage bag from his back pocket, Jesús squatted down next to the decomposing body and went to work. After slipping on work gloves, he ran his hands up and down the limbs, testing their brittleness. Starting with the long legs, he began dismembering the corpse by snapping the body apart at the joints as if breaking kindling.

When Doug and Dodie went into the other room, Madison looked at Pauline with raised eyebrows.

"Would you want to watch," the housekeeper replied, "knowing that's what's gonna happen to you one day?"

Madison shivered. "It is really creepy."

While Jesús worked at breaking up the dead vampire, Pauline unpacked the various containers of animal blood from the cooler. She handed several to Madison. "Here, put these in the freezer." Pauline read the label on one container and set it aside. "I'll keep this one out for their supper tonight. It's wild boar's blood—a particular favorite of Mr. D's. Might make them feel better." Pauline handed Madison the boar's blood, instructing her to place it in the refrigerator. The last several containers went into the freezer along with the first bunch.

When Jesús was done, the body of the once large and bulky vampire had been reduced to the size of two days' worth of kitchen garbage. "At the rate he was going," the knacker noted, "this bag will be filled with nothing but dust by early tomorrow."

Madison couldn't stop her morbid curiosity. "What will you do with him ... with the dust?"

"Depends on whose it is," the odd little man explained. "If friends of the deceased request it, I return it once it's fully decomposed. Otherwise, I scatter it in my garden, in the woods, or sometimes in the ocean. I return it to nature, where it belongs."

When Jesús was done and gone, the Dedhams returned to the kitchen hand in hand. "If you don't need us," Doug told Madison and Pauline, "we're going back to bed." He looked pointedly at Madison. "And you, young lady, should be heading to school. You're not late already, are you?"

Madison glanced at the clock on the wall. If she skipped her shower, she'd make it. "No, I'm good."

"You want something to eat first?" Pauline asked the Dedhams. "Jesús brought some fresh boar's blood."

Doug looked at his wife. Dodie shook her head slowly. It was clear that the Dedhams were truly dead on their feet. "No, thank you, Pauline," Doug said for them both.

"Madison," Doug said, turning to her just before he disappeared into the next room. "Please leave Samuel a message about what happened here today. I'm sure he'll be wanting to discuss it later tonight."

"Should someone wake him?" Madison asked. "I can call Hyun to do it."

"No, let him sleep. There's nothing anyone can do right now, and I doubt any more bodies will show up in broad daylight."

Doug ran a hand through his silver hair. "If it's another vampire doing this, as we suspect, he is—"

"She," Dodie corrected.

Doug glanced at Dodie. "He or she will be tucked in for the day."

"What about Notchey? Should I tell him?"

"Vampires killing vampires is out of his jurisdiction." Doug shrugged in reconsideration. "But if he has the time to give it some thought, run it by him. Never know, he might see something we're missing. And it sure wouldn't hurt to give him a heads-up."

SIX

A nyone know this vampire?" Samuel asked the members of the council seated around the Dedhams' dining table.

Before leaving for her class, Madison had taken Doug's sketch, scanned it, and sent it to Samuel in an e-mail. As soon as he saw the e-mail, he forwarded the likeness off to the other council members with a request to meet at the Dedhams' promptly at ten o'clock. Before the council meeting, Madison had printed off enlargements to pass around the table, hoping the larger picture might jar some memories.

Madison attended some council meetings to record certain information, but not all. Tonight she was asked to sit in and take notes. Even Notchey was asked to attend.

When Madison called Notchey to tell him what had happened that morning, he'd invited her out to dinner. They had gone to Gladstone's in Malibu. While there, Notchey received a text message from Samuel asking him to attend the special council meeting.

"How convenient," Notchey said, showing Madison the message. "I have to take you back home anyway."

"What would happen," Madison asked quietly over their appetizer of crispy calamari, "if the police were called in and found a dead vampire?"

Notchey tilted back his bottle of Guinness and took a long drink before answering. "Hard to say. At first, I'm sure they would think it was just a hoax, or that it was the body of one of those vampirism cult followers with the fake fangs. Of course, the autopsy would be revealing, not to mention interesting."

"What if the body started decomposing right before their eyes?"

"That really spooked you, didn't it?"

Madison shuddered. "Yes. It was like watching one of those nature shows where they speed up time so you can see in minutes what happens over years." She took a drink of her soda. "Have you ever seen a vampire die?"

Notchey remained silent, taking a couple of short nips off his beer bottle while he stared out the window at the darkness that was the Pacific Ocean. Madison's curiosity rose like a thermometer in the desert. It was obviously a question the cop wasn't ready to answer in an instant. She had a choice: drop the question or press. She pressed.

"Well, have you?"

"Yes, I have." He continued staring out at the waves.

"Did it scare you? Or are you too tough a cop to let a silly thing like instant mummification throw you off?"

"Cops are people, Madison." He turned away from the window and faced her again. "Even though we see some pretty horrible stuff, I'm sure a corpse disintegrating on fast forward would scare anyone shitless, including a seasoned cop." He dipped a calamari ring into the sauce and popped it into his mouth, thinking while he chewed. "After, I'm not sure what would happen." He ate another piece of calamari, this time a fried cluster of tiny tentacles. "Although I'm sure if the media got ahold of it, the Dedhams' property would be overrun with reporters, most of whom would be making up shit about either some religious miracle or evidence of the devil at work. It would have to be sold as one or the other so the public could understand it."

"But what about the police investigation?"

Notchey laughed, not a happy laugh but one of wry speculation. "That would be a mess, no doubt about it. And I sure as hell wouldn't want to be the guy filing the report."

There would be no police report. There was no body. The only thing the dead vampire had left behind was an image for Doug's sketch and nightmare fodder for Madison.

When their entrees arrived, Madison wasn't thinking about her grilled shrimp. On her mind was the kiss from yesterday. Notchey hadn't said anything about it. When he had asked her to dinner, she'd wondered if he'd thrown out the invitation to give them a chance to talk. So far, it seemed all he wanted was company for dinner. She wondered if she should say something or just keep her mouth shut. She'd had only two relationships in her life. One had started in her last year of high school and had ended a few years later. The other had been shortly after she arrived in Los Angeles. Both had ended badly. The guy from high school had developed a serious drug problem. The one in LA had turned out to be married. For all of his personal torment, Mike Notchey seemed to be a stand-up kind of guy. Someone dependable, though elusive and filled with secrets. And he wasn't a vampire. Whatever attraction she felt for him, she was sure it was mutual. Or was it? Her track record and background left her doubting any feelings about anything and anyone.

"Mike," she started, pushing a shrimp around her plate with her fork.

He shoveled a piece of salmon into his mouth and chewed, giving her his attention.

She went tongue-tied, wondering how to broach the subject without sounding like a needy, clinging vine. She continued playing with her food.

Notchey pointed his fork at Madison's plate. "Don't you think that shrimp's been through enough without you bullying him?"

She put her fork down and looked at him. After giving her a quick shrug, Notchey went back to eating, returning his attention to the damage he was doing to his own food. Madison picked up the fork again and speared the shrimp, this time stuffing it into her mouth.

"He was a big guy," Doug told the council as they looked over the picture. "Tall and well built, with blond hair just past his jaw line. His beard was darker than his hair, like a dark gold. Difficult to say how old he appeared. His face was very rugged, so he could have been anywhere from his late thirties to mid-forties, maybe even older."

No one around the table claimed to know the vampire in the sketch. They looked from one to the other, shrugging.

"There was nothing to give you a clue as to where he might have been from?" The question came from Stacie Neroni.

"He was naked, just like Keleta." Doug answered. "But he did have the same brand at the small of his back."

"What does the brand specifically look like again?" This time the question came from Kate Thornton.

"A hexagon with an eye in the middle," answered Dodie. Although not on the council, she was allowed to attend since she was a witness. Jerry Lerma, Kate's beater husband, was shut up in the den, waiting for her.

"It looks just like this." Turning around, Doug gave the council the same show he'd given Notchey and Madison the day they'd fished Keleta out of the pool. Colin and Isabella were the only council members not at the meeting, but Eddie Gonzales, Kate, and Stacie all took a closer look. "This is the brand Annabelle Fogle gave me shortly before she turned me."

"Are you sure that's the same brand Keleta and the vampire from this morning had?" Stacie moved closer to Doug's back and squinted, as if burning the brand from Doug's skin into her memory.

"Exactly the same," assured Dodie. She turned to Madison, who nodded in agreement. "Why?"

Stacie resumed her place at the table. "Where's Colin? Does he know about the brand?"

"We're not sure of his whereabouts right now," responded Samuel. "Since our last conference call, he has not been heard from."

"It's no wonder," Stacie snarled.

It was well known that Stacie Neroni and Colin Reddy did not like each other. Madison had once been told by Pauline that it was because of a friend of theirs who had died. She'd once asked

Colin about it, but he'd never answered and had instead grown more sullen as the evening wore on.

"Colin has a brand exactly like that."

Every head turned Stacie's way, both vampire and beater, but it was Samuel who broke the silence. "Are you sure, Stacie?"

"Yes, I saw it once when he had his shirt off. It was a long time ago, but I'm sure it's the same mark."

At the idea of the sexy Colin shirtless, Kate cast an arched brow Dodie's way. Dodie fought to suppress a grin. Stacie saw the exchange.

"Oh, get over yourselves, you two old biddies," Stacie growled. "It was when Colin, Julie, and I were in Mexico years ago and went swimming."

The table went silent as a grave, or as silent as a group of people standing over a fresh grave. Dodie and Kate both had their heads down, whether in embarrassment or from the chastising, Madison couldn't tell. Even the men were looking elsewhere, anywhere but at Stacie, including Notchey. Madison looked at each one of them, her internal radar humming as she tried to get a feel for the reason. Usually lively, the meeting had taken on the same air of discomfort as when someone tells a particularly bad or inappropriate joke.

"What about the brand?" asked Notchey, turning to Madison. "What did he say when *you* saw it?"

Madison didn't care for Notchey's tone or implication. He had a mean streak that came out from time to time, and his question had been underlined with spite. Madison was sure he hadn't made a mistake, that the question had been meant for her.

"It was Stacie, not me," she reminded him, "who said she'd seen the brand. I've never seen Colin with his shirt off, back or front." She stared at Notchey, asking him with her eyes what in the hell he thought he was doing.

"Well," said Samuel, once more breaking the awkward silence with diplomacy, "as soon as someone hears from Colin, let him know I'd like to speak to him. If he knew anything, he should have mentioned it during our conference call. Meanwhile, I want full surveillance on this house day and night. If there's a third body on its way, we're going to be there waiting. Madison, I want you and Pauline doing day watch. The Dedhams will watch all night."

"Absolutely, Samuel," Doug agreed. "We can't have this happening again, no matter who is at the root of it."

Samuel nodded confirmation at Doug and continued with his instructions. "Before you and Dodie go to bed, I want you to wake up Madison and make sure she's on the job. I'll also send Hyun over before dawn, just in case. He can also fill in when Madison's at school. I don't want that back yard unguarded for a moment."

Samuel turned to Mike Notchey. "The information you gave us on Keleta was most helpful; thank you. At least we know he's no more than eighteen months old as a vampire, if that. And we know where he met the woman who kidnapped him. I'm going straight over to Byron and Ricky's tonight to question the boy further about it."

The meeting was about to adjourn when the front door opened. Every head turned to see who came in, half expecting it to be Hyun with a message for Samuel. Instead, it was Colin, standing tall, dark, and handsome in the doorway. He was dressed in his usual black shirt and pants and black leather jacket. His swarthy face was set in stone, and his thick, black hair was windblown. He looked at the gathering with a stony face, offering no greeting or explanation.

Behind him was a gorgeous and very shapely woman with long, wavy red hair. She wore an elegant knit pantsuit the color of copper. Thick gold baubles adorned her neck and ears. Coming around Colin, she entered the room with cocky confidence. Spotting Doug Dedham, she flashed him a wide, perfect smile, but when her sapphire eyes met Dodie's, the smile turned to a smirk. Dodie started to rise to say something, but Doug put a hand on her arm to stop her.

"Annabelle." Doug's voice was a whispered mixture of surprise and wariness.

The woman stepped up to the dining table and placed her designer handbag on it as casually as if she did it every day. Samuel rose at the head of the table and studied her, letting her know he was in charge and she was on his turf.

Annabelle Fogle met Samuel's powerful gaze with a slight but superior smile, letting him know in return that he wasn't the boss of her. "You must be the famous Samuel La Croix I've heard so much about." Her voice was as cold and sparkly as a diamond.

Samuel gave up a tiny, tight-lipped smile of his own. "And you must be the infamous Annabelle Fogle."

The two studied each other like opponents at a gunfight, each waiting for the other to twitch first. The room went silent once again.

With a slight sigh of surrender, Annabelle relaxed. "Actually, the name's Ann now. Ann Hayes."

SEVEN

"ayes?" Doug spoke next, his voice swollen with anger and surprise. "You took my name?" He had risen to stand next to Dodie's chair.

Ann Hayes tossed her glossy hair. "Well, darling, it's not like you were using it anymore. Besides, I wanted something to remember you by." She rolled her stunning eyes. "Thank goodness your name wasn't Dedham at the time. What were you thinking, naming yourself after a town in Massachusetts? I would have thought you'd have more creativity than that." She turned her eyes on Dodie. "Or at least you did when we were together."

Dodie shot to her feet and bared her fangs. "How dare you disrespect me in my own home."

Doug placed his hands on his wife's shoulders and tightened his grip. Everyone at the table was out of their seats, standing at alert.

"Oh, that's right." Ann moved to stand in front of Dodie but remained out of reach. "I'd heard Doug gave you eternal life as a wedding present. How romantic." Ann sneered at Dodie. "Just remember, you mousy old housefrau, who gave it to *him*."

With their speed overwhelming Dodie's strength, both Colin and Doug held Dodie back from attacking Ann. But the usually nurturing Dodie continued to snarl at her opponent like a mad, bloodthirsty dog. Madison watched, fascinated yet pale with fright. Without her realizing it, Mike had put an arm around her waist and was slowly drawing her back, away from the table and out of the fray.

Kate's fangs were out, ready to defend Dodie's honor, while Eddie and Stacie had come behind Ann, ready to step in and break apart the fight. The air was thick and fetid, like bad breath in a confined space.

"Enough!" Samuel's baritone roar filled every crack and crevice of the room with its menacing authority.

Everyone froze, even Ann Hayes. Madison felt warm urine dampen her panties.

"Dodie, sit down," the head vampire commanded. Dodie hesitated, but with a final growl aimed at Ann, she obeyed. Doug stayed behind her, keeping his hands on both of her shoulders like a safety harness.

Samuel turned his milky eyes toward Ann Hayes. "Ms. Hayes, you are a guest here. Remember that and behave accordingly." He indicated the seat at the end opposite him. "Sit there. We have questions we'd like to ask."

Ann looked ready to challenge Samuel's authority to ask her anything, but one glance at the dark figure changed her mind. He'd tolerated her bravado earlier, but it was clear he would not any longer. She'd heard enough about Samuel La Croix to know that he meant what he said and expected nothing less than cooperation. Raising her elegant chin in her only show of defiance, she took the seat at the opposite end of the table.

"Call me Ann, please." She mustered a sweet smile with Samuel as its target.

Samuel glanced at Colin. "Colin, take the seat next to Ms. Hayes." He turned his eyes back to Ann as he spoke to Colin. "Restrain her if you must." He looked around at the rest of the group. "Everyone, take your seats."

After giving Dodie reassuring pats on her shoulders, Doug took his seat next to his wife.

With Colin and Ann added to the party, there were no more seats for Notchey and Madison at the table. Notchey brought two chairs out of the kitchen but set them back away from the table, where the two humans gladly retreated to watch the proceedings from a distance.

With the meeting under control again, Samuel got to the question on everyone's mind. "Ann, did you try to kill Keleta Kibreab and dump him in the Dedhams' pool?"

"Colletta who?"

Samuel opened the file in front of him. It was Notchey's missing persons report on Keleta. In it was a copy of the photo given to the police by Keleta's family upon his disappearance. Samuel retrieved the photo and pushed it down the table. Eddie Gonzales picked up the photo and handed it to Ann.

"Do you know that young man?" asked Samuel.

Ann studied the photo, then dropped it to the table in boredom. "He's cute, but no."

Samuel passed down a print of Doug's sketch, the one of the morning's dead vampire. "How about this man?"

Ann glanced at it briefly before dropping it to the table next to Keleta's. "No."

She turned to Colin, her face ablaze with anger. "Is this why you brought me here? To be interrogated like a common criminal? I thought you wanted my help."

Colin looked at the sketch with surprise, then up at Samuel. "There was another?"

"Just this morning." Samuel shook his head slowly. "But this one didn't make it."

Colin's dark eyebrows met in the center of his forehead like a black hedge. He pushed both pictures back in front of Ann. "Just look at them and answer the questions."

Glancing down at the pictures, Ann shrugged. "Why would I know these men?"

Doug leaned forward. "Because they both had your brand on their backs."

Ann pursed her lips and studied the faces of the two men again before looking back up at Samuel. "Sorry, but you can hardly expect me to remember every man I've turned in the last thousand years." She tossed an inviting smile at Doug Dedham, then turned and did the same to Colin. "Of course, some were more memorable than others."

"You bitch," hissed Dodie.

Madison's eyes widened. She'd never heard Dodie swear, let alone participate in name-calling.

"Oh, come now, Mrs. Dedham." Ann turned a saccharine smile on Dodie. "Just because you've probably never turned anyone doesn't mean the rest of us are celibate in that regard."

Dodie rose from her seat, fangs once more on display. Doug jumped up, ready to step in if needed.

"Order," demanded Samuel, rapping his knuckles on the table. "Dodie, mind yourself, or I'll have you leave the room."

Without taking her eyes off Ann, Dodie put away her fangs and sat down. Doug resumed his seat but stayed alert.

Samuel directed his attention back to Ann. "I don't know what Colin has told you, Ms. Hayes, but we are investigating the attempted murder of that young vampire."

"Yes, I know. Colin told me. He was staked and dumped in a swimming pool."

"*Our* swimming pool," added Doug with emphasis.

Ann turned a plastic smile on Doug. "How interesting. And so you automatically think it's some pathetic trick on my part to gain your attention? You're cute, Doug, but not *that* cute. I've been over you for decades."

Doug narrowed his eyes at Ann. "The last time we saw you, you tried to kill Dodie."

Ann waved a manicured hand in the air. "Pish, posh. Just a little misunderstanding, that's all."

Dodie started to rise, but Samuel, clearing his throat, gave her second thoughts. She settled back into her seat.

The action amused Ann. "Seems Mr. La Croix has you all trained like little lap dogs. How sweet."

Colin leaned in, his mouth close to Ann's ear, but he didn't bother lowering his voice. "Behave yourself, Ann. Killing another vampire in our jurisdiction is serious business."

"Colin is quite right, Ms. Hayes." Samuel stood back up at the head of the table. "We live a civilized life here, and these incidents are unacceptable. So just answer the questions."

With a jerk of his chin, Samuel indicated the pictures again. "Keleta, the young one, was found nearly dead a few days ago in the Dedhams' swimming pool. The other man was found dead this morning in the same place. Both vampires, both with what I understand is your personal brand at the small of their backs."

"Sorry, but if they are my work, I don't remember them."

Samuel didn't let up. "Keleta has been a vampire eighteen months or less. That should be recent enough to be memorable."

Ann's lips curled in smugness. "Then I know he's not mine. I stopped branding about the time the Prince of Wales married Wallis Simpson."

She looked at Colin, then at Doug. "And I'm surprised at the two of you, thinking I would be interested in men like these. This one." She tapped Keleta's photo. "He's too young for my taste. This other." She moved her finger to the unknown vampire. "He appears too rough and uncouth. I only keep company with men of refinement." She turned her intense blue eyes on Samuel. "Someone like you, Mr. La Croix."

Samuel didn't take the bait. "Then how did your brand get on these vampires?"

"I honestly have no idea. Brands are easy enough to have made. Someone obviously is trying to set me up."

"Anyone with a grudge against you come to mind?" asked Samuel.

"I'm sure there's a long list," added Dodie. Samuel shot her a look to not test his patience.

Samuel studied Ann Hayes, trying to read her. Although easy enough to do with humans, vampires were a different story. Sometimes he could get a bead on them, but most often they were able to easily block him. It depended on whether or not they threw up a firewall before he got inside their head. Ann's thoughts were like Fort Knox—secure and guarded.

"I must tell you, Ms. Hayes, if this council decides to charge and try you for one count of murder and another of attempted murder, the consequences could be severe."

Once again, Ann Hayes waved a dismissive hand. "And LA used to be such fun."

EIGHT

W hy am I here?" The question was tossed to Samuel by Madison.

"You are here to observe. Pay close attention to Keleta when he first meets Ann Hayes. Don't take your eyes off of him. If she's lying, the boy's face will tell us. Beyond that, just keep your eyes and ears open."

They were getting out of Samuel's car. Hyun, Samuel's new driver, was holding the door open to the black Mercedes sedan. Where Gordon, Samuel's last driver, had been thick and beefy, Hyun, a Korean man in his mid-thirties, was more on the wiry side. He stood straight in his black suit as he held the door, but his eyes were constantly surveying his surroundings for any possible threat to his employer.

Hyun had pulled the car into the circular brick driveway of a lovely single-story home situated on a quiet cul-de-sac in Beverly Hills. It was the hilly portion of Beverly Hills, not the flat section that was closer to the famous shops and restaurants. The street was steep, and Madison could see that the house was set against a small hill covered with rich vegetation. It was the home of Byron and Ricky, the gay couple who fostered abandoned vampires.

Before they got to the front door, Byron opened it and greeted them warmly. Just as they were entering, Colin's Porsche pulled up to the curb. With him was Ann. Madison had been surprised that Samuel had not invited Ann to ride with them. When she had asked him about it, he'd simply said he needed time away from Ann to think about the problems she presented. He'd made one call from his cell phone. It had been to Isabella, letting her know that Colin had located the former Annabelle Fogle, but asking her to keep snooping around for information on Ann Hayes. For the remainder of the trip from Topanga to Beverly Hills, Samuel had remained silent and unmoving, lost in his thoughts behind his sunglasses until the car came to a stop at its destination.

Byron and Ricky's home was inviting and comfortable. Not huge and sprawling like Samuel's villa or as coldly modern as Colin's condo, it was more like the Dedham house in taste and warmth. Built-in bookshelves lined many of the walls and were filled with more books than Madison had ever seen outside of a library or a bookstore.

"Ricky took Keleta out shopping just before you called," explained Byron as he showed them into the living room. "I called and let him know you were on your way. They should be back soon."

Madison had first met Byron and his partner Ricky shortly after she'd gone to work for the council. Samuel had held a reception for her at his home for the purpose of introducing her to the core of the Los Angeles vampire community. Byron and Ricky were both in their forties, of average build, with brown hair and beards, though Byron's hair and beard were threaded with gray. They looked more like brothers than lovers.

Madison sat on the large sectional sofa. Samuel stood by the sliders that led to the patio. When Ann and Colin came in, they both took seats on the sectional with Madison, though Ann sat on the far side from her. Colin seated himself between the two women and crossed one long leg over the other. He shot a quick glance at Madison, accompanied by a partial wink. Ann saw it and cleared her throat with displeasure.

Ann Hayes had paid Madison little to no mind at the Dedhams'. Now she studied Madison so closely, Madison could feel perspiration beading on her forehead.

"What's she doing here?" Ann smoothed the front of her impeccable pantsuit like a monarch preparing for an audience.

Colin made the introduction. "This is Madison Rose, Ann. She works for the council."

"I thought she was the Dedhams' maid." Ann grinned at Madison. "My mistake."

"Madison is a very valuable asset to both the council and me," added Samuel. He targeted Ann with one of his fierce scowls.

Ann looked Madison over, head to foot, a slow smile stealing across her face like a big cat on the hunt. "I just bet she is, Mr. La Croix."

Afraid earlier to look directly at Ann Hayes, Madison, upon hearing the comment, turned her head and locked her eyes onto Ann's cold blue ones with heat and dislike. The femme fatale vampire stared back a few moments, then increased her smile. "You'd think a human so used to working with vampires wouldn't wet herself so quickly."

Madison wanted to jump the vampiress and beat her hard on behalf of Dodie, as well as herself. Sensing her anger, Colin reached out a hand and touched her arm. It was then Madison realized him putting himself between her and Ann was no accident. It had been planned to keep the peace and to keep Madison from doing something foolish.

Byron filled the awkwardness that followed by asking if anyone wanted refreshments. "Ricky had some fresh Polynesian blood ordered in from Scarlet's for Keleta." Byron shook his head and smiled. "He's positively spoiling the boy." Everyone politely declined.

It wasn't long before they heard a car pull into the driveway and then into the attached garage.

"That's them now." Byron got up, his face relaxed with relief. "They should be coming in through the side door."

Everyone turned to watch the door that led from the garage into the kitchen. From the sofa, they had a clear view. Samuel left his post by the patio doors and moved into a better position.

Keleta was first through the door. He bounded in like a frisky puppy, laughing and chattering in English over his shoulder at Ricky. He was so different from when Samuel and Madison had last seen him. When he saw the room of people, he stopped short, but it was just a moment's hesitation, a blink of shyness that dissolved when he spotted Samuel. A wide smile crossed the young man's smooth, dark face as he called to Samuel in a language Madison didn't understand. Keleta went to Samuel, his hand held out in greeting. The two men shook, and Samuel clapped Keleta on the shoulder as a father would a son.

"Keleta, I've brought some people to meet you." Samuel turned Keleta's attention to the three on the sofa. "You've met

Madison." Keleta gave Madison a quick nod. "On the other side is Ann Hayes, a friend visiting from out of town. And this fellow," Samuel indicated Colin, "is Colin Reddy, one of our council members."

Following Samuel's orders, Madison hadn't taken her eyes off of Keleta from the moment he stepped through the door. She studied his every facial expression, looking for telltale signs that he recognized Ann. She found none. When introduced to Ann, Keleta was polite, almost shy, but he took her offered hand and shook it, followed by a shake of Colin's extended hand.

It was Ann who deftly and creatively broached the reason they were there. "Keleta, have we ever met? You look so familiar."

Keleta studied Ann's face. "I don't think so, ma'am." His voice was lilting yet strong. He formed the formal English words and said them slowly. "If I have forgotten, I apologize. Such a beautiful woman should not be forgotten."

Ann flashed Byron and Ricky an amused grin. "You boys giving Keleta charm lessons as well as vampire lessons?"

Ricky stepped forward. "The charm is all his and quite natural." He looked at Keleta with pride.

"Your English is much better," noted Madison. "You learned it so quickly."

"I study English in school," Keleta explained.

"I think the trauma Keleta experienced blocked some of his memory." Ricky perched on the arm of the sectional. "As he started feeling better, his memory returned, along with his command of the language."

Samuel clapped Keleta on the shoulder again. "Keleta, would you do us a favor and show your brand to Ann? We told her about it, and she is very interested."

Keleta was slow to respond, but he did take off his shirt and turn around. Reaching back one hand, he pulled down the back of his jeans to expose the brand to everyone. Ann moved off the sofa and bent close, studying it with interest. When she returned to her seat next to Colin, she gave Samuel a shrug. "It certainly looks authentic."

Samuel turned to Keleta, who was putting his shirt back on. "Would you excuse us, Keleta? We have some council business to discuss. Maybe you and Madison could visit quietly while we do so?"

"Of course." Ricky stood. "Keleta, why don't you take Madison into the den? You can play those new CDs we picked up tonight."

Although it felt like the kiddies were being dismissed, Madison knew better. If it had simply been council discussion, she might have been asked to stay. It was Keleta they wanted out the way, and bringing her along had provided a suitable age diversion while the seasoned vampires talked. After closing the door to give both parties privacy, Madison settled on the large, comfy sofa in the den. Across from her was a full entertainment center, including a sizeable flat-screen TV and state-of-the-art stereo equipment. The other walls, like those in the living room, were lined with bookcases stuffed with books and mementos.

"What music did you get tonight?" Madison also planned on taking advantage of her one-on-one time with Keleta to see if he would tell her things about his past.

Keleta had his head down, concentrating on unwrapping the CDs. "Usher and the Black Eyed Peas." With his head still down, he stole looks at Madison, as if studying her from behind a curtain. Once the CD was liberated, Keleta stuck it in the player, and Usher's voice filled the room.

Madison grimaced at the volume. "If you turn it down a bit, we'll be able to talk."

Keleta adjusted the sound.

"How are you getting along, Keleta?"

"Ricky and Byron are very nice to me. They are trying to teach me things about this life." He gave Madison an impish grin. "But I already know much."

In a surprisingly quick move, Keleta stripped off his shirt again and plopped himself down next to Madison. Putting an arm around her shoulders, he turned her toward him. His eyes were large and liquid, like pools of rich melted chocolate nestled in white cream. He smiled and moved closer, unleashing his fangs—more white against brown.

Surprised, Madison leaned back but found herself trapped between Keleta and the high arm of the sofa. "What are you doing?"

Keleta placed his free hand on one of her breasts, cupping it through her sweater in his growing excitement. Madison was about to scream when he abruptly stopped and pulled back. He studied her, bewildered. He touched her again, then pulled back once more.

"I am confused." Keleta cocked his head and knitted his brows. "I want to have sex with you and feed, but something is stopping me."

"You're damn right something's stopping you!" Madison put her hands against Keleta's firm chest and shoved him away from her. "Me!"

"No, something else." Keleta didn't seem the least bit perturbed by Madison's rejection as he continued working out the problem in his head. "When I touch you, I cannot do more, though I want to. It's as if I am being restrained with bindings I cannot see."

Madison touched the bracelet on her wrist. She'd never seen it work until now, though she still wondered what would happen if a violent vampire tried to hurt her. Would they be stopped as easily as Keleta?

"It's this." She held up her arm so he could see her bracelet. "It was given to me by the council. No other vampire can harm me when I wear this."

"I remember seeing that before. The day you found me." He shrugged and looked back at her with disappointment. "So you are only consort to the council?"

"Consort?"

He searched for the right words in his jumbled head. "Lover and blood. Am I not saying it correctly?"

Madison thought about Samuel's mistresses. That's what they were, his lovers and food source. That's what Keleta thought she was. She shook her head. "No. I work for the council. I help them with their business."

"You do not have sex with Samuel?" He seemed very surprised. "Is he like Byron and Ricky?"

"No, Samuel is not like Byron and Ricky." Madison laughed softly. "Not at all. Samuel has women … consorts. Many of them."

"But not you?"

Keleta leaned back against the sofa. Madison checked his chest. There was no sign of the wound from a few days ago.

"Very strange," Keleta continued. "Samuel is very power-ful, and you are beautiful." He gave her a look of understand-ing. "You are consort to Colin, then—the other man out there tonight. Yes?"

Her initial fear gone, Madison laughed and again shook her head. "I am consort to no one, Keleta. No one bites me. No one has sex with me."

"How sad for you."

For a brief moment, Madison did feel sorry for herself and her lack of a love life, but she shook it off when Keleta leaned in closer. "You will be consort to Keleta then." He gave her a wide smile, complete with fangs, as if that would seal the deal.

She pushed him back again. "No. I don't wish to be a consort to anyone."

His disappointment was obvious. "This place is so very strange." Keleta retracted his fangs and got up. Retrieving his shirt from the floor where he'd dropped it, he pulled it over his head to cover himself.

"Did you have a consort where you were before?"

"But of course. We all did. Many lived with us for that pur-pose. Anytime we wanted, we could feed or have sex, or both. Not like here."

Seeing a small crack into Keleta's past, Madison started get-ting excited. "You lived with other vampires?"

"Yes." A veil of wariness fell down over Keleta's face. He turned and fussed with the stereo, popping out the Usher CD and replacing it with the Black Eyed Peas.

"Tell me about it, Keleta?"

"They all want to know." He turned back around and looked at Madison. "Byron and Ricky, Samuel—they all ask." He paused, his face clouded over. "Why should I tell you? You are not one of us." He gave her a boyish grin. "Maybe if you were my consort…"

"Forget it, pal. Get your mind off your pants. And your fangs."

Madison patted the sofa next to her, but not right next to her. "Sit down and talk to me, Keleta. We're all just trying to help you. Someone tried to kill you. Just this morning, they dumped another vampire's body in the Dedhams' pool, just like they did you."

At the news, Keleta's eyes grew round, like two bowls.

"But he didn't make it, Keleta. This vampire died."

"Who was he?"

"We don't know." Then Madison remembered something. Thankful she'd brought her bag into the den with her, she dug through it and found a copy of Doug's sketch. She'd brought a few copies along to show Keleta and to leave with Byron and Ricky. She held it out to Keleta, who took it. "But this is a very good likeness."

After studying the sketch, Keleta dropped to the floor and sat cross-legged, his back against a bookcase. His eyes were closed.

"You knew him, didn't you?"

Keleta nodded but did not speak or open his eyes. Madison moved off the sofa and joined him on the large Persian rug that covered the glossy wooden floor, placing herself directly in front of him. Reaching out, she touched his hand.

"Who was he, Keleta? Please tell me."

NINE

Without looking up from his hands, Keleta said, "His name was Parker."

"Was that his last name or his first?"

Keleta shrugged. "We only went by one name at the castle. His was Parker. I was simply called Keleta."

"The castle? Was that where you lived after becoming a vampire?"

He nodded, still not looking up. "That's what she called it. It was a large house that looked like a small castle on the outside."

A house that looked like a castle. Madison stored the information away; she'd ask Notchey about it later. If it was in Los Angeles, he might know about it. "This Parker, was he an American?"

"Yes. But he did not speak like you."

"He had a noticeable accent of some kind?"

"To me, you all speak with accent." Keleta looked up at Madison. The comment could have been said in amusement, but one look at Keleta's face and she knew it wasn't. "The others made sport of him. Called him something." He closed his eyes, then opened them. "A redneck?"

Rednecks usually came from the southern part of the United States, but not always. But with a noticeable accent, Madison was betting Parker was originally from the South.

"How many vampires lived at the castle?"

He shrugged. "Maybe seven or eight of us at a time. Some came. Others left."

"Men and women?" Madison didn't know how long he'd allow her questions, so she plowed through them, keeping her warm hand on his cold one, trying to convey that she was on his side.

"All men, except for the consorts." Keleta looked past Madison, focusing on the wall behind her where there hung an original oil painting of a fruit and flower arrangement. "And her."

"Her? You mean the woman who branded you?"

He nodded, looking back down again.

"Was she the one who made you a vampire?"

Again, a nod.

"Do you think she was the one who tried to kill you?"

Keleta remained silent. Not even a nod.

"How about Parker?" Madison pressed. "Do you think this woman killed him?"

"No. Parker was liked very much. He was a favorite."

"How about other vampires? Any go missing?"

Keleta gave it some thought. "Maybe there were others. I do not know. If a vampire left, he was replaced with a new one."

"Did they say why they were leaving or where they were going?"

"No. They just left or disappeared."

"Why didn't you leave, Keleta? Did you like it there?"

He turned his face to her. His eyes were hard, his jaw set. "No, I did not. But where would I go? I couldn't return to my family." He flashed his fangs. "Not like this. My parents are good people. Christian people." He sheathed his fangs and banged his head gently against the bookcase behind him. "What would I tell them? That I stupidly went off with a strange woman and am now a *sheitan* ... a monster?"

Though not a vampire, Madison understood clearly that everyone who became a vampire had suffered the heartache of leaving those they loved behind. Doug never saw his two daughters again. Colin had yet to talk about his life before turning, but she knew it saddened him and would forever. Madison only knew one person who had turned vampire by choice, and that had been Dodie. Those who were turned against their will were forced to live a different existence in the dark. But even Dodie missed parts of her old life. One of the reasons she cooked so often for Madison and Notchey was to have familiar smells in the house, even though she and Doug could never eat anything besides blood. Colin kept bowls of citrus fruit in his condo to remind him of the past. Stacie Neroni did charity work for the homeless. Kate Thornton had married a beater, even knowing she would outlive him. They all did things to make themselves feel normal and natural, even if they weren't.

Keleta stood up and walked over to a large window that looked out onto the back yard of the house. Exterior lights showed a tidy patio with a table and chairs. The patio was edged with redwood boxes of thickly planted perky flowers. Patio lights illuminated the base of the hillside. Beyond the light, the hill was swallowed up in the dark of night.

"I didn't even know how to feed myself," Keleta continued to explain. "The consorts gave us blood to drink and a body for pleasure. We were taught nothing about being a vampire—at least none of the things Byron and Ricky are teaching me. We were taught to fight. Nothing else. Before I came here, I wanted to die but didn't know how."

"The woman provided the consorts?"

"She provided everything—our clothing, our beds, everything. All she asked in return was devotion and our presence in her bed when she requested it."

"So she made you a vampire so that you could be her consort?"

"I didn't realize it at the time, but now I see clearly. I was no different than the women she provided for us." Keleta took a deep breath and dropped his head in his hands. Suddenly, being a consort didn't seem like such a fun idea to him.

Madison got to her feet and joined Keleta by the window. "We're here to help you, Keleta. All of us. Listen to Byron and Ricky, learn everything you can from them. That's the most important thing you can do right now." She put a reassuring hand on his strong but drooping shoulder. "Who did this to you? What's her name?" When Keleta didn't answer, she added, "Was it Ann Hayes? You know, the woman in the other room?"

Keleta dropped his hands and turned from the window, staring at Madison in surprise. "The woman Samuel just introduced?"

"Yes. If it was her, you can tell me. You don't need to be afraid."

He laughed. It wasn't a happy laugh. "No, Madison, the woman who turned me into a vampire was not the lady out there." He stopped laughing and held up his arms, turning his large, strong hands into fists. "If she were, I would have tried to kill her with my bare hands."

─────────

"So he gave you no name?"

They were back in Samuel's car, just Samuel and Madison, with Hyun up front driving, separated by a soundproof partition.

"No. I asked him several times, but all he said was that they called her Lady. I believe he may not have known her name. I asked about the other vampires, too, but he wouldn't tell me that either. I couldn't tell if he was afraid or protecting someone, though it didn't sound like he was trying to protect her specifically."

"And he has no idea why she wanted him dead or why she dumped him at the Dedhams'."

"None. The last thing Keleta remembers before coming to at the pool was going to bed—with her, I might add."

Samuel took off his glasses and stared at Madison. "She bedded him, then tried to kill him?"

"That's what he remembers."

Samuel turned toward the front and blew out a gust of air. "Man, that's cold. Even for a vampire."

"How could that happen? Do you think she drugged the blood he drank? Is that possible to do to a vampire?"

Samuel went silent for a moment. When he spoke, it was in a low voice, despite the partition. "Have you ever heard of the plant called bloodroot?"

Madison shook her head but gave him her full attention.

"It's a flowering plant found almost entirely in the eastern part of North America from Canada to Florida. Sap extracted from its root resembles blood. While it can be toxic to humans, for vampires it's more of a knock-out drug. It can be administered by adding the sap to our food source or by distilling it into a liquid to be used much like chloroform."

"Does Dodie know this?"

"Of course. She even stocks it in her medicine bag. Had Keleta been unruly the day you fished him out of the pool, she no doubt would have administered it to him."

"So you think that's what Lady used to drug Keleta?"

Samuel shrugged. "Hard to tell. For all we know, there might be other substances that can do the same thing, but in all my years I've only heard of bloodroot—and only in the past few hundred years. Because its growth is not widespread, most vampires in the world have no idea about it."

"And it won't kill a vampire, not even a large dose?"

Samuel turned fully toward Madison and fixed his eyes on her. "There are only three ways to kill a vampire, Madison. Do you know what they are?"

She nodded. "A stake or hole all the way through the heart." She ticked the answer off on one of her fingers. "Beheading." Another finger snapped to attention. "And fire." A third finger straightened, completing the trilogy. "Dodie told me."

"Drugging would certainly explain why Keleta remembers nothing."

"Wasn't he also drugged when he was kidnapped and branded?"

Samuel worked the information around, trying to make connections. "Hmmm, seems this Lady is quite handy with pharmaceuticals. More importantly, I'd wager she's originally from America or has spent a great deal of time here if she knows about bloodroot."

He looked back at Madison. "And what about this Parker fellow? Did Keleta have anything to say about that?"

"Keleta has no idea why Parker ended up dead. In fact, it sounded as if he was one of Lady's favorites."

Silence filled the car's interior again while Samuel thought further about what Madison had told him.

"And he's sure this Lady creature isn't Ann Hayes?"

"He's positive. He did say that Lady was younger than Ann, and while she also has red hair, it's much lighter in color."

"Tomorrow, why don't you fill Mike Notchey in on Parker and this castle building. Let's see if he can provide any clues."

"I'm way ahead of you. I called him while you were saying goodbye to Keleta. I asked him to meet me for a run in the morning."

"Good."

"You know," Madison began, putting her own thoughts in order like cans on a shelf. "If Ann Hayes isn't the one branding these guys, maybe she's being set up, like she suggested at the meeting. Maybe someone knows she has bad blood with the Dedhams and is making it look like Ann's guilty."

"It's a very good possibility. With her arrogance and past history, I'm sure she has a lot of enemies."

Samuel's cell phone rang. He glanced at it, then pressed a button to stop the ringing. He turned his attention back to Madison. "Tell me what you think of Keleta."

"Before or after he grabbed my boob?"

Samuel threw her a look that let her know his question wasn't a joke.

"I thought Ricky and Byron provided that feedback," said Madison, not giving him a direct answer.

"They do, but I'm interested in your opinion. Keleta opened up to you, probably because you're about the same age."

"Which is why you brought me along, isn't it?"

"One of the reasons."

Madison gave it some quick but serious thought. "I like Keleta. Once we got over the consort misunderstanding and started talking about being a vampire and what happened to him, I could tell he was very disturbed and worried about his future. He's also worried about his family and the pain they've suffered not knowing what happened to him." She turned in the seat to look directly at Samuel. "Did you know Keleta was planning on becoming a doctor before this happened? A doctor, just like his father."

"He mentioned something about that to Ricky."

"It's so tragic." Madison sniffed and turned away so Samuel couldn't see the tears welling in her eyes. "Keleta had his whole life ahead of him. A super family—loving parents and two brothers. And now that's all gone." She paused to swallow the lump in her throat. "You've all lost so much, even if you do get to live forever." She thought about Parker. "Well, it seems like you live forever."

"Even the living lose. Look at yourself, Madison. You lost your mother and your innocence, and at a much younger age than most of us become vampires."

As usual, Samuel was right. Losing opportunities and loved ones was a part of life. It sucked, but that didn't make it any less of an occurrence.

They were driving along Sunset Boulevard toward Pacific Coast Highway, heading back to Topanga. Classical music played softly from the car's sound system. As the Mercedes sped along the curving road past very expensive real estate, Madison wondered how best to broach the delicate topic on her mind.

"Out with it, Madison," said Samuel, interrupting her thoughts. "Tell me what's on your mind."

She huffed in frustration. "Why don't I just let you read my mind and save us both a lot of embarrassment?"

"Because it amuses me to see you squirm." He flashed her a smirk. "Besides, nothing embarrasses me, and it would be good for you to learn not to be, as well."

"It's just that this is rather personal. Not for me, but for Keleta."

"That it is."

"Dammit." Madison stamped her foot on the floor of the car. "See, you already know what I'm going to say, so don't make me say it."

"Like I said, it amuses me."

Seeing she was not going to win the argument, which was one-sided to begin with, Madison forged ahead. "Like I told you, Keleta hit on me when we were together."

Samuel stared straight ahead, at least giving her some privacy from his prying eyes. But he still kept a smile plastered on his face. "Are you having second thoughts about rejecting his advances?"

"No, I'm not." Her tone punctuated her words.

"He is a good-looking lad."

"Still, I am *not* having second thoughts."

"Fine, then. Continue."

Madison wanted to ball up a fist and hit Samuel out of frustration. But he would only laugh that off, too. Her only path of action was to push on with her thoughts or forget about them entirely. "Okay, you win."

"I usually do."

Again, she fought the urge to pummel him with her ineffective fists.

Madison took a deep breath before beginning. "I think Keleta should go out on a date."

"A date?" Samuel looked at her, his amusement nearly neon in its intensity. "As in bringing a girl flowers and taking her to a movie?" He was toying with her, and they both knew it.

"Keleta needs to get laid." There it was, nice and blunt. "And I don't think Byron and Ricky are the ones to handle that."

"I'm sure they could provide him with a suitable companion."

"I'm sure they could, too." Her irritation level was climbing, making it more difficult to put into words what she was trying to say. "But that seems so … so clinical. From talking to Keleta, sex seems to be one of the few things he enjoyed from his early days of being a vampire. I think if he saw his new vampire life could be much more rewarding and stable but still contain that one enjoyable part from before, he might be more relaxed about … well … the adjustment."

Samuel wiped the smirk off his face and replaced it with curiosity. "Interesting theory."

Curling one leg under her, Madison twisted in her seat to face him. "Right now you have two very settled, middle-aged guys teaching him how to be a vampire." She held up both hands. "Don't get me wrong. I think Ricky and Byron are super, and they seem to be doing a great job helping Keleta. But because he's so young, I think Keleta needs more than that. I think he needs to go out and have some fun—blow off steam like other horny guys his age. And it's not just the sex. He needs to go dancing, to movies, play sports—all the usual things a guy of twenty-two would do. Even dating. Keleta needs to see that even as a vampire, his life, though bizarre, can still be somewhat normal."

"So, you think we're normal?"

"I think you all work hard at being as normal as possible."

Samuel adjusted in his seat and stared out the window for what seemed like a long time. Madison let him digest what she'd just said. When he turned back to look at her, he said, "I think you've made an excellent point, Madison."

She was pleased that her idea was well received. "I think Colin should handle that part of Keleta's adjustment. He'd be perfect at it."

Samuel gave it a bit more thought. "I think Colin is an excellent choice. He knows all the hip clubs and activities. And while he's at it, he can take you with them."

Madison frowned. "Are you that determined to pimp me out to Keleta?"

Samuel's laugh was as thick and rich as fine coffee. "No, not at all. It's just that Keleta isn't the only one who needs to be shown the fun, young side of life."

"I have fun," she protested.

"Uh-huh." Samuel took out his cell phone and started sending a text message to someone. "I'm sending Colin a message that you have something important to discuss with him about Keleta."

"Me?" Madison's mouth fell open in protest. "That's *your* department. You're the head vampire. I'm just an assistant—a peon beater."

"It's your idea and a very good one. Take responsibility for it." Samuel read an incoming message.

Madison leaned over to try to read the display. "That was fast."

"Colin wants to know what time is good for you tomorrow, early in the evening or later?" Samuel glanced at her. "I suggest early. If Colin wants to take Keleta out tomorrow night, there will still be plenty of time after you speak to him."

Madison leaned against the back of the leather car seat and crossed her arms in front of her in a sullen display. "Tell him tomorrow, after he rises."

"Done." After a pause, Samuel relayed to her Colin's next response. "He says to come by his place around seven."

"His place?"

"You know where it is, don't you?"

"You know I do."

Samuel punched his device, sending the confirmation off to Colin on the other end. "There, it's all set. His place will give the two of you more privacy for such a delicate chat."

Madison thought Samuel seemed way too pleased with himself, and it bugged her.

When they arrived at the Dedhams' home, Hyun opened the car door for them. Samuel slipped on his sunglasses and got out first. He offered his hand to Madison, helping her out of the car. He was like that—a frustrating tease one moment, an elegant gentleman the next. He walked her to the door, passing Madison's car, which was parked in the circular drive.

"You need a new car," Samuel told her.

Madison studied her car. She'd picked it up in Idaho before moving to LA. It was over ten years old, with enough dings and dents to give its finish a pimply look. It ran well enough if she kept watch over it. It had been cheap, and she'd paid cash for it. "Nothing wrong with the one I have."

Samuel wasn't convinced. "You need something more dependable and fitting your position with the council."

"I've already overhauled my wardrobe at your bidding."

"Yes, Colin told me that the two of you went shopping recently. He has quite an eye for the latest fashion, doesn't he?" He ran his eyes up and down Madison's usual jeans and sweater. "Though I haven't seen much evidence of your shopping spree."

"Hardly seems necessary to drag out the new stuff when I'm just hanging out or going to school."

His eyes moved back to the car. "Why don't you pick out something you like and let me know. The council will cover it."

"I can afford a new car if I want one, Samuel. You guys pay me very well, and the Dedhams refuse to let me pay room and board."

"The council will still pay for the car, and you can continue squirreling your money away." Samuel turned serious. "As I've told you before, Madison, vampires never know when they must disappear. If that happens, you need to be prepared to start over." His demeanor changed back to playful. "I do hope you're not still keeping your money in a tampon box."

Madison shook her head, remembering how she used to do that before coming to the Dedhams' home. Hiding money was a habit she'd developed from years of foster care, when she didn't know when or where she would be moved. Years of distrust had been layered one on top of the other like a lopsided cake.

"No. Doug has invested the money I had left from my great aunt Eleanor, and I'm building a healthy bank account thanks to my job with the council. Though I still keep ready cash, just as I'm sure you do." She fixed him with a knowing eye.

He smiled at her accurate assumption. He did have a sizeable stash ready to move with him at a moment's notice. All smart vampires did.

"Samuel," Madison began just before she pulled out her door keys, "is Keleta going to make it? I mean, will he be able to live as a vampire, or will he be … you know … terminated?"

Under the outside light, Samuel took her left hand, bent over it, and kissed her knuckles. "You have such a tender heart, Madison Rose. Tough and tender, that's you." Continuing to hold on to her hand, he said, "It's still early, but both Byron and Ricky seem to think the boy is salvageable and could have a lot to offer the vampire community in time."

Madison gave a noticeable sigh of relief. "I'm glad."

Samuel turned her hand over and studied the palm, running an index finger over her plain and solitary lifeline. When he looked up at her, a wide grin spread across his face like freshly hung laundry.

"Too bad you don't have a bloodline, Madison. You'd make an excellent vampire."

TEN

Mike Notchey picked Madison up at six forty-five for their run. Madison had crawled out of bed at six thirty.

"Long night?" he asked as soon as they were on their way.

"Yeah." Madison buckled her seat belt and slouched in the seat. "Got home around one. Bed by one thirty. An early night by council standards."

"We could have skipped the run. I could have met up with you later to get the scoop."

"The run energizes me, and I do okay on five hours of sleep."

Notchey half laughed. "Tell me that in another ten years—even in five."

On the way to the trail, Madison got him up to speed about Keleta.

"You have any ideas about this 'castle'?" Madison asked just as they were getting out of the car and warming up.

"Not off the top of my head, but I'll look into it. I do know of a place up in Glendora that looks like a castle, but I doubt that's it."

"And," she added, "Samuel wants to get me a new car. Any idea what model I should get? I'm thinking a hybrid of some kind."

Notchey grunted.

They ran in silence, with Notchey keeping a better pace with her than before. He was quickly getting used to the hilly trail. When they returned to the parking lot, Madison didn't have to wait for him. He'd arrived with her, though puffing harder and sweating more.

"Nice work, Notchey. I didn't have to leave you in the dust today."

He produced a water bottle, twisted the top off, and handed it to her. "Pretty soon, I'll be waiting on you."

She took a drink. "I doubt it, old man." She giggled and shook her water at him, splashing it in his face.

"'Old man'?"

Notchey grabbed for the bottle, but Madison quickly twisted it out of his reach. She followed the movement back around, hitting his head with another spray of water.

"So that's how it is," he said with a grin.

Using both hands, Notchey playfully made a grab for the bottle, but Madison deftly hopped out of his reach. After folding himself into a slight crouch, he leapt at her with surprising agility, trapping her against the front fender of the car. He grabbed the water bottle and tipped it over her head, with her own hand still grasped around it.

"Old man, my ass." Notchey laughed and released the bottle. He didn't move away but kept her pressed against the car.

Madison shook her head, soggy and chilly in the morning air, sending a small spray at Notchey. They were both laughing when Notchey clutched her waist in his hands and brought his mouth down hard on hers. Dropping the plastic bottle, Madison grasped his shoulders in her hands and responded.

Ignoring the early morning cold that nipped their sweaty bodies like fire ants, they kissed deeply before Notchey pulled back. He stared into her face as if seeing a stranger, then broke away from her. Without a word, he opened the passenger door for her and started around the car to the driver's side.

Madison walked the few steps to the passenger side but didn't get in. "What's going on, Mike?"

He didn't look at her. "You're cold and wet. I need to get you home."

"Oh, no." Her voice was thick with hurt and aborted passion. "I'm not buying that. Every time we get close, you do this. You break it off and act like I have a contagious disease."

He glanced at her, then looked away. "Get in the car."

Madison slapped the palm of her hand against the roof of the car. "No! Tell me what's going on." She shivered. Reaching into the car, she grabbed her warm-up jacket and slipped into it. "See, I'm all warm now. So what's the problem?"

Notchey looked around. It was shaping up to be a very gray day with possible rain. The overcast sky matched his foul mood. There were fewer cars in the parking lot than usual, the threatening weather keeping many of the morning runners home warm in their beds. He wished he'd done the same.

"Why can't you just leave it alone, Madison," he said to her over the top of the car. "I won't kiss you again. Fuck, I won't touch you again if it's going to lead to this shit."

In spite of herself, Madison started to cry. Steeling her shoulders, she sniffed back the tears and strode around the car to

Notchey. "One minute you want me, the next you act like you're disgusted by me. Are you still hung up on why I was arrested in Boise? I told you that was a long time ago, and I never once turned a trick."

"I said forget it." He turned to climb into the car, but she stopped him.

"No, Mike, I won't forget it." She grabbed his sweaty tee shirt and hung on, keeping him from getting into the car. "What is going on?"

"You really want to know?"

"Yes, I do."

He broke free of her grip and spun around, his face distorted in anger. "You may not have done tricks then, but what about now?"

Madison staggered back from the naked ferocity in his voice. "What in the hell are you talking about?"

"Now, Madison. I'm talking about now. Your new clothes. A new car. Fancy nights at Samuel's."

"I paid for those new clothes with my own money." Her protest fell on deaf ears.

"You just fucking Samuel, or is Colin getting his share, too?"

Madison couldn't believe her ears. She took a step toward Notchey, her face hot with indignation. "There is *nothing* going on between me and Samuel—or Colin. I work for them, and we're friends. That's it."

Notchey shook his head. "I've seen the way those two look at you, Madison. I've seen vampires look at women like that before. They've had you, and they want more. You'll belong to them until they've had their fill. Then they'll toss you aside like garbage."

"You're insane!"

"Am I?"

"Yes, you are. You're *certifiable*. If you don't believe me, ask the Dedhams."

"Vampires will lie for other vampires. They will always protect their own against us."

Madison leaned against the car, limp with emotional exhaustion. Looking over at Notchey, his revulsion tattooed on his face, she knew she would never be able to change his mind. It was as set as dried concrete.

"I thought you were different, Mike. I thought you liked me. Valentine's Day. The running. The dinners. You even gave me a Christmas present." She looked at him, her eyes puffy and blinking against the cold. "Was that all an act? Were you just playing me to find out information about the council?"

Notchey moved to stand in front of her, his eyes hard, stabbing into her like an awl. "It's not an act. I do like you—more than I should. More than I want to." He lifted his hand up to her face but held himself back, as if the feel of her skin would burn him. "Don't be fooled, Madison. Blood and sex, that's all vampires are about. Blood, sex, and power." He withdrew his hand. "And I'll be damned if I'll take leftovers from the likes of them."

Notchey moved to get into the car. "Now get in," he ordered. "So I can take you home."

"No." Madison stood straight and backed away from the car. "I'm not going anywhere with you."

Notchey was halfway in the car, one foot still on the pavement. "Get in the car, Madison."

"Get the hell out of here, Notchey." She spit the words at him. "I'll find my own way home."

"Come on, now. It's gotta be at least two miles, and you're tired from our run and your late night."

"Two miles," she repeated with scorn. "Enough time for me to infect you with vampire lust and suck your dick dry, just like I do the vamps."

Notchey blew out a gust of breath as he tried to rein in his own emotions to reason with her. "I'm sorry, Madison, but it's how I feel about the matter. I thought I could ignore it, but I can't."

As his words slapped her, she recoiled and took a few more steps backward. "I said, I'll find my own way home, *cop*."

Notchey finished climbing into his car and started the engine. He backed it out of its parking space and pointed it in the direction of the road. Rolling down his window, he called to her, "Last chance."

In response, Madison raised a middle finger.

After she watched Notchey's car disappear, Madison sat down on a nearby bench. She was in shock. Notchey believed she was sleeping with the vampires, at least with Samuel and possibly Colin. She'd always found both of them sexy and attractive, especially Colin. She'd even been kissed by Colin, and it had been hot, no doubt about it, but she couldn't get beyond knowing that same mouth sucked blood out of people. She was attracted to Mike, too. She found him solid and smart, even funny in his own odd way. She wanted someone like him. Someone alive and with a heartbeat. She wasn't drawn in to the glamour, power, and wealth of the undead. She wanted someone like herself—screwed up, maybe, but at least if Notchey bit her it wouldn't be as a food source.

Madison hugged herself. She was chilled in spite of her jacket, and her face stung from her tears. The dew on the bench was beginning to work its way through her leggings. She had to get home. Getting up from the bench, she started walking toward the road when a black SUV drove up and lowered its window. Inside was one of the young women she often saw running in the morning. She had strawberry blond hair pulled back into a ponytail. She looked to be in her late twenties. Madison recalled she usually ran with a man. Today she was alone.

"Do you need a lift?" the woman asked.

"Thanks, but I'm fine."

The woman jerked her chin in the direction of the road. "I saw the fight you just had with your boyfriend. Looked like a beaut."

"He's not my boyfriend. Just a … a friend." Madison wondered if she even wanted him as that anymore.

"Uh-huh. You can see I'm alone today. We fought this morning, too. Must be something in the air or the stars, or some shit like that."

Madison smiled at the remark.

"Come on," the woman said, seeing Madison's cheerier look. "Get in. I'll drive you home. Think of it as a girls-bonding-over-assholes thing."

This time, Madison laughed softly and put both of her hands on the edge of the woman's window. "Thanks anyway, but I don't live very far. Maybe the run will burn off my anger before I get home."

"Sure?"

The invitation was tempting, but Madison was a bundle of nerves. The run would do her good, even if she had finished a strenuous workout just minutes before. She also wasn't in the habit of taking rides from strangers, male or female.

"I'm sure, but thanks for being so nice."

"Anytime." The woman started to leave, then braked after moving forward a foot. "Hey," she said, hanging her head out the window. "Maybe we could run together sometime. I'll look for you."

"That would be great," Madison told her, already feeling better. "Thanks."

"My name's Julianne—Julianne Jaz."

Madison pointed at herself. "Madison Rose."

After waving goodbye to Julianne, Madison started again for the road. Once there, she broke into a steady jog. She could do two miles standing on her head, and she'd made a new friend. Mike Notchey could just piss off.

ELEVEN

By the time she ran home from the trail, it was drizzling. Madison was tired, both inside and out, with the cold penetrating through to her core. Before going up to take a hot shower, she checked the pool from the kitchen window. No body. There hadn't been one when she'd left for her run either, but she was getting skittish about vampires floating in the pool. The last thing she wanted was to go three for three.

She nodded through the patio doors to Hyun, who was guarding the place. He'd arrived shortly before she'd gotten up for her run to take over the watch from the Dedhams. Madison would be on duty with Pauline until she went to school.

"Miss Madison," Hyun called to her.

Opening the patio door, she stuck her head out, her teeth chattering. "I'll be back as soon as I shower."

Hyun was seated at the patio table, a mug of steaming coffee in front of him, along with a folded newspaper. Also in front of him was a gun, ready to be grabbed should the need arise. He wore black trousers, a black turtleneck, and a dark gray tweed jacket. On his wrist was a protective bracelet similar to her own. His glossy black hair was short and spiky. If the damp chill of the drizzly morning bothered Hyun, he didn't show it.

"There's been a change of plans." Hyun spoke with a slight accent and the clipped cadence of a man saturated with military discipline.

Putting her shower on hold for a few minutes, Madison looked at the driver/bodyguard with curiosity and stepped outside. She hugged herself against the cold. "You might as well tell me now."

"Mr. La Croix wants me here all day. He doesn't want to leave you and Mrs. Speakes on your own, especially Mrs. Speakes after you go to school."

"But vampires sleep during the day. It's the nighttime that's the real threat."

"He wants to be careful. There's a gap on Thursdays from the time Mrs. Speakes leaves until you return from class, so he asked that I stay all day."

"Okay. Whatever Samuel thinks is best." She started to go into the house, then stopped. "Have you had breakfast? When I come back downstairs, I can whip you up something." She felt her insides clench as she made the offer. On running days, she'd gotten into the habit of making breakfast for Notchey, and she looked forward to it. It had morphed from a simple meal into a fun time over eggs before he went off to work and she got ready for school.

"Thanks, but I've eaten." Hyun looked at her without expression. It was his working face. Samuel's last bodyguard had worn the same look. "I'd appreciate it if you'd just keep the coffee coming."

"Do you know where the bathroom is? With all that coffee, you'd better."

"Just inside the door, to the left." There was no humor in his voice, just a robotic monotone delivering facts unencumbered by frills. She'd half expected Hyun to produce a portable urinal.

With a nod, Madison left to go upstairs and shower.

When she returned from school, Hyun wasn't at the patio table but walking the perimeter of the Dedham property. When he saw her, he made his way to the patio.

"Everything okay?" she asked him.

"Fine."

Hyun looked just as fresh and alert as when she'd left him earlier in the day, except now he was wearing sunglasses. The drizzle had disappeared by late morning, leaving in its wake a glorious California day, even for February. Madison, on the other hand, felt like a dishrag that had been tossed under the sink and left to mildew. The day had taken its toll on her, from not enough sleep to the fight with Notchey to the long day in the classroom.

"Would you like me to spell you?" she asked.

"I'm good. I'll be going shortly after the Dedhams get up." Hyun looked directly into Madison's face but revealed no emotion. "You look like you're ready to drop."

"I am very tired."

"Why don't you take a nap. I'll be fine down here."

"You sure?"

For the first time, Madison saw the barest hint of a smile on Hyun's face. "It's my job to protect you, not the other way around."

Madison thanked him and started to leave. A nap was exactly what she needed. She wanted to be alert tonight for her meeting with Colin. Before going back into the house, she turned around.

"Hyun, did you work with other vampires before coming to work for Samuel?"

If the bodyguard was surprised by the question, he didn't show it. "Yes. I've worked for one other."

"Have you ever seen anything like this? I mean, vampires being murdered and dumped in swimming pools?"

Hyun paused briefly before answering but never turned his face away from hers. "I've seen much worse, Miss Madison. Much worse."

"In general or regarding vampires?" Before he could answer, she added, "Oh, and please drop the Miss. It's just Madison."

"Both. It's fairly civil here. In some parts of the world, vampires hunt both humans and other vampires." He hesitated slightly, but his face remained impassive. "Just for sport."

A cold hand clutched her heart at the thought of being hunted like an animal. "I was told it was like that here before Samuel came."

"Yes, although California was not near as barbaric as some other areas of the world. Mr. La Croix is quite famous throughout the entire vampire nation. I am honored he chose me to serve him."

"Do you mind my asking these questions?"

"Not as long as you understand there are some things of which I cannot speak."

Madison nodded. She'd ridden in Samuel's car enough to know the privacy partition wasn't always in place. As Samuel's driver, Hyun overheard a lot of juicy information. "I do understand." She took a minute to phrase her next question. "Did you see the tattoo on Keleta's back?"

"No, but Mr. La Croix told me about it. He asked if I had ever seen anything like it before."

"Had you?" Madison leaned forward, hoping it was territory Hyun would discuss.

"Yes. On a couple of male vampires."

"Where?"

"At my last employer's."

"How about Ann Hayes? Had you ever come in contact with her before?"

"Yes. She was a frequent guest of my last employer. The male vampires with the tattoo were part of her entourage."

Tired as she was, Madison tried to fit the information together like a cap to a bottle. "And Samuel knows this?"

"Of course. I told him as soon as I recognized her."

Madison squinted at Hyun. "Did she recognize you?"

"I do not believe she did. Ms. Hayes is not the type to pay attention to the hired help."

"Humph." That sounded like Ann Hayes. "Hyun, who did you work for? Was it someone local?"

Without moving his mouth, Hyun laughed, the sound coming from inside his throat like someone digging to get out. "No, Madison. I worked for His Majesty King Leopold."

He said the name as if she should automatically recognize it, but she didn't. Too embarrassed by her lack of knowledge of vampire hierarchy, she thanked Hyun for his time and went into the house.

Upstairs, Madison did not head straight to her nap. Instead, she turned on her laptop. Notchey had said he'd look into buildings that could be taken as castles, but she wasn't about to wait around for him. Not after this morning.

Starting with Google, Madison searched for castles in California. The most obvious—Hearst Castle—topped the list of results. There was a winery and a castle-sized hotel that was for sale. She also found references to the Sleeping Beauty Castle in Disneyland and the one in Glendora that Notchey had mentioned. One link led her to a site that featured all the castles in California. She had no idea there were so many. Most were open to the public for tours, one was available for a weekly rental, and some were closed. There even two that were still private residences, but those were located in Northern California.

Keleta had said the castle was a large building that looked like a castle. Most of the ones listed online were either real castles or looked like castles, but Madison's gut told her Lady would not choose to set up shop in a building so publicly known. Keleta's castle was probably in Southern California in order for Lady to transport the bodies easily, and it was most likely in a rural area or someplace where the natural vegetation afforded a lot of privacy—like the part of Topanga where the Dedhams' house was located, or someplace similar. Madison wasn't familiar with all the local areas that fit that description. She'd ask Notchey. Notchey again; well, that convenient source wasn't available any longer. She didn't need him anyway. Whatever he knew, she could find out on her own. It would take her longer, but it wouldn't be impossible.

She leaned back in her chair and tried to think of how she could find out about large properties close to Los Angeles but still relatively private. Applying her fingers to the keyboard, she searched for a particular realtor's information. She'd seen the company's name on signs around the area where Samuel lived. If that realty agency did business in that high-end neighborhood, someone at that office might know of properties, available or not, of the size she was searching. Once she'd located the phone number, she made the call. A woman answered.

"Hello, my name is Madison, and I'm calling about a very specific type of property." Madison sat up straighter to give her voice more authority. "I was hoping you or your agency could help."

"Is this for yourself?"

"No, it's for my employer. Actually, it's for a special project he has in mind."

"And your employer is?"

"He wishes to remain anonymous at this time. I'm sure you understand." Madison knew if the realty agency dealt with ultra-high-end properties, the woman wouldn't be put off by an anonymous buyer in the least. In Los Angeles, with its celebrities and entertainment executives, such initial tactics were business as usual when feeling out a deal.

"I certainly *understand*." The woman's emphasis told Madison the realtor was hooked and hungry for a Moby Dick–sized commission. "What is it your employer is looking for specifically?"

"A very large property and house. Something close to Los Angeles and very private. The home should be able to comfortably accommodate..." Madison paused just long enough to make a guestimate of how many people Lady might have had living at the castle. "Oh, about twenty adults, including staff."

"Twenty adults." The woman paused, but her composure never slipped. "Will this be a commercial endeavor? We do have a very capable commercial division."

"No, private. My employer is looking to open up his residence to friends for indefinite stays." Madison's words flowed through the phone like olive oil. She'd learned to lie growing up like second-hand clothing being dragged from house to house; the finesse she was learning at the feet of the vampires.

"He plans," she continued, "to open the home to his various artistic friends. You know, a quiet and private place where they can get away and write and paint and be brilliant without the stress of day-to-day life impeding their craft."

"Oh, like a patron to the arts." The woman's voice brightened at the thought of the next Harper Lee or Van Gogh being nurtured in a home she'd found.

"Yes, exactly." Madison paused as she thought of what else to add. "Oh, and he prefers classic European architecture. In fact, he has a slight thing for castles. It's not a dealbreaker, but it will help."

"There might be several properties on the market at this time that could meet your needs. I would be happy to do some research on their availability and get back to you."

"That would be lovely. Thank you." Madison twirled a strand of hair around her finger. "And even if something is not for sale, please let us know about the property. My employer can be quite persuasive when he finds something he wants."

"What about a lease? Would he be interested in leasing if I found the right property?"

"I'm sure he'd be interested in anything you find that fits his need."

"Wonderful," the woman gushed. Madison gave the woman her cell number and hung up.

She yawned. Fighting the urge to stretch out on the bed, Madison continued her Internet search, this time for a King Leopold. The search brought up Leopold II of Belgium, a monarch who visited atrocities upon the people of the Congo and maimed thousands of its children, as well as information on Leopold I, the first king of Belgium. She also searched for vampire royalty or vampire kings and came up with nothing but references to fiction and TV shows.

With each new bit of information, her eyes grew heavier.

———————

"Madison."

Madison stirred but didn't open her eyes. Dodie jiggled her shoulder again. "Madison, dear, wake up."

Raising her head slowly from the desk, she squinted at Dodie. Her neck ached, and her face felt numb. "What time is it?"

"After six. Don't you have an appointment with Colin tonight?"

Madison moved her chin in what passed as a weak nod. "Yeah, but I'd rather go back to bed."

Dodie smiled down at her. "I don't think napping with your head on your desk constitutes sleeping in a bed."

Straightening up, Madison stretched. "Thanks for waking me up. I was doing some research on the computer and must have fallen asleep."

Dodie picked up an article of clothing from a nearby chair and folded it. "Take your time getting ready. I'm sure Colin won't mind if you're a tiny bit late."

Madison stood up and groaned, her body stiff from being hunched over the desk.

Once Madison's head cleared, she caught on that Dodie was stalling. She'd picked up several pieces of clothing and folded them—some twice.

"Something wrong, Dodie? You're folding my dirty laundry."

Dodie looked at the shirt in her hand, shook her head, and put it down. She sat on the edge of the bed. "Has something happened between you and Mike? Something unpleasant?"

Madison shrugged and moved to her closet, pretending to pick out something to wear that night.

"Madison, what is it?"

"What makes you think we had a fight?"

"I never said fight—not specifically."

Madison didn't turn around. She knew Dodie had a special insight into people's thoughts and feelings. It wasn't of the same caliber as Samuel's mental eavesdropping, but she was very accurate. "Okay, then. What makes you think something *unpleasant* happened?"

"I called him and asked if he wanted to come by tomorrow night for pot roast. He turned it down. First time in all the time we've known him he's turned down my pot roast."

"Maybe he was busy."

Dodie got up and walked over and put a tender hand on Madison's arm. "I respect the fact that you don't want to tell me, dear. And I won't pry. But if you need to talk, I'm always here."

Finally, Madison looked at Dodie. "I know that." She gave the older woman a small smile of affection. "Maybe I will. But first I need to sort it all out myself."

"Like you, Mike has had a hard life, but I know he cares very deeply for you. Never forget that."

Madison wasn't so sure. Pushing aside her own thoughts and happy to change the subject, she studied Dodie's outfit—chiffon evening pants with a silver sequin jacket. "You look lovely. You and Doug going out tonight?"

"Yes, we are. Samuel has invited us to dinner. There's a new vampire restaurant over in Hollywood off of Melrose. It's supposed to be very chic. Keleta will be joining us."

"Keleta? You guys hoping a nice environment and a full tummy will loosen his tongue?"

"That and a little grandparently attention." Dodie shot Madison a sly grin. "Hyun will stand guard while we're gone."

Whatever the motives behind taking Keleta to dinner, Samuel and the council generally did their skullduggery in style. If he wasn't careful, by the end of the meal, Keleta would be pouring out his deepest secrets, including those he didn't know he had.

"You guys have a nice time. I'll be anxious to hear what Keleta tells you."

Dodie walked over to the closet and pulled out one of the new pieces Madison had bought on her shopping spree with Colin. The tags were still on it. "Why don't you wear this tonight." She handed it to Madison. "It will look smashing with your new leggings."

After planting a light kiss on Madison's cheek and reminding her to eat some supper, Dodie left.

Madison looked down at the garment in her hand. It was a slate-gray cashmere tunic with a wide ruffle circling the low and daring neckline and going down the front to the hem. It felt sensuous and delicious against her skin. She'd loved it in the store. So had Colin.

It was about time she starting wearing her new clothing—clothing she'd paid for herself. Retrieving a small pair of cuticle scissors from the bathroom, she snipped off the tags as if applying the guillotine to Mike Notchey's neck.

TWELVE

Colin Reddy's two-bedroom condominium was on one of the top floors of an elegant high rise on Pacific Coast Highway in Santa Monica. It had a killer view of the ocean. Looking out the wall of windows at night gave one the feeling of floating in space. Madison stood before the windows and lost herself in the black void.

"You seem a million miles away." Colin came up from behind and handed her a heavy mug of hot, aromatic tea. It was a special blend he obtained from a tea shop located in a mall in Century City. He couldn't drink it himself but loved brewing it to fill his home with its spicy bite. "Have you eaten? I can order something in for you."

"Thank you, but I had supper at home." She smiled to herself. "Dodie reminded me." Madison often forgot that when she spent time with vampires, she might go a long while before she had an opportunity to eat. Samuel always kept food in his home for his human friends and guests, but Colin never did.

Colin leaned against the wall, his eyes resting on Madison. Born to an English nobleman and his Indian mistress, Colin had thick, black, wavy hair, penetrating dark eyes, and expressive eyebrows. His face was ruggedly handsome, made even more so by his closely cropped beard. Tonight he was dressed in his usual black jeans, along with a black silk shirt worn loose and half unbuttoned. The sleeves of the shirt were rolled up, showing off his sinewy forearms. His feet were bare. He was tall and lean, with wide shoulders and a sullen bad-boy attitude that only added to his looks.

"And what did you have?" he asked.

Madison took a sip of tea and looked at him over the rim. "You want to know what I had to eat before I came here?"

"Yes, I do." He flashed his eyes at her but didn't offer a smile. "Humor me. It's as close to real food as I'm allowed."

"Okay, if you insist. But I warn you, it was pretty boring."

She moved from the window to the large black leather sofa and sat down. Beneath her, the leather felt like soft cotton. Colin's condo was gorgeous but stark, like a set for an interior design studio. Even the large, expensive oil paintings on the wall were void of much emotion. The furniture was either black leather or black lacquer, the area rugs were textured muted tones over a glistening slate floor, and the counters in the kitchen area were granite. On one large wall hung a huge flat-screen TV that beckoned for action like a junior movie screen. Beneath that, a cabinet held top of the line video and audio equipment and an eclectic selection of music from around the world. Classical jazz currently floated from it as soft background music. On the coffee table and the counter were tasteful bowls filled with citrus fruits, some pierced with whole cloves. Colin, sensitive to smells, kept them as a reminder of his past human life, similar to the spicy tea. It was an immaculate masculine haven, cold and beautiful, like Colin.

"I had a grilled cheese sandwich and tomato soup."

"What kind of cheese?"

"Sharp cheddar."

"Thank god. For a moment, I was afraid you were going to say that American rubbish."

"Have you ever tasted that *American rubbish*?"

"Of course not."

She pointed an index finger at him. "Then don't knock it till you've tried it. I grew up on the stuff."

"I rest my case."

She laughed and placed the mug on the heavy glass top of the stone coffee table in front of the sofa. "This new?" She indicated the coffee table.

"Yes." He walked over to the table. "You like it?"

She studied it closer. "It looks like a real headstone."

"Actually, it's made of several. I heard about an old graveyard being dug up for development and called about buying some of the stones. Unfortunately for its residents, the cemetery wasn't old enough to be considered historical, but it was old enough that it had fallen into neglect. I took the stones to a chap in Venice. He made the table for me." Colin crouched down and ran a hand over the faded engraving on one of the outside stones.

"It's fascinating," she admitted, "in a disturbing sort of way."

"Rather like me?" He granted her a crooked smile. Colin Reddy didn't smile much, but when he did, he could charm the undies off a nun.

"Get a grip, Reddy." Madison, keenly aware she was far from being a nun, crossed her legs and moved to the purpose of their meeting. "I was talking to Samuel about Keleta, and he thought I should bring it up to you."

Colin moved to the sofa. Sitting on the end cushion, he lounged back against the arm and faced her, one long leg stretched out on the floor, with the other bent up on the cushions. "I'm all ears."

Picking up her mug, Madison focused on her tea rather than facing him while she explained her idea about Keleta. Holding the mug helped steady her shaking hands. She was physically attracted to Colin, and the delicate topic wasn't keeping her internal temperature at bay. Usually when they were together, it was out in public or with the other vampires.

"So basically," Colin said when she was finished, "you want me to get Keleta laid." It was the same phrase she'd used with Samuel, and hearing it now from Colin, it seemed so primal and nasty, but not necessarily in a bad way.

She turned to him in frustration. "What I want is for Keleta to see that his life isn't over—that as a vampire he can live a full and satisfying one. I want you to show him a good time."

"Same sort of thing, isn't it?" Colin sat up slightly and eyed Madison's chest. "By the way, that sweater looks smashing on you. I was afraid I'd never see it outside the boutique."

Madison squirmed and softly tugged at the neckline, wishing it wasn't quite so low. Her cleavage, round and perky, peeked through the folds of the ruffles.

She stood up. "I think you've got the right idea, so I'll leave it up to you."

"There's a private party in Brentwood Saturday night. I'll take him."

"A vampire party?"

"For the most part. There will also be quite a few hot vampire-friendly beaters in attendance, both male and female."

Vampire-friendly, Madison knew, was code for beaters who hung out with vampires and could be trusted to keep their secrets. Many got high on providing sex and blood to the undead.

"You should come, too. You can wear that sizzling ruby silk halter top and leather pants we picked up."

Madison knew exactly which outfit Colin meant. When they'd gone shopping, he'd helped her pick out conservative but elegant clothing suitable for when she accompanied Samuel on council business. They'd also picked up better casual clothing like the tunic she was wearing tonight. Colin had also insisted she needed a couple of outfits for nightclubs. In the end, she'd given in.

"Will Miriam be there?"

"I hope so." Colin flashed his slow, sexy half smile again. "She'd be perfect for showing Keleta a good time."

Miriam was a former member of a vampirism cult. A few months ago, she hadn't even known real vampires existed. She had a big crush on Colin, and once she discovered who and what he was, she left the cult to party with the real thing. Madison had seen her at some of the parties and clubs she'd gone to with Colin, and it was plain to see Miriam still had the hots for him. Though he never said anything, Madison suspected Colin saw Miriam from time to time.

"You mean you'd share her with Keleta?"

"Miriam is a free agent, and an adventurous one at that." Colin put both feet on the floor and stood up, his chest nearly touching Madison's. "If I didn't know better, I'd say you were jealous."

"Don't be stupid. I am not jealous. I just want to make sure Keleta has some fun."

Colin laughed. "Trust me, with Miriam, Keleta will have a bloody good time." When Madison scowled, he took hold of her upper arm. "And you might be interested in knowing that Miriam is a university graduate and owns her own business."

"Which is more than I have," Madison jerked her arm away. "Right?"

"I didn't say that. What I am saying is you're either a snob or jealous." He cocked a thick eyebrow at her. "I prefer the jealous theory myself."

Madison stalked to the window and looked out. Why were the men in her life being so difficult today? *Just leave,* she told herself. *You've discussed Keleta, there is no need to hang around.* But she couldn't make herself move for the door.

"So Ann Hayes is the one who turned you into a vampire." Madison spoke to the night sky, keeping her back to Colin.

"You're jealous of her now, too?"

Pivoting on one foot, Madison swung back around. "I am not jealous of anyone, Colin Reddy. Get that through that thick, undead head of yours. I just want to figure out who's behind all this."

Madison left the window and went back to the table to collect her tea. She took a big gulp of it before continuing. "She must have some idea who's copying her brand."

"If she does, she's not saying." Colin held out his hand for her mug. "Let me make you a fresh cup."

Madison took another gulp and handed him the mug. He took it into the kitchen area on the other side of the granite counter. "I grilled her pretty well, but Ann is insisting she has no idea who is doing the branding or the killing."

"Do you believe her?"

Colin put a kettle of water on the stove and retrieved a fresh mug and tea from the cupboard. "I believe she is not the one behind this. Whether I believe she has no suspicions of her own, I'm not so sure. But I have no doubt that Ann is doing her own investigation even as we do ours. She's too narcissistic to allow anyone to use that brand, even if she's no longer using it herself."

Comfortable talking about the situation involving Ann Hayes, Madison took her seat back on the sofa. "And you have no idea who the dead vampire is?"

"None. If I did, I would have told the council immediately."

Colin brought Madison her fresh tea. The mug was warm and comforting in her hands. He sat back down on the sofa and leaned against the arm, as he had before, and watched her as she blew over the surface of the hot liquid.

"You want to ask me about Ann, don't you?" he asked.

She put the mug down on the table and turned to him. "Yes, but not if you're going to accuse me of being jealous."

Colin ignored the remark. "I met Ann, though she was known as Annabelle then, while traveling in India. My mother died when I was around ten. I was raised and educated along with my father's two legitimate sons until he died when I was about twenty-four. At that time, I was given a decent sum of money by my father's wife and told to disappear or something unfortunate would happen to me. I took the money and left."

"But why would she do that?"

"I was older than my two half brothers, and the Duchess was afraid I would try to lay claim to my father's title and lands. And even if I didn't, my future would always be in question and tainted by my bastard status. So I took the offered purse and set out to find my own fortune. I was well educated and highly trained as a soldier. It was easy to find work over the years, no matter where I went. Eventually, I made my way to India, where I tried to find my mother's people."

"Did you find them?"

"No, I never did. But in Bombay I did find Ann." Colin half smiled to himself at the memory. "She was beautiful and exciting. An older woman with much to teach a young man so far from home."

"Did you know she was a vampire?"

"Not at first, though I did suspect something was different about her. While we made love, we never slept together. She was never up during the day. When I asked about her, her maid simply said she was not seeing anyone."

Colin stood and wandered over to the counter. Picking up a clove-studded orange, he held it in his hand and squeezed gently. "The idea of her being a vampire never crossed my mind. I didn't believe in such creatures, and if I had, they would never in my wildest imagination have been as alluring or as beautiful as Ann. After about a month, I became restless. I didn't like being kept around like a pet and told her I was moving on. That night, while making love, she told me what she was and bit me for the first time."

"You must have been scared out of your mind."

"On the contrary, I was totally captivated. Once Ann showed her true self to me and left restraint behind, I only wanted her more. Like a powerful narcotic." Colin paused before adding, "Not unlike what the fair Miriam feels."

"Your point is taken." Madison had heard before how some humans were nearly addicted to the combination of sex and being bitten. She'd met some. Miriam had been that way even before she knew about vampires. In some of the vampirism cults, sex and blood sharing between members was seen as a religious experience or rite.

"Ann and I went along like that for another spell before she explained about bloodlines and pointed out that I had one. When she asked if I wanted to be a vampire, I eagerly said yes."

Madison sloshed her tea. "You *wanted* to become a vampire?"

With one hand, Colin grabbed a paper towel from the kitchen and brought it to her. "Absolutely. Power, sex, eternal life—a difficult gig to turn down, don't you think? Especially for a bloke like me—a half-caste bastard without family or future." Colin looked directly at her as he spoke. "You'd be surprised how many vampires became this way by choice."

"Until now, Dodie was the only one I knew."

"Knew of, you mean." Colin shook his head with slow amusement. "Isabella Claussen is another. And Stacie Neroni. And Ricky turned Byron at his request."

Madison's mouth sagged open more with each name. She snapped it shut. "But the branding—is that normal?"

Raising a finger on the hand not holding the orange, Colin pointed at Madison. "That part Ann didn't share. I knew nothing about the branding until I found myself drugged and tied facedown on a bed, with a hot iron being applied to my back." His voice turned bitter. "I'd seen more than my share of men being branded for punishment or as slaves, and I wasn't about to be branded myself. Not by choice."

It wasn't making sense to Madison. "I don't understand why she did it, especially if you were willing to become a vampire."

"With Ann, everything returns to her ego. No matter where I went in the world, for eternity I would always be her property, at least in her mind." Colin squeezed the orange again. This time, Madison picked up the sweet, oily scent as it escaped cracks in the rind. "After the brand healed, she turned me into a vampire."

He walked into the kitchen, deposited the broken orange in the sink, and washed his sticky hands.

Madison got up from the sofa and stood at the counter watching Colin dry his hands on a towel. "How long did you stay with her after that?"

He shrugged. "A few decades, maybe more. We traveled the world and took many lovers between us, all human. Even took lives, though Ann wasn't one for wanton bloodlust, and I had seen too much of it in my own travels for it to be an attraction."

Colin had admitted to murder as easily as if he'd told Madison he'd just taken out the trash. Her shock must have showed because Colin came out of the kitchen and stood before her, his hands gripping her shoulders in a vice. He shook her gently. "All vampires kill, Madison. At some point, all of us have killed and will kill again. It's in our nature. Even your precious Doug and Dodie have human blood on their hands."

Madison's thoughts went to Bobby Piper. She'd seen the Dedhams kill Bobby. They'd done it to save her life; that's how she'd met them. Mike Notchey, too, had warned her about forgetting that the vampires, for all their wealth and external sophistication, were really just unnatural monsters with wild animal instincts.

She pulled away from his grasp. "I do understand that, Colin. I've seen the Dedhams kill and feed. Remember?"

She walked back to the windows and stared at the blackness beyond, wishing she could step out and fly into the night—to feel weightless, inside and out. "I'm not naïve. I know I'm only alive by the council's good graces and that my situation could change at any time. It's like walking a tightrope above the Grand Canyon." She turned to him, her arms crossed, her face tight with emotional stress. "Every day it's like that." After staring at Colin a long moment, she turned back to the view.

Colin approached. Standing behind Madison, he placed his hands once again on her shoulders, this time gently. He kissed the top of her head.

"There are days," he told her, his voice barely above a whisper, "when I wish you'd never come to us. Not that I wanted Piper and his pals to kill you, but sometimes, Madison, I wish you'd been able to live your life in ignorance of all this."

She leaned back against him, taking comfort, if not warmth, from the solidness of his physical presence.

"Me, too," she said softly, keeping her eyes straight ahead.

Moving his hands from her shoulders down her arms, Colin slowly wrapped them around Madison's front, enfolding her in a cocoon. He nestled his face in the crook of her warm, long neck and ran his beard along her smooth skin. Madison closed her eyes. When Colin kissed her neck, she sighed.

Then he bit her.

She froze, her next breath caught in her throat. He hadn't bitten her with his fangs but with his lips, but it was enough to remind Madison who—or what—had her in a tight embrace.

Colin kissed and nibbled Madison's neck a few more times. When he stopped, both of them looked straight ahead, not at the view but at their reflections in the window.

"Do you want me to stop?" he asked in a whisper that caressed her ear.

Loosening Colin's arms, she turned within them until she could stare up into his dark eyes. In response, she tilted her mouth up toward his in invitation. He returned his RSVP by bringing his own mouth down on hers, first with softness, testing her decision. For the second kiss, his mouth came down on hers with no holding back.

THIRTEEN

For all his usual sullenness, Colin was a playful lover. As their mouths locked and tongues danced, they both laughed without breaking the connection. He reached under her top and tweaked and tickled her body. Madison squirmed with unselfconscious delight.

When Colin started pulling the tunic over her head, Madison stopped him with a coy look. "I thought you liked this on me."

He grinned. "Perhaps, but I think I'd enjoy it more off."

Once her top hit the floor, Colin deftly dispatched her bra and pushed her up against a nearby wall as his mouth found her naked breasts. Madison shuddered and moaned and wrapped one of her long legs around one of his. Grasping his thick hair, she pulled him closer to her as he nipped, kissed, and licked her chest as he had her neck.

There was no doubt in Madison's mind that Colin knew how to please a woman. No wonder Miriam followed him around like a lovesick puppy. Thoughts of Miriam quickly vanished as Colin yanked on Madison's leggings and swore under his breath.

"Bloody things are stuck to you like paint."

She kicked off her shoes and wiggled out of the pants with a smile on her face. "Well, you picked them out."

"Next time, remind me to get something with easier access, will you? Maybe one of those Hawaiian muumuus or some other equally ridiculous item."

They studied each other a moment before their mouths met again, this time with a fiery hunger. Colin grabbed both of Madison's wrists and pulled her arms high above her head while his mouth devoured and his tongue tasted. When Madison's breathing changed to short, fast breaths, he unleashed his fangs and traced her elegant neck with them from her ear down to her right nipple. She could feel their sharpness playing with her trembling flesh, taunting her with their danger.

Colin worked his way back up to her neck, then pulled back to look at her flushed face. "You frightened?"

It took her a minute, but slowly she shook her head. "No."

He grinned, his fangs made even more terrible by the gesture, and grazed her lips with his own before moving them across her cheek to her ear. "Liar."

She cried out when he nipped her right earlobe. It stung like a quick cut from a sharp paring knife. As her warm blood trickled down her neck, she held her breath. Colin moaned and flicked his tongue at the small drip, licking it clean from where it strayed up to its source. Clamping his mouth against her lobe, he nursed on the small gash and tongued her ear until Madison felt her eyes roll back into her head with pleasure.

"Delicious," he whispered.

When he stopped sucking, Colin sheathed his fangs and broke away, moving back several feet.

Baffled and confused, Madison covered her exposed breasts and looked at him, unsure of what to do, worried that it was Mike Notchey all over again. Was Colin disgusted by her, too? He didn't seem to be until now, but why the sudden change? As humiliation overtook her passion, her eyes drifted to the floor and her discarded clothing. She reached for them.

"Don't," he told her. "I simply want to look at you." His eyes scanned her up and down, taking their time, drinking in every physical feature. "You are so beautiful."

Madison nearly collapsed with relief. This man—this supposed monster—wasn't going to reject her at all. He wanted her. And she wanted him. She lowered her arms and stood looking back at him.

"So, luv." He approached her. Reaching out an index finger, he scooped up a droplet of blood that had fallen from her ear to her neck and licked it off his finger tip. "How do you like vampire foreplay so far?"

When Madison laughed, Colin took it as a good sign. He playfully lunged for her and started to pick her up. She held up a hand to stop him.

"Don't tell me," she giggled, "that you're going to sweep me off my feet and carry me into the bedroom like in some romance novel."

He narrowed his dark eyes at her and flicked a piece of her hair from her face. "Yes, I can see you are far too much of a realist for that cheesy move."

Without another word, Colin grabbed her by the wrist and slung her over his shoulder like a sack of potatoes. "This better?" He slapped her bottom with affection.

"Much."

After roughly depositing her on his king-sized bed, Colin stepped back. The only light in the room came from an amber torchiere in the corner and what little filtered in from the living area. Without taking his eyes off of her, he pulled off his shirt and undid his jeans, dropping them to the floor.

She studied his body with appreciation, as he had done hers. "Do all vampires go commando?"

He flashed her an arrogant look. "Only the really cool ones."

Naked, he pivoted like a fashion model. "See. All the same equipment, in all the same places as those beater blokes." He approached the bed.

"Turn around," Madison told him when he reached her. "I want to see the brand."

He hesitated but did as she asked. At the small of his back, just above his firm bottom, was the same brand she'd seen on Keleta and Parker. The skin was a different color at the site and slightly raised. She traced it with a fingertip. Putting a hand on Colin's hip, Madison raised herself up and kissed the brand. Under her touch, she felt Colin's muscles clench, then relax.

Colin moved to the end of the bed. Bending over, he grasped each one of Madison's ankles and yanked her to him at the edge. She gave a yelp of surprise, then broke into giggles.

With a hand on each of her legs, starting with the ankles, he moved his hands up her legs in a firm, slow caress, keeping his eyes on her. His touch was cool and dry yet still created a heat she couldn't ignore. When his hands reached her hips, he latched his fingers around the thin band of her bikini panties and slowly started pulling them down, retracing his earlier path down to her ankles. Once he'd removed them, he tossed them on the floor by his own clothing.

Madison never took her eyes from Colin's face. She had always known he found her sexually attractive, but tonight he was studying her, touching her, with more intensity and in a different way than he ever had before. She'd expected a vampire to make love in a rough and forceful manner, but Colin was adept and caring in each touch of her flesh. She'd seen him with Miriam once, and he hadn't been this gentle with her. He'd ravished her, and Miriam had loved it, turning into an animal right along with Colin. With Madison, Colin was taking his time, enjoying each delicious moment as much as she was.

Still, she was nervous. Colin was going to bite her; she knew it and was torn inside about it. She closed her eyes and tried not to think about it. Notchey had said the vampires only cared about sex and blood and power. Colin had said as much himself. Maybe Notchey was right, but they had the power and he didn't. Notchey had already condemned her, so why not enjoy the sex he was so sure she was getting?

Colin kissed the inside of her thigh, the soft, fleshy area just below her crotch, and Madison tried to forget about Mike Notchey and what he'd said. She sighed and opened her eyes.

From between her legs Colin looked up at her. He kissed her flesh again and tongued the area. "Right here," he told her, licking the area again as if swabbing it. "Right here is the best place to bite."

"Not on the neck?"

He sat up on his knees and gave her a small smile. "No, the best is right here." He touched her inside thigh, sending a charge through her body. "It's sweet and won't show." He moved between her legs, lowering his body over hers, and bent to kiss her breasts. "But not for a first time."

Colin kissed his way up to Madison's mouth, coming down on it harsher than before, consuming her with his growing passion. She responded under his touch, but it wasn't with the fever of before. Her body wanted him more than she'd ever wanted a man, but her mind was splintered with worry planted by Notchey and fertilized by her own self-doubt.

Colin stopped kissing her. He didn't move away but hovered over her, his mouth still above hers, their lips barely touching. His body covered hers like a blanket. Their intimacy so close to completion, she could barely breathe. Her eyes were closed tight.

"I thought you wanted this," he said, his lips touching hers as they moved.

"I do." Madison didn't open her eyes. She squeezed them tight to shut out thoughts of Notchey and the fight they'd had. What he'd said about the vampires haunted her like a dead relative.

Colin hesitated, studying her tight face and shut eyes, then kissed her again. After a moment, he stopped and shook his head in frustration. He rolled off her to his side. "You're going to have to work with me, Madison. I may be dead, but I'm really not into necrophilia."

Her eyes snapped open, and she turned her head in his direction. They were nearly nose to nose. "What?"

Rolling onto his back, Colin covered his eyes with an arm. "Christ, I made a hash of that."

Madison jumped out of bed. "If that means you screwed up, yeah, you did." She looked around for her clothes. "Unless in the vampire world calling your lover a corpse is a term of endearment." She stopped scavenging to fix Colin with an angry eye. "I'm sure the maid Miriam is a lot livelier than I am in the sack."

"Don't be like that, Madison." Colin had turned on his side to watch her huff and puff around the room. He patted the bed. "Come on back to bed."

Remembering that her clothes were in the other room, Madison picked up Colin's shirt and slipped into it. She eyed the bed and Colin with a lustful but wary eye. Instead of returning to the bed, she sat down in a nearby reading chair and curled her long legs up under her.

Colin got off the bed and came to her. Kneeling, he took her hands in his. She looked away. "I'm sorry I said such an awful thing. Truly, I am. It's just that I was so frustrated with your change of heart. And at such an … inopportune time."

"I didn't change my mind, Colin." She still didn't look at him.

"Yes, you did." He tapped the bracelet on her wrist.

Madison glanced down at the council's bracelet. It was nestled against two colorful beaded bracelets she'd picked up while combing the shops on Venice Beach.

Confused, she looked at Colin. "I don't understand. This is supposed to protect me."

"And it's working," he said in a wry tone. "Certainly against me."

"But I want this, Colin."

"And so do I, very much. But while your mouth is saying yes, your heart and mind are saying no." He tapped the bracelet again. "And that is what this reads."

"What is it, some sort of voodoo?"

Colin shrugged. "Not sure. It's one—"

Raising a hand, she cut him off. "Don't tell me: it's one of those mysterious things vampires just learn to accept. Dodie tells me that all the time."

"Dodie's right. I'm four hundred years old, and I'm still learning."

He took her hands in his again. "Tell me, Madison, what changed your mind from the living room to the bedroom? Is it because of what happened to you as a young girl?"

She shook her head and pulled her hands out of his. It was bad enough Samuel could read her mind, and sometimes Dodie could sense what she was feeling, but now this bracelet ... It had protected her against Keleta's advances and now against Colin, even though physically she wanted Colin. Her head had been filled with doubt planted by Mike Notchey—crammed with worry about being used by the vampires. Had the bracelet weighed and considered that?

When she didn't answer, Colin stood. "It wasn't just the bracelet that made me stop." He picked up his jeans from the floor and began pulling them on, covering his nakedness. "Whether you realize it or not, you were just lying there, frozen and immobile, like you were resigned to a fate worse than death. Hardly the vibes a bloke likes when making love to a woman."

"Necrophilia," she spat out. "I got your drift."

He zipped his pants. "It was an unfortunate choice of words on my part." He sat down on the bed facing her. "So what did change your mind? Was it the idea of being bitten?"

Madison reached up and touched her ear. It still stung but was no longer bleeding. She shook her head and curled up into a tighter ball. "No, I ... I ...." She looked at him. "It's nothing."

"It's not *nothing*, Madison." Colin's voice took on an edge of impatience. "Something changed your mind, and quickly."

"Something was on my mind. It diverted my attention. That's all."

Colin wasn't buying it. "I may not be able to read minds like Samuel, but I know when someone's not telling me the whole truth."

Madison got up and walked over to the bed. Trying to push Notchey from her mind, she ran her fingers through Colin's thick hair and bent down to kiss his lips. His hands instinctively grasped her hips and held her. When the kiss was over, he buried his face in her middle and stayed that way a moment before pulling away.

"Nice try, Madison, but your kiss wasn't the same as it was before." He pushed her a few inches away but still hung on to her hips. "It felt more like a duty just now than passion. Tell me what's going on."

She extricated herself from his grasp and went back to the chair. If she had to tell him, she wanted distance between them. "Why do you want me, Colin? Am I just another conquest, like Miriam?"

"You are not Miriam. Not by a long shot."

"That's right. I don't have her education or own a business."

Colin shook his head. "You need to stop this jealousy. It's very unattractive." He stood up and paced the room, raking a hand through his hair. "Vampire mysteries be damned. Women are the real mysteries. As long as I've lived, I've never understood them."

"No," Madison reassured him. "This isn't about jealousy or even about Miriam." She took a deep breath. "All my life, people have used me and discarded me. I don't want that to happen anymore."

He stopped pacing and turned to her. "What makes you think I'd do that to you?"

"Once you have my body and my blood, what's to stop you?"

Colin was at a temporary loss for words.

"Then again, you've already had my blood, both you and Samuel," she continued. "He told me you shared the blood those creeps took from me last October with him." She shot him a disgusted look. "What did you do? Toast my future with vampires with Waterford crystal goblets?"

A slow grin crossed Colin's face. "It was Baccarat, actually."

She scowled. "And now you want more."

"Yes, I do." His words were blunt with honesty. "And you want it, too. Or at least you did out in the living room." He took a few more steps, then turned to her, his face screwed up in irritation. "I should have just taken you in the heat of the moment, but I wanted your first time to be special. Stupid me."

"Mike Notchey thinks I've been screwing you all along. Said he can tell by the way you look at me. He didn't believe me when I told him I wasn't."

"So tonight was revenge sex?" Colin stood in front of Madison, looking down at her in disbelief. "You and Notchey having romantic problems of your own, so you're getting back at him with me?"

"There's nothing going on between me and Notchey."

Colin let out a short, dark laugh. "Like hell. Just as he's watching me, I'm watching him. He wants you in his bed, same as I do."

"Lucky me to be such a popular girl," Madison hissed. "Notchey also thinks I'm doing Samuel—that the two of you are sharing me, much as you share Miriam with everyone."

"Would you stop bringing up that tart's name!"

The room went silent. Madison stayed curled in the chair like a disgruntled porcupine. Colin flopped down on his back on the bed and stared at the ceiling.

"So," Colin said, breaking the silence. "What was your plan?" He sat up and fixed his dark eyes on her, the earlier affection gone, though they still smoldered with desire. "After me, were you going to hop into Samuel's bed—let him also bite and feed off of you? Was that how you were going to teach Notchey a lesson?"

"That's so unfair." She uncurled. Swinging her legs to the floor, she stood. "I went to your bed because I wanted to, Colin, no matter what this damn thing says." She shook the wrist with the bracelet at him. "Mike put doubts about you in my head, yes. Am I worried about being used and dumped? Yes. But I came to you willingly." She ripped off the bracelet and threw it to the floor. "There. Now there's nothing to stop you."

Colin shot off the bed with blinding speed and grabbed the bracelet. Pushing Madison down on the bed, he climbed on top of her, his fangs out and close to her face. "Don't you ever take this off again. You hear me?"

Frightened by his anger, she nodded her understanding. He sat up, lifted her left arm and roughly shoved the bracelet back onto her wrist. "Never!" He got off the bed and plopped himself down into the chair she'd vacated, dropping his head in his hands.

Sobbing, Madison got off the bed and dragged herself into the living room. Stripping off Colin's shirt, she collected her clothing and started to dress. She was nearly finished and her tears had stopped when Colin entered the room fully clothed. He was wearing a black pullover sweater, along with boots and a leather jacket. He held her panties aloft in his fingers.

"Don't forget these." He tossed them to her. "Or are you going to start going commando, too?"

Madison stuffed the panties into her bag. "I'm not cool enough for that." She tossed her long hair back over one shoulder and stood up to put on her own jacket. "There's no need for you to walk me out."

"I wasn't going to." His voice was stiff as he picked up his motorcycle helmet. "I'm going out." He pulled out his cell phone and punched the keypad. "Hey, Miriam, it's me." He looked directly at Madison while he spoke. "Feel like a booty call tonight?" He listened, then laughed. "See you in fifteen minutes." He ended the call.

"You pig," Madison shot at him.

"Just living up to people's expectations, luv."

FOURTEEN

When Madison returned home, it was around eleven. Samuel's car in the driveway meant Hyun was still on guard. The sight of the Dedhams' vehicle meant they were home from their evening. She'd hoped the Dedhams were still out on the town with Samuel and Keleta. Her plan had been to go to bed before they returned and avoid prying eyes. Entering the kitchen from the driveway side door, she spotted Hyun through the window, seated at the patio table still keeping his post. Seeing him, Madison realized she'd forgotten to ask Colin about King Leopold and Ann's connection to him.

She opened the patio door and poked her head out. "You're here almost as much as I am these days."

Without interrupting his scan of the yard and woods beyond, Hyun told her, "They're inside. They'll be glad to see you."

"The Dedhams or Samuel, too?"

"All three." He gave her an odd look. "You okay?"

"I'm fine."

Madison slipped into the bathroom off the kitchen to check her face and immediately saw what had put Hyun on alert. Enough time had lapsed since she'd left Colin's that her eyes weren't swollen from crying, but her mascara was ruined. Pulling a small washcloth from a nearby cabinet, Madison wet and soaped up one end, then carefully dabbed at the smudges around her eyes. It wasn't great, but it was better.

She checked her ear. Dried blood had crusted around the wound. Using the soapy cloth, Madison gently wiped the area, being careful not to open it up again. No doubt the vampires in the other room would pick up on this—they could smell fresh blood a mile away—but she wasn't going to help them out.

Much to her surprise, she'd liked having her ear nipped and sucked. It had been exciting in combination with Colin's other attentions, and she wondered if really being bitten by him would bring the same excitement, only intensified. Madison made a face at herself. Colin was probably screwing and biting Miriam right this minute, the bastard. Then fine—let him. She had other things to worry about, like who and why someone was dumping vampires into the Dedhams' pool.

Running her fingers through her long hair, she made sure it covered her ear, then turned on her heel and stomped out of the bathroom, hoping her anger would mask her hurt.

The Dedhams were entertaining Samuel in the comfort of their den. A small fire crackled in the fireplace, lending a cozy atmosphere to the room. Doug was tending the fire when she walked in.

"Good," Doug said, putting the poker down and turning to her. "We were hoping you'd come home soon."

Dodie and Samuel were in conversation. Samuel was seated in one of the large leather club chairs, and Dodie was on the sofa. They stopped talking and turned to her. The three of them were still in their evening clothes, though the men had loosened their ties.

If the vampires sensed or noticed anything unusual about Madison or smelled the blood on her ear, they kept their opinions to themselves in mannerly behavior, though Madison did catch meaningful looks being tossed between Dodie and Samuel.

Madison leaned against the door frame. "Kind of an early night for vampires, isn't it? Wasn't the restaurant any good?"

"It was grand," answered Doug. "We had a wonderful time."

"Come on in, dear," invited Dodie, "and visit with us." She patted the sofa seat next to her.

"Actually," Madison replied, "I'm quite tired. I think I'll go to bed."

Samuel fixed her with a knowing look. As usual, it annoyed Madison. "Don't you want to know what we learned from Keleta?"

Her curiosity won over her desire to be shed of vampires for the rest of the night. "Yes, of course." Madison took a seat in another club chair opposite the sofa. "Were you able to find out the identity of Lady?"

"Unfortunately not," Doug answered as he took the seat next to Dodie.

"But," Dodie added with a smile, "we did learn a lot about his family. Keleta is such a charming young man and so bright."

During the exchange, Samuel stared at Madison with his penetrating eyes. She tried to block him out but she was too tired to concentrate on the effort. Instead, she stared back at him with a knitted brow, silently telling him in colorful language to back off. He tilted his head back and laughed. Doug and Dodie locked eyes, Dodie letting Doug know with a few quick blinks that she couldn't tell what was going on.

"Have you decided yet," Madison asked, "if Keleta is salvageable?"

"It's looking good," Doug told her. "So far, Ricky and Byron's reports have been very encouraging."

"True," Samuel added. "Unless something happens to change our course, I believe we'll be able to acclimate the boy sufficiently."

Dodie seemed as pleased as Madison with the news. "And he seems so eager to learn. From what little we've learned, maybe being dumped in our pool was the best thing that could have happened to him since becoming a vampire."

Doug agreed. "It certainly sounds like he was given a second chance."

Madison tried to appear relaxed and wasn't sure if it was working. Inside, she felt edgy, like she was trying to walk across razor wire. "Any more word on Parker?"

"No," Samuel answered. "Nothing, but I'm glad you brought him up. I'm sending you out of town tomorrow to do some research on Parker's identity with Joni Langevoort. It might give us a lead on this Lady."

"Tomorrow?"

"Yes. You don't have any classes tomorrow, do you?"

Madison shook her head.

"The council will fly you up to San Francisco late tomorrow afternoon. We would have sent you tonight, but there are no direct flights this late. Eddie Gonzales will meet you at the airport and drive you to Marin."

"That's north of San Francisco, isn't it?"

"Yes." Samuel explained. "Joni is a former council member and an expert in vampire genealogy. You'll be working with her, tracing vampiric lineages to see if this Parker shows up. I'm thinking you should start with Ann Hayes and branch out from there."

"Can't we just send her Doug's drawing and see what she comes up with?"

"It's more involved than that. Besides," Samuel insisted, "as I told you earlier, I want you to learn how to use her database for the future."

Doug reached out and tapped Madison's arm. "Think of it like one of your classes—a crash course in Vampire 101."

"Can't I drive up instead?" Madison asked. "If I leave early in the morning, I'll be there early afternoon."

"It's only an hour flight." Samuel paused and considered Madison. "Are you nervous about flying?"

"No, not at all." She shuffled her feet.

"You've never flown before, have you, dear?" Dodie gave her a small, encouraging smile. "Don't worry, you'll be fine. Doug and I fly all the time."

"Get used to it, Madison," Samuel told her in a direct manner. "There may be a day when you'll be required by the council to travel a lot longer distance than a few hundred miles. Do you have a passport?"

She shook her head.

Samuel turned to Dodie. "Why don't you and Madison work on getting her a passport as soon as she returns. She should have one, just in case we need her overseas."

"Certainly, Samuel," Dodie responded.

Madison swallowed and nodded. It wasn't that she didn't like flying, she'd just never had the opportunity. Until coming to Los Angeles, she'd never been out of Idaho, and she'd driven from Boise to Los Angeles. The idea of getting and needing a passport excited her.

"You'll only be gone one day," Samuel continued, giving Madison her assignment like a general laying out a battle plan. "You'll leave tomorrow afternoon, work all night with Joni, and return Saturday. There's an important party Saturday evening I want you to attend, so I'd prefer you to return Saturday afternoon."

"The party in Brentwood?" Madison asked, afraid it was.

Samuel nodded. "Yes."

"Colin said something about taking Keleta to it."

"Splendid. Although you'll be attending with me."

Madison squirmed. She didn't want to go to the party with anyone. She didn't want to see Colin, especially at an event where he might have Miriam hanging on his arm. "I'm not much into parties."

"Which is exactly why I want you there. I need your keen observation skills. Whoever tried to kill Keleta might be at that party or have people in attendance. Keep your eyes and ears open, especially around Keleta. He seems afraid to tell us any more than he has. He even seems worried about what he's told us so far. If he sees someone he knows, he'll probably give off some sort of reaction. I want to know about it immediately."

"Will Ann Hayes be at the party? She might also be a help. Seems like whoever is doing this is setting her up."

"Ann is the one throwing the party. She's hoping to flush out the person behind this or, at the very least, get some information."

Samuel looked at Doug and Dodie. "May I have a minute alone with Madison?"

"Of course, Samuel," said Dodie. The Dedhams got to their feet and filed out the door.

When they were gone, Madison said, "It doesn't matter if they leave. They can hear everything anyway."

Samuel got up and sat on the edge of the coffee table, directly across from Madison. "I didn't ask the Dedhams to leave to keep something from them, but to give us some privacy."

He reached out and brushed Madison's hair back away from her ear. Then he touched the wound. She flinched. "Wasn't Mr. Reddy very hungry?"

"Why don't you tell me? You're already fishing around in my head. It's getting so I can feel you rooting around up there like a pig after truffles."

"Nice metaphor."

"I try."

Samuel chuckled. "You seem more innately hostile than usual. Would you like to talk about it?"

"Why? You already know what's bugging me."

Samuel took a deep breath. "Yes, I do, but I ask you anyway because I think it's good for you to express your feelings. My knowing doesn't help you sort things out. You discussing how you feel does."

Madison swatted his hand away from her ear. "Are you my shrink now, besides my boss?"

"I'm someone who cares about you."

"You know, Samuel, that's swell of you, but I've had a very emotional evening." Madison got wearily to her feet. "Hell, I've had a rough day, starting with daybreak. I just want to go upstairs and go to bed, especially if you're expecting me to work all night tomorrow night."

Samuel stopped her by grabbing each of her wrists in his hands. "Madison, Mike Notchey is right. Vampires do care about blood and sex and power. But it's not all we care about, at least not the more evolved among us. We are capable of strong feelings, including love and loyalty." He pulled down on her wrists, encouraging her to sit again. She stayed upright.

"Mike has a bit of a love-hate relationship with us—with vampires. On one hand, like you, he's very close to the Dedhams, and he helps the council as much as possible. But several years ago, his sister fell in love with a vampire and disappeared."

"What?" Madison sat down hard, her bottom giving off a soft *thud* against the leather.

"I'll bet he's never mentioned her to you, has he?"

In shock, Madison could only shake her head.

"It's true. Libby became the mistress of a vampire, much like Kai is to me, but this vampire didn't treat her very well. Mike knew nothing about vampires until that happened."

"Is she ... you know."

"Dead? We don't know. The council banished the vampire from California for some illegal practices having nothing to do with Libby. She chose to go with him, despite Mike's best efforts.

When he tried to stop her, he got into a nasty scuffle with the vampire and a couple of his beater companions."

Madison listened with sharp ears and interest. "Is that when he got shot and nearly died a couple of years back?"

Samuel nodded. "Yes. But it's been seven years now, not just a couple."

"Notchey made it sound more recent."

"To him, the pain of losing Libby probably feels like yesterday. As I understand it, they only had each other—no other family."

Samuel's last words sunk into Madison's head with familiarity. Mike Notchey was alone in the world, just as she was. When she thought about it, the news didn't surprise her. He had the same chip on his shoulder and prickliness she did—a constant shield raised against the outside.

"Mike killed one man," Samuel continued, "and wounded two others before nearly being killed himself. Rather than tell the authorities what had really happened, Mike passed it off as a drug bust gone wrong, which in reality it could have been. You see, the vampire was the head of a large drug ring, something the council does not tolerate. The wounded men kept their mouths shut about their leader out of fear and went to prison. Since then, Mike's been staying close to us, hoping to hear some news about Libby. He also works hard to hold the line between vampires and the living."

"I had no idea." Madison's personal sinkhole was forgotten, replaced by genuine sadness and pain for Notchey. "His behavior makes more sense now, though I still don't like his accusations or that he didn't believe a word that came out of my mouth."

"Mike Notchey cares about you. He's worried you'll fall into the same ugly situation as his sister."

"Fallen," Madison corrected. "Notchey accused me of sleeping with both you and Colin—present tense."

Samuel touched her ear again; this time, she didn't pull away. "Yet despite our best efforts, you're sleeping with no one, not even the good detective."

"Notchey won't touch me as long as he thinks I've been with you or Colin."

"And who do you want, Madison? I know you have feelings for both of them."

"Them? And what about you? Aren't you going to throw your hat into the ring?" She looked boldly at the head vampire, challenging him. "I've always had the feeling you wanted to add me to your harem. Or are you willing to share me like one of those vampire groupie girls?"

"I don't share. What's mine is mine." Samuel put a hand under her chin and fixed his milky eyes on hers. "More importantly, you're worth more than that—a lot more. And it is about time you started realizing it, no matter what your background. Inside here," he tapped her head with his other hand, "and inside here," he tapped her chest over her heart, "you have what it takes to rise above whatever life hands you, past or future."

She looked doubtful. She wanted to believe him, but it was difficult. A lifetime of being beaten down couldn't be erased in thirty seconds with a handful of pretty words.

"Those vampire groupies," Samuel continued, "those girls like Miriam would never have been approved to work with the council. Nor would I waste my time mentoring any of them."

"Is that what you are, my mentor?"

Still holding her chin, Samuel leaned forward and kissed Madison. It was the first time he'd ever kissed her mouth. It was soft and tasty like a fresh peach. Madison didn't pull back but leaned into it. When it was over, Samuel slipped a hand around the back of her neck and drew her to him again, this time for a longer, deeper kiss.

"There," he said, when their lips parted company. "Now tell me honestly, did that send shivers down your spine?"

Madison leaned back in her chair. "Don't be silly."

"I'm quite serious." Samuel got up and walked to the fireplace. He leaned against the mantle and faced Madison. "Did it?"

She cast her eyes down, unable to look at him when she spoke the truth. "I'm sorry, Samuel, but no."

"Don't be sorry about the truth, Madison, especially when I'm trying to make a point."

His words coaxed a smile from her. She lifted her head to see that while he was serious, he was also smiling.

"Okay, now," he continued, seeing her relax. "Did Colin's kisses send shivers down your spine?"

She nodded. "And everywhere else."

Samuel fought to suppress a grin. "And what about Mike Notchey's kisses?" Samuel paused, scrunching his brow in consideration. "You have kissed him, haven't you?"

"Yes, I have. Just this morning and not for the first time. And, yes, his kisses did curl my toes."

Samuel walked back to her and sat down on the edge of the table again. "Now that we've gotten that out of the way, let's talk again about what you want."

"Wait. You don't find me attractive?" Madison sunk lower in the chair. "You mean I'm being rejected by three men in one day? That's a new personal low, even for me."

Laughter rumbled from deep inside Samuel's chest. He flashed her one of his killer smiles. "Madison, I find you very sexy and physically attractive, but I have no trouble finding women to share my bed—women whose toes *I* curl." They shared a smile before Samuel continued. "What I have difficulty finding is dependable friends, especially women. You are much more valuable to me as a close friend. I think you feel the same way, deep down, about me."

Madison understood Samuel's words were high praise and that he didn't offer friendship lightly. "Thank you, Samuel. A friend and a mentor?"

"Precisely." He stood. "Although who knows what the future will bring." He held out a hand to Madison. She took it and stood up in front of him.

She shrugged and took a deep breath. "I honestly don't know, Samuel, about the two of them, though I suspect you'd prefer me with Colin. In fact, you set that up tonight, didn't you? That's why you insisted I speak to him about Keleta and go to his place to do it. Dodie even picked out this sweater for me to wear. You two in cahoots?"

"It wasn't a setup, Madison. I'd simply hoped that by putting the two of you together with such an intimate topic, nature would take its course. I think Dodie was probably thinking the same way." He glanced at her ear again. "And it seems it did, up to a point."

"What you didn't factor in was pig-headed behavior on both our parts."

Samuel laughed again. "You always make me laugh, Madison. It's another reason why I like having you around."

"Glad I'm the court jester—though I didn't see *that* on my job description."

"Yes, I would prefer you to be with Colin, because he's one of us, and it would be simpler for me, as head of the council, to have you emotionally engaged in such a way. But Mike Notchey is a solid man with a good heart, and once he irons out his misconceptions, he will be good to you."

Samuel stroked Madison's cheek. "Colin and Mike are very much alike. Maybe that's why you can't make up your mind. Both are good men with tragic pasts that haunt their present and dictate their behavior, even when it's bad. Both have had to kill and live with the consequences. Both know deep loss." He pulled out his sunglasses but didn't put them on, just held them as he carefully composed his words. "I'm afraid the road to love will be rather rocky, whichever path you take. And," he said with another smile, "considering your personality, it won't be a smooth ride for the man you choose."

"Gee, now give me the bad news."

Samuel started for the door but stopped and turned. "Another thing that would be good for you, but perhaps not so great for the council, is to make some friends, living friends, your own age. I know it might be difficult considering your work and living circumstances, but I think it would be healthy. Maybe there's a classmate or two you can go to the movies or shopping with once in a while."

"I didn't make friends easily before I came here; what makes you think I'm any better at it now? Besides, I thought my loner status was one of the things you guys liked about me."

"Skilled at it or not, it would be very good for you to spend more time among the living." He paused, then added, "And I trust you to be discreet, or I wouldn't suggest it."

Madison thought about the people she met at school. There were a few she thought she might like to know better. Then her thoughts turned to Julianne. "There is a woman I've met while running in the morning."

"Splendid. Give it a try, Madison. You might surprise yourself."

Samuel was about to say more when his cell phone vibrated. With his free hand, he retrieved the phone from inside his suit jacket.

"Yes," he said into the phone. As the call continued, Samuel's stance stiffened. He asked few questions of the caller but listened a great deal. "Someone will be right there," he said just before ending the call.

Samuel flung open the door to the den. "Doug, Dodie: get Hyun and come on back in."

"What's happened?" Madison asked, but he only held up a finger telling her to wait.

As the Dedhams and Hyun came rushing into the den, Samuel made a call. "Colin," he said when the call was answered. "Get over to Stacie's as soon as possible. There's been another murdered vampire."

"What? Where?" asked Doug, speaking the questions on all their minds.

"At Stacie's house. Another one was killed and discarded."

"In her pool?" asked Madison.

Samuel turned to her. "Stacie doesn't have a pool. He was in her bathtub."

Dodie couldn't believe her ears. "They broke into Stacie's house?"

"Sure seems that way." He turned to Hyun. "Get the car." Hyun took off.

"Colin's going to meet me over there. Dodie, I want you to stay here in case someone decides tonight's the night to dump two bodies. Doug, you come with me, and bring your sketchpad."

Samuel looked at Madison, unsure what to do with her. "I should send you straight to bed since tomorrow night you'll be up all night, but I want you to come with us. I want you to check this vampire over and record every detail about him to tell Joni. You'll ride with Doug. I'll send the two of you home as soon as possible."

As much as Madison didn't relish seeing Colin so soon after their encounter, she was very curious about the latest dead vampire.

Samuel sensed her hesitation and turned to her. "Will that be a problem, Madison?"

"No, Samuel, it won't be."

FIFTEEN

Doug pulled the Dedham's Range Rover into Stacie Neroni's driveway and parked next to Samuel's black sedan. Next to the car, Hyun stood on alert. Madison had taken time to change into a heavy sweater and jeans, which put their arrival several minutes behind Samuel.

Madison got out and surveyed the area. The house was entirely hidden from the street by tall, mature trees, and the house itself was the color of aged wood, helping it to blend in with its surroundings. Coming down the street, she hadn't noticed any other houses close to the road's edge.

"Everything okay, Hyun?" Doug said to the bodyguard.

"Seems to be, Mr. Dedham. I did a quick walk of the perimeter but found nothing."

"Boy," Madison said to Doug as they walked to the bottom of the staircase leading to the door, "this place is even more secluded than yours."

Doug looked back toward the street but saw only inky night. "The people who own homes in this area are rabid about their privacy. I believe several well-known celebrities live on this road."

Stacie's house was built into a hillside not far from the Dedhams'. From the main part of the driveway to the front door, it was a good climb up winding stairs.

"Where's the back door?" Madison asked as she and Doug started up the stairs.

"It's around back, up at the top. You either have to walk up the drive or drive up and park in front of the garage."

Madison eyed the steep drive that curved up a hill and disappeared behind the house. "Those are the only two entries?"

"As I recall, there's another door inside the garage that leads into the house through the laundry room. I would have parked closer, but Jesús will need to get his truck up there." Doug indicated Samuel's car. "I'm sure Samuel had the same idea."

"I don't mind the climb, though I'll bet whoever broke in and dumped the body drove up to the back. These steps would be hard carrying dead weight."

"Unless the killer had an extra kick of strength," Doug noted.

"You mean like Dodie?"

"Exactly. Even I would have a difficult time carrying a grown man up these stairs. A couple of people could do it, but it would be very awkward with the way the steps zigzag."

Madison stopped at the top landing and looked back at the dark road. "And a car could quietly come onto the property and no one from the street would notice or probably care."

"You're becoming quite the detective, Madison. Notchey giving you lessons?"

"Humph. Just making sensible observations."

They found the downstairs empty and followed voices up the inside staircase to what looked like the master bedroom. Stretched out on an area rug was the dead vampire, his eyes hollow orbs. His face and head were clean shaven. A short stake had been driven through his well-developed chest. He looked much younger than Parker but older than Keleta. Kneeling next to him was Samuel. Stacie was sitting on the edge of the bed. They stopped their discussion when Doug and Madison entered.

"He has a brand just like Parker and Keleta," Samuel told them as he turned the body on its side to show them the mark. The vampire's back also sported some intricate ink work. "He also doesn't appear to be a very old vampire, as he's showing no signs of rapid deterioration."

Doug pulled up a small chair from next to a dresser and positioned it near the body. Opening his sketchpad, he pulled out a pencil and got to work.

Madison studied the naked body on the floor, then pulled out her cell phone. It was a new smart phone—a Christmas gift from the council. She aimed it at the body and took a couple of photos.

"Those might be very hazy," Stacie told her.

"Still, it might be worth a shot." Looking at the photos, Madison could see what Stacie was saying. The first two photos showed the body clearly, but it was outlined in a fuzzy haze, as if someone had tried to erase it from the outside in. She showed the photos to Stacie.

"Actually," Stacie told her, shooting her eyes from the photo to the body on the floor, "those are pretty good. Another indication this guy hasn't been a vampire very long."

"What do you mean?"

"The older the vampire, the less clear the photograph." Stacie pointed to the fuzzy edges surrounding the body. "On an older vampire, the entire body might be fuzzy or even just a shadow. Depends on the age of the vampire."

Curious, Madison aimed the phone at Doug. He saw her and mugged for the camera. When she looked at the photo, she nearly gasped in surprise. She could see him, but his likeness was very faded, like an old photo that had been left out in the sun. She turned to Samuel and got off another shot.

"Would you quit playing around," Stacie snapped at her, "and get back to checking out the body. I'd really like it out of here as soon as Jesús arrives."

"I'm trying to set a frame of reference between the ages and how faded the photos are," Madison explained.

"That's very smart of you, Madison." Samuel looked over her shoulder at his own photo, or what little there was of it. He had been leaning next to a chest of drawers made of pine when she'd taken the shot. In the photo, the chest was as clear and solid as it was right in the room with them. Next to it was a hazy figure, an outline, like an apparition caught in the middle of a haunting.

Madison laughed. "I could put this on the web and claim it's a photo of a ghost. People would believe it in a New York minute."

Samuel looked at her in surprise. "You don't believe in ghosts, do you?"

"Why not?" she replied, half in jest. "Four months ago, I didn't believe in vampires. Who knows what else is out there that goes bump in the night?"

"Ghosts," Stacie scoffed. "Next you'll be telling us you believe in Santa Claus."

Quickly, Madison took a photo of Stacie. "You're the youngest vampire here in the room, right? I mean, except for the dead guy. About how long?"

"I've been a vampire forty-three years now." Stacie stopped short. "Wow, if I hadn't been turned, I'd be eighty-one years old now."

"And terrorizing the staff in some old-age home, more than likely," teased Doug as he continued to sketch.

Her sample photos taken, Madison went back to looking at the dead vampire. Besides the empty eye sockets and that he was dead, there was something disturbing about him, something that scratched her brain like a loose piece of wire. "It looks to me like this guy was some sort of gym rat. Look at that six-pack and those arms."

Stacie paced off the stretched-out body. "He's also not very tall. Maybe only five foot seven or eight, max. Compact and fit."

Madison got an idea. "Can you turn him over again, Samuel, but more on his front. I want to take a photo of those tattoos. Since he's not an old vampire, they might come out okay."

"Yes," added Doug. "It might also be a good idea for me to make a quick sketch of them. They seem rather distinct."

Before turning the body over, Samuel pulled out the stake. It made everyone wince.

Madison bent to study the hole. "There's not much blood. I noticed that with Parker, too. Is that normal?"

"Yes," answered Samuel. "Vampires don't have as much blood in their systems as the living, nor do we have a heartbeat to pump it out. Also, this fellow was probably killed elsewhere and brought here."

It was difficult to tell if the tattoos on the back of the dead vampire were one art piece added to over time or a mishmash of a bunch of tats on a limited space. They only appeared on his back—none on his arms, legs, or chest.

Madison traced a delicate hummingbird with her index finger. Next to it was the logo for Harley-Davidson. The hole the stake had made went through a turtle, taking out its head. "It's as if he limited them only to where they wouldn't show unless he chose to show them."

Stacie took a closer look. "Makes you wonder what he did for work before he became a vampire. Maybe he couldn't have any tattoos showing."

"You two need to move," Doug told them, "if you want me to sketch those things. As it is, I'll only be able to get a general sense of them on paper. There are just too many."

Madison took several quick photos and moved out of the way. "Make sure you get that one on the edge up by his left shoulder." She pointed to a tattoo the size of a Ping-Pong ball.

Samuel took off his glasses and leaned in for a closer look. "Those are fangs. And female lips."

"Yep." Madison traced the outline as she had the hummingbird, as if reading it by Braille. "Wonder if that's a new or old tattoo?"

Doug kept sketching. "If the brand hadn't been placed so far down on his back, we might have missed it with all this other stuff."

Samuel put his glasses back on and took a few steps back. "Vampires can't be tattooed. If they are, the marking disappears shortly after it's made because of our fast healing process. This man was probably involved with a vampire before he was turned. Maybe he had one as a lover."

"Possibly Lady herself." Everyone turned to find Colin approaching the door. "I couldn't help but overhear the conversation."

After a nod to everyone, Colin crouched down near Madison and looked the dead vampire over, front and back. Colin was wearing the same clothes but smelled freshly showered. Madison stood up and backed away, then caught Samuel looking at her.

"Ever see him before, Colin?" asked Samuel.

"Maybe. Possibly around some of the clubs, but I don't have a name or remember who I might have seen him with."

Much like Isabella Claussen acted as the council's ambassador around the world, Colin was the council's eyes and ears on the club circuit, particularly the nightclubs that attracted and catered to vampire worshipers. There were several such groups, also known as covens, in the Los Angeles area. Colin made it his business to be familiar with them all, though none of them knew he was the genuine article, the very being they worshiped and sought to be. He also kept an eye on the clubs that catered to real vampires and their human companions.

"You know," Madison added, "there's something familiar about him to me, too, but I can't place it."

Doug looked up at her. "Maybe at school?"

"He hardly looks like Joe College," Stacie quipped.

Doug grinned at her. "Don't judge a book by its cover, Stacie. You don't exactly look like an attorney."

"Oh, yeah? So what's an attorney supposed to look like? Perry Mason?" Stacie stuck out her chin and folded her arms. "What is this, 'bag on Stacie' night? Isn't it bad enough I have a dead vampire in my bedroom?"

Everyone laughed. "Better yours than mine," shot back Colin.

Stacie cured her lip in a snarl. "Let's not get started on what goes on in your bedroom, Reddy."

Colin and Madison shot each other dirty looks, then quickly looked elsewhere, hoping no one else had caught the exchange.

Colin stood up and went to Stacie. "Samuel said you found him in your bathtub?"

"Yeah. Creeped me out, walking in and seeing him there."

Considering everything vampires saw and did on a daily basis, Madison found Stacie's choice of words amusing, but she kept it to herself.

"There was no sign of forced entry, either," Stacie added. "They must have picked the back lock."

Madison cleared her throat. "Don't tell me: security systems are out of the question for vampires. Right?"

"You don't see one at our house, do you?" asked Doug. "Can you imagine what the police or security company would think if the alarm went off during the day and they found Dodie and me upstairs sleeping?"

Samuel, who'd been in the bathroom having another look around, stepped out with the rest of them. "I have one. But there is always a live person on my premises at all times, especially after I retire."

Unlike the Dedhams, who employed Pauline Speakes to come in for a few hours each day, Samuel employed a middle-aged couple who lived in a guesthouse on his property and worked for him full-time. Foster and Enid were small, dark people who spoke broken English. The wife took care of the house while her husband managed the grounds. Enid always beamed when Madison emerged from Samuel's guest wing because it meant she would be able to put her considerable cooking skills to work on breakfast. She loved cooking for Madison as much as Dodie did. Hyun lived in a very large apartment over the four-car garage.

Madison turned to Stacie. "Do you have a housekeeper or someone here when you're sleeping?"

"My secretary, Barbara, is here most of the day. She works in an office I have downstairs. She arrives after I go to bed and generally goes home shortly after I wake up." Stacie glanced at everyone as she spoke. "My housekeeper comes in only two days a week. Like I told Samuel earlier, tonight I went to a movie with friends. I left here around eight and got home just past eleven."

"Well," Doug said, "at least we have a short window of time during which it could have happened. At our house it probably occurred after we went to bed."

Colin went to the window and pulled back the room-darkening drapes. He stared out into the night, digesting the facts. "Sounds to me like someone was watching you, Stacie, to see exactly when you left the house." He turned back. "Maybe we have this all wrong. Maybe it's not Ann Hayes out to hurt the Dedhams or someone out to set Ann up. Maybe it's someone out to target us—the council."

Samuel glanced at Doug, then turned to Colin. "It's an idea that came up tonight at dinner, even before Stacie called me."

Colin turned to look at Samuel. Stacie and Madison were all ears.

"Keleta didn't say much tonight at dinner," Samuel continued, "but from what little he did say, we started wondering if we're thinking too small by only looking at the Dedhams as the target.

At least it's another theory. Now I'm thinking it's a stronger possibility." Samuel walked over to the bed and sat down. Crossing one leg over the other, he got comfortable. His collar was open, his tie long gone. "Think about it: I doubt anything like this could happen at Colin's condo. The security is too tight, and there are too many neighbors who might see something. There's always someone at my property. The remaining council members live in the northern part of the state, making it difficult to transport a body over a distance. Only the Dedhams and Stacie here would be easy targets for someone watching their patterns."

"What about Kate Thornton?" Madison asked. "She lives in Southern California."

"Yes," Samuel admitted, "but out nearly to Riverside." He brushed at some lint on his trousers. "Still, we might want to warn her and Jerry, just in case."

Finished with his sketching, Doug stood up and stretched. "We may be barking up the wrong tree here, but it pays to be careful."

"Exactly," Stacie agreed. "We can't have anyone finding these bodies except us. Can you imagine the nightmare of trying to explain this to the police?"

"Speaking of police," said Samuel, "we should give that sketch to Mike Notchey to see if he can locate a missing persons report on this fellow like he did for Keleta. Although without a name, it might be very difficult."

"I'd like a copy of the tattoo sketch." Colin left the window and walked back over to look at the body again. "As well as the sketch of the face. People this covered with body art usually have it done at a favorite spot. There are a lot of tattoo shops in Los

Angeles, but it wouldn't hurt to start checking out some of the more popular ones."

"Great idea, Colin." Samuel stood up and faced Madison. "Scan copies of the sketches as you did with Parker, and get them to everyone on the council first thing in the morning. Right now, though, I'd like you to e-mail those photos to me. I'll send them on to Ricky and have him show them to Keleta immediately. They're clear enough to help."

Madison nodded and began e-mailing the photos from her phone. "Am I still going up to Marin tomorrow?"

"It's more important than ever," Samuel told her. "And remember to take copies of the sketches of both Parker and this guy with you."

"Marin?" Colin asked, turning to Samuel with surprise. "You're sending her up to Joni?"

"Yes," Samuel told him. "Just for a day. Joni has been working hard on the genealogy database, and I want Madison to get familiar with it. Seems like the perfect time with all this nonsense going on."

Colin turned his gaze to Madison. She returned it without a flinch. "I agree," he finally said. "I think it would be good for Madison to get away right now." He looked at Samuel and quickly added, "She could be more of a help on the research end than stomping around tattoo parlors with me."

SIXTEEN

Shortly after Jesús arrived at Stacie's house and confirmed that the dead vampire was a young vampire, as they'd suspected, Samuel sent Doug and Madison home. Before she went to bed, Madison scanned the sketches and downloaded the photos and sent them to all of the council members. Samuel had texted them earlier about the latest development and let them know the sketches would be coming. He'd also texted a message to the council and Madison saying Ricky felt from Keleta's reaction to the photos that he knew who the latest dead vampire was, but claimed he didn't. Byron and Ricky were going to work on Keleta to get him to talk.

As tired as she was, Madison had trouble sleeping, awakening just after daybreak. Restless, instead of turning over and going back to sleep, she got up and put on her running clothes.

Once at the park, Madison was happy about her decision. The morning was shaping up to be beautiful and clear. She had just parked her car and was heading to the trail when she saw Julianne jogging toward her, obviously done with her run. She was with a different running companion—a tall, young man with dark hair and brown skin. He wore a Dodgers cap like Julianne's.

"I'll be with you in a minute," Julianne told the guy, tossing him the keys. He headed for the SUV while Julianne stopped to speak to Madison.

"I was wondering if you'd be here today," she said to Madison. "Have trouble getting out of bed this morning?"

"A bit. I had to work very late last night."

"And you're alone today. I'm sorry about that."

Madison shrugged. "Yeah. I haven't seen or talked to Mike since yesterday morning. I think we both need some cooling-off time." She tossed her head in the direction of Julianne's companion. "I see you have a new running partner. He's pretty cute."

Julianne laughed and looked over at the SUV. "Yeah, he is. Not the brightest bulb on the tree, but he is fun." She looked back at Madison and winked. "Men are like busses, Madison—miss one, another comes along."

Julianne started to walk to her car, but Madison stopped her. "Julianne, you've been so nice. Maybe one day we can meet for lunch or something?" They were difficult words for Madison to spit out. She wasn't used to making overtures toward people she didn't know, but she did need friends her own age, and Julianne seemed like a good place to start.

A wide smile crossed Julianne's lovely face, and her blue eyes brightened with interest. "I'd like that, Madison. I really would. I get so wrapped up with my career, I seldom take the time to relax with girlfriends."

"I know what you mean. I go to school and work. In fact, I'm going out of town tonight for my employer."

"Tell you what, then. Let's dump the clowns and run together Monday morning. We can talk more then."

Madison was excited at the prospect. "Great. Usual time, around six thirty?"

"Hang on," Julianne said and ran to her vehicle. She returned with a piece of paper on which she'd written her phone number. Handing it to Madison, she said, "That's my cell. Call me if something comes up. Otherwise, it's Monday morning for sure."

———

Buoyed by her successful chat with Julianne and her invigorating run, Madison attacked the rest of her morning in high spirits. She packed for her trip, did some schoolwork, and even managed a nap—a nap cut short by the ringing of her cell phone. She reached over to grab the phone from her nightstand.

"Hello." Madison's voice was thick with sleep as she answered the phone on the fourth ring. One more and the call would have gone to voice mail.

"Ms. Rose," the caller began. "This is Nina. Nina Weinberg, the realtor. Did I catch you at a bad time?"

Madison sat up and shook off the fog of sleep. It was the realtor she'd spoken to the day before. "No," Madison said in a hurry. "Not at all. Did you find something already?"

"I may have. I made several calls yesterday to some colleagues. As I suspected, there are quite a few properties that meet your size requirements on the market right now, but only five that might suit your employer's architectural tastes and privacy needs. Two are currently being leased, but both leases are due to be up soon. Of the remaining three, two are unoccupied." She paused. When Madison didn't say anything, she continued. "If you'd like,

I could show you three of properties tomorrow. The leased properties are not available for showing except by special arrangement, but we could drive by those if you have the time. If they are suitable, I'll arrange for a showing."

"I have to go up north on business this weekend." Madison got out of bed and walked over to her laptop. "Do you have information on the properties you can e-mail me? I can show them to my boss. If he's interested, he may want to do his own drive-by before taking it further."

When the realtor hesitated, Madison rattled off her council e-mail address. If Nina Weinberg checked the root address, she would find an impressive website on the foundation that was a front for the California Vampire Council. The foundation was real, but its true business was that of handling the affairs of the vampires.

"I'm sorry," Nina told her, "but could you hold on a moment? I have another call, and I'm in the office alone right now."

"Of course. No problem." Madison was savvy enough to smell the polite lie for what it was, a way of buying enough time for the woman to check the website. Nina Weinberg was cautious. Madison liked that.

"Thank you for your patience, Ms. Rose," the realtor said a minute later. "Let me gather up the information on those properties and send them right over to you."

"I really appreciate it. We can look them over this weekend in between meetings." The lies once again came easily, and Madison started to feel guilty about the commission the realtor would never see.

While she waited for the e-mails, she finished preparations for her trip. There were still several hours before she had to head to the airport, and Madison intended to make the most of that time. Sensing Colin would be concentrating initially on the more popular tattoo parlors in the trendy areas, she had intended to check out some of the shops in her area and along the beach communities. She also knew he wouldn't be starting his search until dark. Before her nap, Madison had done online research on tattoo parlors in Los Angeles and made a list of those within a reasonable driving distance to target before she left. She'd noticed that most parlors didn't open until at least two in the afternoon and stayed open quite late. Her plan was to hit them shortly after they opened, before they got too busy to chat. But now with the realtor sending information on possible castle-type properties, she was changing her plans.

She didn't have to wait long before the e-mail from Nina Weinberg came through. Included were addresses and photos of the properties. Each looked like a perfect fit—large, secluded, and European in appearance. One even looked like a modern rendition of a castle. Madison concentrated on the occupied properties first. It was possible that Lady and her crew had left the area recently. It was even possible that they were not in one of the houses on the list. But Madison felt it was too quick for Lady and her sizeable household to pack and leave, and since the bodies had all been dumped geographically close together, she also felt chances were good they might be close by. If it weren't daytime, she'd run over to Byron and Ricky's and show the photos to Keleta, but by the time they arose she'd be on her way to the airport. If she found something viable, she could always e-mail the information to Samuel to show Keleta tonight.

"I'm going out for a bit and taking the Range Rover," Madison called to Pauline, who was transferring laundry from the washer to the dryer.

The Dedhams had two vehicles and put both at Madison's disposal. She plucked the keys to the Range Rover off the key rack near the door and was about to leave when she stopped short, remembering something.

She stepped into the laundry room. "I just thought of something. If I leave, you'll be here alone. Hyun isn't coming by until he drives me to the airport. Should I call him and see if he can come by now?"

Pauline shook her head. "Nah. Hyun called me earlier to say that Samuel didn't think we needed round-the-clock guarding any longer, at least not in the middle of the day. He wants us to be on guard but thinks if anything happens, it will be after dark." She set the timer on the machine and turned her attention to Madison. "You gonna be gone long? I still hate to leave the Dedhams alone under the circumstances. Sounds like whoever is doing this is watching people's houses. Might be vampires; might not be."

"Not too long. I want to check out something having to do with Keleta."

Pauline eyed Madison up and down, taking in her black tailored slacks, white silk shirt, and tweed blazer. It was a different fashion statement than her usual jeans and sweater and let the housekeeper know whatever Madison was up to, it required a professional appearance. "Tell you what. I'm due to leave in two hours, but I don't have any special plans for tonight. How about I stay an hour or two longer. Will that give you enough time?"

Madison considered the timing and the distance she had to cover. "I think it will be plenty." She glanced at her watch. "Besides, Hyun will be here in about four hours, so I'll have to be back." She paused. She had grown to love the gruff Pauline, who stood before her squat and thick and full of street smarts, as much as she had the Dedhams. "Are you sure you'll be okay here alone?"

Instead of answering, Pauline walked over to the kitchen counter. Opening a drawer, she pulled something out and turned to Madison. In her dark hands was a large handgun.

Even though the gun wasn't directed at her, Madison jumped back. "Where did you get that?"

"It's mine," the housekeeper said casually. "Had it for years. I brought it from home as soon as all this nonsense started." She put the gun on the kitchen counter. "You run along and try to get to the bottom of this. The sooner someone does, the sooner things will return to normal around here." Pauline closed one brown eye and fixed the other on Madison to give her next words extra meaning. "I happen to be a big fan of *normal*."

Madison was going to make a crack about there being nothing normal about working for vampires, but one glance at the gun and she changed her mind.

SEVENTEEN

Fortunately, all three of the homes were on the west side of Los Angeles. Not having to drive through the sprawling city would save time. The first was the closest to the Dedhams. Madison had wanted to take the Range Rover over her own car for a few reasons, the most important being it had a GPS. The other reason was the areas these homes were located in no doubt had high security and private patrol vehicles. If spotted, the Range Rover would give her a much better image than her old, beat-up car. It also might not look so out of place. More and more, she was thinking Samuel was right about her getting a new car.

She drove first to the property in Calabasas. It took her close to thirty minutes to get there. Following the GPS instructions, she wound through a neighborhood lousy with huge mansions until it alerted her she was at her location. The house was situated to her left. Madison pulled over and stared up at a ten-foot wall and an equally high iron gate. To the left of the drive was a call box. Security cameras were posted at the top of the wall on each side of the drive.

Getting out of her vehicle, she approached the gate and peered through the bars. At the end of the long drive sat the house listed in the property description. It was solid and stately— a mini Buckingham Palace, even though there was nothing mini about it. All it lacked were palace guards in red uniforms and tall, funny hats.

Madison had studied the photos of each property posted at the links Nina Weinberg had provided her. She remembered reading that this house had five fireplaces, custom chandeliers, and both indoor and outdoor pools. She couldn't imagine the elegant house beyond the gate serving as a frat house for newbie vampires, with the mysterious Lady as house mother, mistress, and pimp to them all. But, as Madison reminded herself, vampires were unpredictable and seemingly with endless funds.

"May I help you?" asked a male voice without a body.

It took Madison a moment to realize the sound was coming from the box at the gate.

"What do you want?" The disembodied voice was more stern the second time around.

"I...I...," Madison moved closer to the intercom, which was extended toward the driveway on an angled pole so that people driving up would not have to get out of their cars to speak with the guard. "I received this address from a realtor. She said it was on the market."

"*You're* intending to buy *this* house?" Now the voice was smug. Madison looked up at the surveillance camera closest to her, glad she'd foregone her usual casual attire. Her first inclination was to show it her middle finger, but she restrained herself.

"I am scouting it for my employer," she explained in an authoritative voice laced with forced superiority. "He is the one who may very well buy this house."

"Sorry, miss." The voice ratcheted its attitude down a notch or two but still wasn't chummy. "Your realtor will have to make an appointment to show it to you. Them's the rules. No exceptions."

"I understand. I just wanted to see it myself before we went to all that trouble—to make sure, at least from the outside, it's what he's looking for."

"Well, you've seen it, so please move along."

She drove next to a property located in Topanga. The final property was in Encino, as far away from the Dedhams' as the house in Calabasas but in a different direction. This time, the GPS directions took her deep into a wooded area. Even with the satellite help, she missed her turn and had to find a spot to make a U-turn and try again. Finally, she spotted the road. She had seen it as she'd passed. It was a decent size and paved, but she hadn't seen the street sign so hadn't trusted the GPS when it directed her to turn right. Coming back from the other direction, she spotted the street sign, along with a larger sign marked Private. Seeing no gate or wall shutting folks out, Madison turned down the road and slowly followed it deeper into the woods. Every now and then she spotted a paved drive shooting off the main road and the occasional huge house peeking through the trees off in the distance. Some of the drives were walled and gated, some were not. The GPS told her to keep moving, so she did.

"Arriving at your destination on the right," the voice from the GPS cheerily informed her just as she reached the end of the private road.

Before Madison was another gated drive. There was no wall. The density of the bushes and trees formed a natural barrier hindering unwanted vehicles from passing. At the gate was a speaker with a buzzer similar to that at the first house. Madison looked around and spotted a security camera mounted in a nearby tree and pointed at the gate. Two other security cameras kept lookout from different angles.

Her shoulders sagged. All of these properties would have heavy security. She'd be lucky if she got close enough to see the front door or an ornamental shrub. Madison kicked herself. What did she think she would accomplish by running around from property to property? There were hundreds of such places in this part of Southern California. Nina Weinberg's handful of locations might have only scratched the surface. If the right property wasn't for sale, it might go totally missed by the realtor. The tattoo parlors might be a better way to use her time. She dug around in her purse, then swore to herself. She'd left the list of her targeted tattoo shops on her desk. The only list she had with her was the one of the five properties she'd printed out.

"In for a penny, in for a pound," Madison said out loud. She closed her eyes in warm yet painful memory. It had been one of her great aunt Eleanor's favorite sayings. The woman always had a bag full of folksy phrases—something to fit almost any occasion, like a box of generic greeting cards. Every now and then, one would pop into Madison's mind or out of her mouth—souvenirs of the last time she'd been happy as a child.

With the words hanging in the air like moisture on a humid day, Madison picked up the property descriptions and read further on the house behind the gate in front of her. Rather than one big house, this property was a compound containing several buildings—a large main house and two guesthouses for starters. The main house contained a media room, catering kitchen, solarium, six bedrooms, and eight bathrooms. There was also a garage for six vehicles, parking for at least a dozen more, a detached office or studio, staff housing, a greenhouse, and a stable for horses. She'd printed out the photos as well. Even in black and white, they were impressive.

Madison glanced up from the property description and photos and studied the gate. It was difficult to believe everything listed on the paper in her hand lay just beyond the sturdy but unimposing gate.

Getting out of her car, she approached the gate with caution, not really sure what she would or could do, half expecting a voice to snap at her from out of the blue. She pushed on the heavy metal gate. It didn't budge. Looking up into the security camera, she hit the button below the speaker on the intercom. A few seconds later, a woman answered.

"It's about time you got here." The voice sounded young and harried but not angry.

A second later, Madison heard a thick metallic *clink,* and the gate began to slowly swing open. She scrambled back into the Range Rover, driving through the gate as soon as it was wide enough. Once beyond the gate, she still couldn't see any buildings. She continued down the paved drive, framed on either side by more thick trees and bushes, thinking this would be a perfect place for Lady to stash her stable of male vampires and consorts. It occurred to Madison that it would also be a perfect place to ambush and trap ignorant spies.

The road seemed to go on for a long time before finally opening up to a circular drive, beyond which was a gathering of buildings that looked like a Mediterranean village separated by stone pathways. The landscaping was abundant with flowers and blended in nicely with the natural wild vegetation on the outskirts. The main building had two large round turrets. The place reminded Madison of fancy vacation villas she'd seen in glossy brochures.

Getting out of her vehicle, Madison approached the large carved wooden door of the main house and rang the front doorbell. From somewhere behind the buildings she could hear children squealing in play. It was a clear indication that she probably had the wrong place.

A woman answered the door wearing worn jeans and an oversized tee shirt. In one hand was a stuffed toy. Her blond hair was pulled back into a loose ponytail with curly strands trespassing around her pretty face. Even without makeup, Madison instantly recognized Gwen Maddox, the lead actress on very popular TV medical show.

"You're supposed to deliver the cake to the kitchen entrance," the woman told her, almost sounding out of breath. Before Madison could get a word out, Gwen's eyes focused on the Range Rover and Madison's empty hands. "Wait, you're not from the bakery." Her face turned from surprised to wary to angry. "You skanky paparazzi. How did you find this place?" She started to shut the door.

"No, wait," Madison quickly squeaked out. "I'm not with the press. Really."

The actress stopped the door from slamming, granting Madison a few seconds to explain herself.

"Look," Madison said in a rush, "I'm sorry for the intrusion, but I'm scouting property for my boss and was told this was on the market. You buzzed me in before I could say anything at the gate."

The door opened a few more inches while the woman studied Madison. For the second time in less than an hour, Madison was glad she'd worn some of her new clothes. She really did look like a professional assistant to an important tycoon.

Gwen's body relaxed as she made up her mind. "Forgive me. It's been a hellish day," she explained. "My husband's entire family is arriving in a few hours for dinner. The cook's in a snit, the nanny's sick, and the kids are driving me insane. On top of that, my husband's plane hasn't even landed."

Madison would have liked to have gotten a photo and an autograph for Dodie, who was a huge fan of Gwen's show, but she knew the timing wasn't right.

"It's okay. I should have set up an appointment, but I didn't want to bother the realtor unless the property was exactly what Mr. La Croix was looking for. Seeing this place," Madison said, glancing around, "it's lovely but not exactly what he wants."

Madison studied the famous face. "I'm sorry to have bothered you, Ms. Maddox. Good luck with your dinner." She started for the Range Rover, then stopped. "And trust me, I'll tell no one about this place or who owns it. My boss is very private, so I know how to be discreet."

"Wait," the woman called to her. "This is definitely on the market, and it's a real gem. We just need something a bit larger. What sort of place is your boss, Mr...."

"La Croix." Madison filled in the blank. "Samuel La Croix."

Larger. Madison scanned the front of the house and the other buildings within her vision and couldn't imagine needing something bigger. She knew this wasn't Lady's castle but stepped back toward the door.

"He's looking for something that resembles a castle. I think the realtor recommended your home because of the turrets."

"A castle," Gwen repeated.

"Mommy," called a reedy voice from somewhere in the house.

"In a minute, Callie," Gwen called back over her shoulder before returning her attention to Madison.

"You know, there are a few properties like that around here. Several years ago, we went to a party at the home of one of my husband's business associates. The main house looked like it'd been shipped over from England or Scotland, or someplace like that, stone by mossy stone. Our realtor brought it up to us when we started looking for a new place. We nixed it because it's not really kid friendly, but it's very impressive."

Madison's interest sharpened. "So this place is for sale?"

"Not officially, but it was our understanding that the owner was toying with the idea of unloading it. He lives in France most of the time. It's been leased out for the past few years."

"Do you know the address?"

"Not exactly, but it's over in Calabasas off of Cold Canyon Road, right where Wonder View and Timpangos meet. Very nice area. You know it?"

Madison nodded. Nice, indeed. "I was looking at a property earlier not far from there."

Madison stepped toward the front door and held out her hand. Gwen Maddox transferred the stuffed toy from her right hand to her left and shook Madison's offered hand briefly but with warmth.

"Thank you very much, Ms. Maddox, for both your time and information."

At that moment, the intercom by the front door buzzed. Gwen pushed a button.

"Bakery," a voice announced. "We have a cake you ordered."

Gwen pushed another button releasing the front gate, then turned to Madison, who was making her way back to her SUV. "Would you like to stay and help me with the kids?" she called. "I pay very well and will reimburse you for any dry cleaning."

From Gwen's strained smile, Madison couldn't tell if she was serious or joking—maybe a bit of both.

EIGHTEEN

As she drove away from the house, Madison passed the bakery van coming in. She smiled at the man driving. He was a young Latino with black slicked-back hair and sunglasses. He grinned back and blew her a kiss, probably thinking she was flirting with him. He had no idea that by being late, he'd done her a solid.

Back at the main road, Madison checked her watch to see how she was doing on time. The other house on her list was in Encino, farther away. After a short debate, she decided to head back to Calabasas to see if she could find the castlelike mansion Gwen Maddox had mentioned.

Retracing her earlier route, she took a right on Mulholland Highway. When she reached Cold Canyon Road, she veered left and continued on the twisty roadway as it wound through the hills. She'd remembered passing Wonder View earlier, both coming and going from the first mansion, but before leaving the private road in Topanga she'd keyed the intersection of Wonder View and Timpangos into the GPS just to make sure she didn't miss it. Time was ticking away, and she didn't want to take advantage of Pauline's gracious offer to stay beyond her usual hours. She also had to get back home and change into something more comfortable for traveling.

The intersection of Wonder View and Timpangos was less of an intersection and more of an elbow in the road where one road turned into the other. Just before the bend, set back from the road about a dozen yards on the Wonder View side, began a high wall made of pale gray stone with evenly spaced, groomed shrubbery running in front of it. It ran straight, then followed the curve in the road. The drive and gate were on Timpangos, and the wall continued well past the massive gate of intricate, open scrollwork.

Unlike with the other houses, Madison didn't pull up to the gate and try the buzzer. She didn't want a repeat of being turned away and doubted she would luck out as she had at the Maddox home. Instead, she drove a bit past the structure looking for a place to stash her vehicle. Along both sides of the road were stands of trees and thick natural vegetation. In spite of carving massive estates out of the countryside, the builders of the mansions in the area had managed to leave much of the original wild foliage along the road intact. In short order, Madison found a small turnout on the opposite side of the street. It was close to the main gate of the house but not so close as to appear obvious. After making a U-turn, she pulled into it as far as the Range Rover would go and climbed out, hoping a security patrol didn't drive by before she got a peek through the gate.

As she had slowly driven by in search of parking, Madison had noticed two security cameras mounted on either side of the gate. Both were trained on the driveway by the box, enabling them to see both the driver and any front passenger of an approaching vehicle. Her goal was to avoid those cameras so that she could get a longer look at the property before being noticed.

After crossing the street, she tucked in close to the shrubbery hugging the wall, trying her best to keep flat without the bushes clinging to her tweed jacket. Slowly she approached the gate, keeping out of camera range. She didn't know if this house had a full-time guard monitoring the cameras' security screens, but she was going to assume it was the same as the first house.

When she got close to the gate, Madison noticed that there was a gap of a few feet between where the cameras were trained on the security intercom and the gate itself. She sent up a soft prayer that if there was a guard on duty, he wasn't rotating the camera lens like a gaming joy stick. Taking a deep breath, she inched forward. The shrubbery stopped where the wall met the wide pillar that held the gate. She moved away from the bushes. Putting her back against the left stone pillar, Madison peeked her head around the edge and peered through the ornate iron bars.

Gwen Maddox had been right, the home did look like a mini medieval castle plucked from a storybook.

The large stone edifice matched the gate and was closer to the gate than the first house had been. There was still a large circular driveway edged with low-standing manicured shrubs, but there was less distance between the front gate and the actual house. In fact, the front gate almost spilled right onto the wide circular drive. Madison wondered if, although still grand, this estate did not have the same amount of acreage as the other houses she'd seen. With land so costly, it was common in Southern California for huge homes to be placed on smallish lots—or at least small by rich people's standards. The shortened drive also allowed Madison to get a very good view of the wide front steps and entrance. To the left and right of the house, she could see evidence of smaller buildings built in the same matching weathered stone, probably the garage and guesthouse. A few cars were parked in front or to the side of the main entrance. While a couple were nice cars, some were not, which Madison thought strange. If the older, less attractive vehicles belonged to maids and other staff members, they would normally be parked around the back of the house. Then she noticed something else different from the other houses. This estate didn't look quite as cared for as the other properties. On first glance, its appearance could even be called immaculate, but overall the property had a sense of abandonment or lack of emotional investment, like a marriage where neither party cared anymore but still kept up appearances. It was still beautiful—the lawn was mowed and the trees and shrubbery trimmed—but the beauty came from the architecture, not from any warmth or sense that this was a home. Madison wondered if it was because it was a leased property.

She leaned forward to study the gathered vehicles, trying to memorize each for details and wishing she could see license plates. She still didn't know if this was the house Keleta had been kept in, but it didn't hurt to take notice of everything possible. Pulling out her cell phone, Madison began snapping photos through the bars of the gate. She'd show them to Keleta as soon as she could.

She was snapping photos of the cars when the front door to the mansion opened. A woman walked out dressed in jeans and a light-colored pullover sweater with a long scarf around her neck. She was slim, with long, curly dark hair and took the steps at a quick pace. Just as she opened the door to a silver Honda Civic, another young woman appeared at the door. She was dressed in a gauzy pastel robe. Her long blond hair was tangled, giving her a just-rolled-out-of-the-sack look.

"Where are you going, Libby?" the woman in the robe called to the woman getting into the car.

"Just out to run some errands," Libby called back. "I'll be back in a hour or so."

The woman at the door looked nervous, glancing over her shoulder back into the house. She pushed her messy hair out of the way and turned back to Libby. "It's getting late. Make sure you're home before they get up."

Madison felt her ears widen like satellite dishes. Libby. Though not a rare name, it wasn't that common either. Leaning as far as she dared, she focused in on the conversation.

"They'll be hungry, and you know how she gets if we're not all here."

"I told you not to worry," Libby replied in a hurried voice. Waving to her friend at the door, she climbed into the car.

Madison, forgetting about security patrols and the unsure footing of her high heels on the pavement, ran back to the Range Rover. She barely had time to buckle up and start the engine before the gate opened and Libby's Honda pulled out onto the road, heading in the direction from which Madison had come just a few minutes before. Madison pulled out and followed.

Libby turned left onto Cold Canyon Road, then made a quick right on Piuma. When Libby reached Las Virgenes Road, Madison was surprised when she took a right. She had assumed Libby would turn left and make her way the few miles toward Malibu, where there were plenty of shops and restaurants.

As she drove a safe distance behind Libby, Madison kept running the brief exchange between Libby and the other woman through the corridors of her mind. The word *hungry* had definitely been used. So had a reference to people getting up late in the day, and the specific mention of a *she* who was in charge. Had Madison stumbled upon Keleta's castle via the helpfulness of a hassled TV star? Of course, she argued with herself, it could also mean the others in the household generally slept late. And most people were hungry when they first got up. It could be that *she* was the leader of a rock band who played gigs late into the night and demanded that her entourage be in attendance when everyone rose and got ready for their next performance.

It could also be that *she* was Lady, and *they* referred to the male vampires she kept around for kicks or whatever purpose they served. If that was the case, there was a good chance Libby and her friend back at the house were two of the consorts Keleta had mentioned.

Libby. Consorts. Had Madison unwittingly stumbled upon Notchey's missing sister as a bonus? Madison struggled with both the excitement and the dread that crowded for her attention. If the Libby driving in the car ahead of her was Notchey's sister, she'd been living in the Los Angeles area and had not contacted her brother—meaning there was a good chance she did not want to see him or have him know she was here.

Madison had asked Keleta if the women at the castle were enslaved in any way—kept there by force for the vampires' enjoyment. He'd been emphatic that they were not—that the women were employed and could leave anytime they wished, and in the short time he'd spent at the castle, several did come and go, though a few had been there the entire time he'd been in residence and appeared to have been with Lady quite a long time. He'd also said that most of the regular or favorite consorts lived at the castle, though some came in and out on a part-time basis or when called in by Lady.

Madison watched the taillights of the Honda ahead of her light up as it slowed for a curve. Libby had gotten into her car and driven off without any indication that she was sneaking out or escaping.

Continuing to keep her distance, Madison followed Libby up Las Virgenes for nearly five miles until she turned on Agoura. Up ahead was the freeway on-ramp. Again, Madison was surprised. Instead of getting onto the freeway, Libby pulled into the parking lot of an L-shaped strip mall.

Madison continued down Agoura a half block then doubled back, entering the same parking lot from a different angle. She kept to the far end of the lot, pulling into a space that allowed her to watch Libby enter a Starbucks. Madison's gut told her Libby was meeting someone. Either that or she had a big-time hankering for an overpriced designer coffee.

Looking around the inside of the Range Rover, Madison spotted a black wool bucket-style hat Dodie kept in the vehicle. It sat low on the head, with a brim that was thin in the back and widest at the front. Scooping up her long hair, Madison twisted it up on top of her head and stuck the hat over it. She pulled the front brim down low enough to hide her eyes without obscuring her vision. Even though it was a sunny day, it was February and a slight chill hung in the air. The hat would not look out of place. With one final deep breath, Madison made her way into Starbucks.

The scattered tables were partially filled, several occupied by individuals working on laptops. Libby was at the counter ordering her drink. Madison got in line two people behind her. When her drink was served, Libby took a seat at a small table next to a tall, square trash container on the other side of the room. She sipped her beverage without taking her eyes off the main entrance.

Madison posted herself at a table on the other side, next to a window, keeping watch on her prey without getting too close. She studied Libby, looking for any resemblance to Notchey. Though she looked pale and tired, Libby was a lovely woman with an angular face, large dark eyes, and full lips.

They'd only been seated about five minutes when Madison glanced out the window. Surprise nearly made her drop her coffee. A car she recognized had pulled up, and an equally recognizable figure got out and headed for the coffee shop—Hyun, Samuel's bodyguard.

Madison shook off the surprise and put her brain in gear. She glanced over at Libby. She was sitting straight, her eyes bright and fixed on Hyun as he made his way through the parking lot toward the coffee shop.

Madison shuddered to think what this meeting might mean. Hyun might have known all along the identity and location of Lady and withheld the information. Or he might be working for Samuel as a plant for Lady. Or Hyun was involved in the deaths of the vampires. Any one of the possibilities would be reason for the council to put him on trial, especially the last two.

Madison quickly picked up her drink and rose. She wandered over to another table, pretending to glance at an abandoned newspaper. Hyun was nearly to the door when she spied a small table on the far side of the trash receptacle next to Libby's table. The occupants of that table were leaving. Picking up the newspaper, Madison scooted over to the table, smiled at the folks leaving, and claimed it for herself, sitting with her back to the trash container. She wouldn't be able to see Hyun and Libby, but with any luck she might be able to hear them. If she was wrong and Hyun wasn't there to meet Libby, Madison might be able to connect with him herself and let him know what she'd discovered.

A second later, she heard Hyun's voice behind her. "Libby." The name was said low and with longing, followed by the sound of several kisses. Hyun took the empty seat at Libby's table, the chair next to the trash container, separated from Madison only by a block of plywood and used paper cups.

Like creative lying, eavesdropping was another skill Madison had learned in foster care. The smart kid always found ways to listen in undetected on adult conversations. Otherwise she'd never learn what was coming around the bend to smack her world around. Most often the talks had nothing to do with her or the other kids, but once in a while it did, and forewarned was forearmed.

"Libby," Hyun repeated, his voice sounding like he was saying it for the first time. Madison pictured him clutching Libby's hands across the table. "I'm so glad you called. I was afraid after the last time you'd never see me again."

"That was my intention, Hyun." Her voice was clear and strong but not hard.

Silence followed.

"You want some more coffee?" Hyun asked.

"No. I'm good."

More silence. Madison got antsy while the couple brooded about their personal issues.

It was Hyun who broke the silence. "I love you, Libby. I have for years, and I'm very sorry about our fight."

"I know that, Hyun. And I love you. Very much."

"Then leave Lady."

When Madison heard Hyun's words float her way over the top of the trash can, she nearly leapt from her seat with an *Aha!* The house on Timpangos *was* the castle, and the "she" referred to by the other woman *was* Lady.

"Soon, Hyun. I don't want to argue about this again."

Hyun sharply scooted back, hitting the trash container, which, in turn, hit Madison's back. "I'm beginning to think you don't want to leave."

"Listen," Libby said, her voice becoming a low feline growl. "You knew when you met me at Leopold's that I was a V-girl and what that entails." She paused long enough to adjust the tone in her voice. "We need to stick to our original plan, Hyun. Between my work as a V-girl and your former runner days, we almost have enough saved to go anywhere we want and live well. Now that we're both back in the States, it's all falling together. You just have to be patient."

Madison heard Hyun let out a deep sigh before he spoke again. "Libby, leave Lady now. If you love me, change the plans and leave her right this minute. We have enough money. If you're afraid of Lady, La Croix will help protect you. I'm sure of it."

"But that's why I wanted to see you, Hyun. I have decided to leave earlier—at the end of May." Libby's voice turned upbeat. "I've already told Lady that I'm retiring on my thirtieth birthday. That gives me enough time to train one of the other girls to be head consort." She paused, then added, "She was happy for me and wished me well. We're meeting tonight to decide who should take my place."

"No, Libby. Now. You must leave *now*." Hyun's mood turned demanding but his voice remained low. "Trust me when I say all hell is about to rain down on Lady. And when it does, I don't want you caught in the middle."

"What are you talking about?" Libby became alarmed.

Their side of the trash can grew silent. Madison wondered if Hyun was deciding how much to tell Libby, if anything, to get her to leave Lady.

Hyun cleared his voice. "Have any of the male vampires gone missing lately from Lady's household?"

"Missing? No. A couple have left, but that's normal. Happened all the time at Leopold's. You know that."

"At Leopold's it was normal for vampires to come and go. But is it normal for very young vampires to leave and go off on their own?"

"What do you know?" Libby's voice grew alarmed.

"A couple of vampires have shown up dead in the past week. And the local vampires believe Lady is behind it. If she is, it's just a matter of time before they find her and bring her down."

"You haven't told them where the castle is, have you?" The question was asked with hushed urgency.

"No, I haven't, and when Samuel La Croix finds out I knew all along where it was, who knows what he'll do to me. But I had to get you out of there first."

"Those could have been any vampires, Hyun. What makes you think they're from the castle?"

"They all had brands at the small of their backs."

"But Lady isn't the only one who brands before turning. I know, I've seen the same brand on other vampires, many much older than Lady."

"Yes, me too. But these were very new vampires. All except one." He paused. "What do you know about a boy named Keleta?"

"Keleta?" The surprise in Libby's voice was monumental. "He's dead?"

"No, but he was left for dead. How about a young, bald vampire, heavily muscled, with tattoos all over his back?"

"Duff?"

"Duff?" Hyun's question echoed Libby's. "Wasn't he the guy who bit you so badly a month ago that you needed stitches?"

"Yes, that's the one." Libby's words were full of bile. "If he's dead, then good. He deserved it. Keleta's a good kid. The girls all liked him. He was polite and treated us well. But Duff was a different story. As soon as he became a vampire, he started brutalizing us, even when Lady told him not to. A few mornings ago, he and Lady came back to the house just after dawn. Duff was totally amped up about something and demanded to be serviced before he retired. He savaged one of the new girls so badly she died. She was barely eighteen—a runaway from Oklahoma he had picked up in a bar about a month ago and turned into a consort. I thought Lady sent Duff away because she was angry."

Madison was appalled and couldn't help wondering what had been done with the poor girl's body. Had the knacker come and taken it away, hiding it from the authorities as part of his service to the vampires? And, if so, had it been Jesús? Or had the vampires simply dug a hole in the woods and dumped the girl like garbage? She shuddered. Last October, Doug and Dodie had killed someone to save her life, and the body had disappeared.

About the same time, the council had executed a couple of beaters. Madison had no idea how their bodies had been handled. This was the sinister underbelly of the seemingly urbane council.

"No, Libby," Hyun said, "I think Lady killed him. Killed him and dumped him at the home of one of La Croix's council members."

More silence while Libby digested all the horrible information. "You said a couple of vampires were killed. But Keleta's alive, right?"

"There was a second dead one. All we know is his name's Parker and he was part of Lady's entourage."

"Parker?" The gasp in Libby's voice was so loud Madison didn't have any trouble hearing it. "That's impossible. Lady would never have killed him. Parker was different. For starters, she didn't turn him. And they were a couple."

"Do you know who branded and turned Parker?"

"He was already with Lady when she recruited me from Leopold's court to manage her consorts. But I got the idea they'd been together several years. Are you sure it was Parker?"

"Keleta identified him."

"Lady told us Parker had gone out of the country on business for a while. He'd done it before, so we had no reason not to believe her." Libby paused. "They had been arguing a lot lately, but they'd done that before."

The silence on the other side of the trash container was so long and thick, Madison wondered if Hyun and Libby were speaking in such low voices she couldn't hear them. Finally, she overheard Libby say in a sweet voice, "Let's get our favorite room over at the motel and spend what little time we have left today not talking."

"You're not understanding the serious nature of this situation, Libby. As soon as La Croix and his crew find out where the castle is, they will invade it and take Lady out. Trust me on this. That council is serious about not having anything disrupt their business and way of life, and someone dumping bodies in their midst definitely disrupts their agenda."

"I do understand, Hyun. I also understand that I want to be in your arms right now. I want to feel your body next to mine before I have to go back."

"You don't have to go back. Leave your car here and come back to my place. We can start our life together right this minute. They will never know where you went, and if they do, you'll be safe."

"I'll be quite safe. Even if Lady is killing vampires as you suspect, she's never harmed a consort. She treats us much better than she does the men in the house."

"If Lady is trapped, she'll kill to save herself. Killing is in her blood. It's part of all vampires, even those who wear thousand-dollar suits and have box tickets at the opera."

Madison's thoughts immediately went to Samuel, and she knew that was exactly who Hyun was thinking about when he said the words.

"If there's that much danger, then I have to go back and get the other girls out. And I'll have to be very discreet about it, which will take some time. I'll start right away, right after they go to bed tomorrow morning."

"Meet me tomorrow, right here. But make it an hour earlier if you can. Until this is over, I want to see you with my own eyes every day to make sure you're safe."

"Let's make it in the room instead of here," Libby told him, "and let's start right now."

"I have to take someone to the airport for La Croix." Hyun paused. "But that's not for another hour or so."

Madison whipped out her phone and quickly typed out a text message to Hyun. A second later, she heard Hyun's phone beep.

"What is it?" Libby asked.

"How odd. It's a message from the girl I have to take to the airport. She says someone else is taking her. Talk about timing, huh?"

When Madison had come into the coffee shop, she'd silenced her phone, so when Hyun wrote back asking if she was sure, she got the message without alerting them of her presence. *YES*, she wrote back with flying thumbs. *AND HE'S PICKING ME UP, TOO. SO DON'T WORRY ABOUT THAT EITHER.*

"I still don't have a lot of time, Libby, but that just bought me a bit more."

"I have to get back soon, too, so let's not waste time talking."

NINETEEN

Madison watched out the window of the coffee shop as the two lovebirds walked across the parking lot hand in hand to the motel next door. She hoped for the next hour or so they could forget about vampires and death and get lost in each other's arms.

As soon as they were out of sight, she called Notchey. He answered on the first ring, which surprised her. After their fight, she was worried he'd blow her off.

"Can you take me to the airport?" she said as soon as he answered.

"When?" If he was miffed by not receiving a cordial hello, he didn't let on.

"In about an hour."

"What's going on?"

"Samuel's sending me out of town tonight on council business, and I want to see you before I leave."

After a pause, Notchey said, "Sure, why not? See you soon." He hung up.

Madison wasn't sure what she was going to say to Notchey. She didn't want to dredge up the details of their fight. He could either believe her or not. And she wasn't sure she wanted to alert him to Libby's whereabouts. Hyun's Libby still might turn out not to be Notchey's sister. She never heard a last name mentioned in all her eavesdropping. She could have even driven herself to the airport and parked her car there overnight, but something made her want to be near Notchey, and she needed to speak with him about Duff.

She left the coffee shop and went to her vehicle. From there, she could see the motel. Hyun and Libby had just left the office and were heading for a room on the first floor at the far end of the parking lot. Once they were inside, she climbed into the Range Rover and drove it through the motel parking lot. Slowly she passed by the rooms on the first floor until she reached Hyun and Libby's. She made note of the room number.

As soon as she'd returned home from her search for the castle and Pauline went on her way, Madison changed into jeans, a thick sweater, and boots. It would be much cooler up north than in Los Angeles. The Dedhams had just gotten up when Notchey arrived. Dodie seemed genuinely pleased, though puzzled, to see that he was taking Madison to the airport.

"I thought Hyun was taking you," Dodie had asked when Madison did a last check in her room to make sure she hadn't forgotten anything.

"He was, but I need to talk to Notchey, so I told Hyun he didn't have to bother."

"Hopefully you and Mike can iron out your differences." Dodie stared deep into Madison's face while she spoke. "What's troubling you, dear? I see quite a bit of darkness behind those eyes of yours."

"Just a lot of loose ends. I'm thinking a lot about Keleta and what happened to him, and whether or not we can get to the bottom of things before more bodies show up." Madison hoped Dodie hadn't picked up on her thoughts about the castle and Libby. She wasn't ready to share that information until she thought it through better.

Dodie patted her arm. "I'm sure we will. Don't you worry." Dodie reached into the pocket of her trousers, pulled out a small cylinder, and held it out to Madison. "I want you to take this."

Madison took the object, noting that it was a small, slender plastic vial with a spray pump. "What is it? Breath spray or a portable stain remover?" She laughed and looked at Dodie. Noting she was very serious, Madison stopped being a smart ass and paid attention.

"Samuel mentioned to me that he told you about bloodroot." Dodie tapped the container in Madison's hands. "This vial contains bloodroot juice. Keep it with you, and don't be afraid to use it if the need arises. Just spray it in a vampire's face and run. It will take a few seconds to work, depending on how much they inhale and how fast, so you'll want to make sure you are out of reach until then."

"But I thought my bracelet would protect me."

"It will, but there might be times you'll need to subdue a vampire. It's just a precaution. You will probably never need to use it, but since you now know about it, I thought it made sense to give you some. By the way, don't open the container. The cap's on nice and tight, but the juice stains everything it touches. This container is also small enough that it should pass airport security if it's tucked into your bag."

Madison was surprised. "You think I might need it around Joni Langevoort?"

"I think I'd feel better if you had it with you no matter where you go."

———

The ride to the airport started off in an awkward silence lasting nearly ten full minutes. Madison had questions for Notchey but wasn't sure how to broach them without also touching on their fight, followed by the possibility of him throwing her out of the moving car.

"You hungry?" Notchey asked, finally breaking through her thoughts.

"Yeah, a little. I was running errands most of the day and didn't have time to eat." She looked at her watch. "Not sure I have time now."

"Your plane's not for a couple of hours, and check-in and security should be easier since you're flying first class and only have a small carryon."

"How do you know I'm flying first class?"

"Samuel and the council always fly first class." He glanced at her. "Unless they're making their employee fly coach."

Madison looked at her ticket again. It was first class. "Nope, first class." She laughed. "First time on a plane, and I'm going first class. How's that for catching a break?"

"You've never flown before?"

"Nope."

"You nervous?"

"Not really." It was the truth. With so much else on her mind, the fear of flying was pretty low on her list.

"There's a Denny's right before the airport. If traffic doesn't bog us down, there should be time for us to grab a quick bite before you need to check in." He looked over at her with a grin. "Does that sound good, or is that too pedestrian for a first-class traveler like yourself?"

"Right now, I'd trade down to coach for a Super Bird sandwich and a Coke."

For the next few miles, Madison filled Notchey in on Duff. She pulled out the copy of the photos and sketch she'd made for him.

"You're sure his name is Duff?" he asked her.

"Yes, but I don't know if it's a nickname or not. Sounds like a nickname."

"Okay, I'll see what I can do. Duff might stand for the last name of Duffy or something similar. Did Keleta ID him?"

"No. Keleta looked at the photos and clammed up. I found out his name just this afternoon tracing a lead."

Notchey glanced at her, his brows knitted in worry. "I don't want you going off on your own on this. Last time you did, you nearly got killed."

"Don't worry, I think I've gone about as far as I can with what I know. You and the vamps can do the real digging while I'm up north."

"That's probably another reason why Samuel's getting you out of Dodge—so you won't go snooping around. Smart of him."

A few miles later, Madison asked a question that she hoped would eventually segue into what she really wanted to ask Notchey.

"What's a V-girl?"

Notchey didn't look at her. He kept his head straight, his eyes on traffic, but his knuckles protruded, stretching the skin on his hands as tight as spandex, as he gripped the steering wheel. "Isn't that something you should ask Samuel? Or even the Dedhams?"

"I want to ask you. Is it a hooker who caters to vampires?"

"Is this why you asked me to take you to the airport, to rehash a fight that should never have happened? Look, I was out of line before. I'm sorry."

"Answer my question, Mike."

"Wow," he snapped in a mocking tone. "You called me *Mike*. I must be in deep-shit trouble. Call me *Michael*, and I'll think you're my mother after receiving a call from the school principal."

"You think I'm a V-girl, don't you?"

"No, I don't." He took a deep breath. "*V-girl* or *V-boy* is slang for those who are hired by vampires to provide sex and blood and often companionship."

"Hookers."

"Technically, yes. But in the vampire culture, it's a legitimate occupation, much as Pauline is a legitimate housekeeper. The more formal title is either *courtesan* or *consort*."

Madison gave it some thought. "So the beaters who provide blood at Scarlet's for the vampire diners, are they also V-girls or V-boys, just without the sex?"

"No. They're called *farmers*." He glanced over at her. "Farmers do not provide sex, although I understand some of them started as consorts. Both farmers and consorts are extremely well paid, although consorts are the highest paid. And consorts are hired by only one party or a specific group at a time. They do not have numerous clients or turn tricks like a prostitute. They are not allowed to."

"So Kai would be considered a V-girl?"

"Definitely, though Samuel hates that term, so be careful using it around him. He thinks it sounds cheap and disrespectful."

"I do, too." Madison's thoughts drifted to Miriam. "How about someone who hangs around the vampires for fun? Would she be considered a V-girl?"

"No. She's a groupie—a girl just out to have a good time. She probably doesn't even realize she could turn it into a well-paid career. Groupies aren't respected, no matter how much fun they provide."

"How do you know so much about this?"

He cut his eyes to her. "If I'm going to work with the vampires, I need to know about them, don't I?"

"What's a runner?"

"A runner?" Mike thought about it before answering. "Not sure I've heard that term before."

"It's something I heard in passing—it might not mean anything."

They were traveling south on Pacific Coast Highway. Madison looked out her window at the ocean as it played peek-a-boo between the close-set buildings, wondering if she really wanted to hear the answer to her next question. "So what do you think I am?"

Another deep sigh came from the driver's side of the car. "I thought the vampires were wooing you with their glamorous and fast lifestyle." Notchey shot a look at Madison. "One step away from becoming a V-girl."

She swung her eyes away from the beach to Notchey. "If it's a legitimate occupation, as you claim, why would that bother you?"

Notchey shifted in his seat but remained silent, his jaw now as tight as his knuckles.

Madison turned in her seat until she was facing Notchey. She put one hand on the head rest behind him and leaned in close, her brows knitted together, her eyes steely. "I want you to listen to me, Notchey, and listen good."

"Good, we're back to *Notchey*," he quipped. "Always a good sign."

"If and when I decide to have sex with a vampire, whether it be Samuel or Colin or even some other vampire yet to be determined"—the image of Colin's naked body invaded her thought process, but Madison beat it back—"if and when that happens, or even if and when that happens with a beater, it will not be any of your business, unless it happens to be you. And it will be because I care about that person, not because of what he has or can give me. You got that?"

Notchey glanced at her and nodded.

"Say it, Notchey. Say you understand."

"Absolutely. I understand."

They rode along in more silence until Notchey turned the car onto Lincoln Boulevard, and then Madison threw out the real question she'd been wanting to ask. "Was Libby a groupie or a V-girl?"

Notchey snapped his eyes in her direction and stared at her.

"Look out!" she screamed.

Notchey braked just in time to avoid hitting the car in front of them that had stopped for a light. The two of them jerked forward as far as their seat belts would allow, then slammed back against the seats as the car came to an abrupt stop.

"What in the hell is going on, Madison?" Notchey yelled once his heart returned to a normal rate.

"Quit yelling at me and I'll tell you."

A vein in Notchey's left temple rose to the surface. "What do you know about my sister?"

"Only what Samuel told me," she explained. "He read my mind shortly after we had that fight. He told me about her and how what happened to her was influencing your behavior toward me. Is that true?"

"If the almighty Samuel says it, it must be true."

"There's no need for your sarcasm. Samuel cares about you. He cares about both of us."

Notchey remained silent until they were almost at the airport. "There's time for that Super Bird, if you still want it."

Once seated in Denny's on Century Boulevard, Notchey was still as stone. Madison remained quiet, waiting for him to decide if he was going to talk about Libby or the weather. It wasn't until the waitress took their order that he said anything more.

"Libby was a groupie who fell in love with a piece of shit vampire. I didn't even know the bastards existed until she came to tell me she was leaving town with one." The waitress brought a Coke for Madison and coffee for Notchey. "Did Samuel tell you everything? Or do I need to recount the gruesome details?"

"He told me. I'm really sorry."

Notchey looked down into his coffee cup and shrugged. "It's been a long time. She's probably not even alive." His shoulders might have said *no big deal*, but his voice cracked, giving up his true emotions. "She was about your age when she took off with him. Our folks died in a car crash coming back from a weekend in Vegas. Libby had just started college and was living with two other girls. I had just become a cop. It was her roommate who introduced her to the vampire scene a few years later. It was there she met Gus—Gus Himmel."

Their food came. Madison dug into her turkey and bacon melt with gusto while Notchey picked at his prime rib sandwich.

"Do you have a photo of Libby?" Madison asked between bites.

Notchey took out his wallet and produced a photo. Madison wiped her hands on a napkin before taking it from him. It was an old photo of a young woman in a traditional graduation headshot. It was a photo of the woman who'd gone off to the motel with Hyun.

Now it was Madison's turn to lose her appetite as she struggled between her mind and her heart about what to do. Her first impulse was to bring Notchey relief by telling him immediately that his sister was alive and in Los Angeles. But she knew he'd demand to know where and would make her life hell if she refused to tell him. There were several reasons why she felt she shouldn't. She knew if she told him Libby's location, Notchey would storm the castle to rescue her, whether or not she wanted or needed rescuing. Libby had also been in Los Angeles awhile and had not contacted Notchey. She could still be angry with her brother for the gun fight that had resulted when he tried to stop her from going off with Himmel. She also might have written him out of her life for another reason. Either way, Madison decided not to tell him yet. She wanted to know more about Libby and her situation first.

"Samuel told me that the council has tried to find Libby for you."

Notchey had taken a half-hearted bite from his sandwich. He chewed and swallowed. "Yes. He's put inquiries out, but nothing has come back on her. Himmel turned up dead about two years after they left the country—the result of a fight with another vampire. We don't know if Libby was still with him at the time or not."

"If she wasn't with him, is there any reason why she wouldn't contact you?"

Notchey stared across the booth at Madison with hollow eyes. "The only reason I can think of is that she's dead."

"Maybe she feels you might not want her back in your life after what happened. After all, you almost died."

Notchey balled his fist and gave the table a sound smack. Her soda and his coffee jumped in unison. "And I'd gladly take another bullet if it would bring her back."

TWENTY

The fire in the large stone hearth beckoned to Madison. She moved toward it, holding her hands out to the warmth. She and Eddie Gonzales were in the great room of a sprawling log cabin located deep in the woods in Marin County in Northern California. They had just shaken the light rain off their jackets and left them on a wooden coat rack in the outside foyer before entering the main part of the house.

"Joni," Eddie called out, walking deeper into the room.

The cabin was a two-story, with the great room split—half of it stretching up to the roof's rafters, the other half situated under the second-story balcony that looked out over the open section of the main room. To the right of the front door, a staircase led up to the balcony. From down below, closed doors leading to the various upstairs rooms could be spotted lined up like soldiers for inspection. The inside walls and floors of the cabin gleamed with shiny wood and smelled of pine. On the glossy floors, thick area rugs with intricate designs were used to mark off specific areas such as living room, dining room, and even a small library and reading area. The furniture was rustic and sturdy.

The trip from Los Angeles to San Francisco had been uneventful. After finishing dinner, Notchey had dropped her off at the departure gate. Since she'd never flown before, he flashed his badge at an airport cop so he could leave his car parked curbside while he guided Madison to the line for first-class check-in.

"I'll be here to pick you up tomorrow," he told her before saying goodbye. "If your flight changes, just call or text me." He kissed her lightly on the mouth. "Thanks for calling," he told her. "I really appreciate it." He touched her face. "Really."

As Notchey walked away, Madison continued to wrestle with her decision to not tell him about Libby. She thought about calling Samuel to let him know the castle's whereabouts, but didn't for almost the same reason she didn't tell Notchey. Samuel would send his people in there to confront Lady, and who knows how many innocent people would be hurt.

"Joni," Eddie called again. He moved toward a large hinged door just beyond the massive oak dining table. Opening it, he peered into the next room. Finding no one, he turned and faced Madison, giving her a shrug.

Eddie Gonzales was a short, pudgy man with the sort of features one easily forgot. He was a CPA by trade, both before and after turning into a vampire. He appeared to be in his late forties and was gay. He and Stacie Neroni had formed a lucrative partnership. Utilizing her legal skills and his accounting background, they helped vampires maneuver the intricate estate planning and investment issues faced when people live forever. Eddie Gonzales was also in charge of the northern part of the state.

With California being such a large state, the council had divided it up into territories—south, north, and central. Isabella Claussen, who made her home in Morrow Bay when not traveling for the council, oversaw the central area. Doug Dedham was her backup when she was out of the area for large stretches of time. Each of the territorial leaders had two or three vampires under them who helped govern locally. Joni Langevoort, Madison had learned from Samuel, while once on the council, was now one of Eddie's assistants.

"I guess she stepped out." Eddie returned to Madison. "Why don't we make ourselves comfortable until she returns." He glanced at his watch. "I hope she gets back soon; I have a dinner engagement."

Madison and Eddie had just settled on the sofa across from the fire when they heard footsteps on the second floor balcony. Turning, they watched a sturdy man with flowing blond hair and a close-cropped blond beard come down the stairs, taking them two at a time. He wore well-worn jeans and an open light-blue chambray shirt. He came toward them, a welcoming smile on his face. On his right upper chest opposite his heart were two sets of deep fang marks. One was crusted over. From the other set, half-congealed blood oozed thick as toothpaste.

"Joni will be right down," he told them as he pulled something from his jeans pocket and used it to bind his hair back into a ponytail. "Is it still raining outside?"

Eddie got to his feet and faced the man, not speaking. Madison noticed the hungry eye he was casting on the firm, blood-specked chest of the guy in denim and moved the conversation along before the accountant forgot his manners and tried to poach on Joni's private stock.

"Yes," Madison replied.

The guy grabbed a leather jacket draped over the back of a chair and casually slipped into it. With a nod to them both, he disappeared out the front door. When he was gone, Eddie let out a deep breath. Madison was sure if vampires could perspire, Eddie would be sweating like a menopausal woman in a sauna.

Before Eddie could retake his seat, they heard another set of footsteps on the second-floor balcony.

"Sorry I wasn't available when you arrived." A woman leaned over the upstairs railing and called down to them. Her voice was laced with a slight accent. "Be down in a jiff."

In the blink of an eye, she was standing next to the sofa. She kissed Eddie affectionately on both cheeks. "I was just grabbing a little snack to hold me over until dinner."

With two fingers, Eddie dabbed at a spot on Joni's left cheek. "You missed a spot, darling." He licked the blood off his fingers. "Very nice," he said with approval. "Nothing like good old-fashioned country cooking."

"You still seeing that sweet Japanese boy?" Before Eddie could answer, Joni looked over at Madison and winked. "It's Eddie's personal take on sushi."

Eddie glanced at his watch again. "Speaking of which, I'm meeting him very shortly, so let me make the introductions and get out of here."

He indicated for Madison to approach. She stood up and joined the two vampires.

Joni Langevoort was a middle-aged, petite woman with a lush figure. She wore her dark blond hair in a single long braid down her back and was dressed in a denim skirt, a red pullover sweater, and short Ugg boots.

Eyeing Madison, Joni leaned toward Eddie. "I think she's afraid I'm going to gobble her up as I did that fine young man."

The two vampires shared the laugh. Madison didn't join in. She was too busy trying to take Joni's measure. Madison was used to the good-natured ribbing vampires often displayed with one another and often with her, but she didn't know Joni Langevoort and wasn't sure she liked the idea of spending a day or two alone with a strange vampire. Inside her head, Madison kept reminding herself that Samuel would never willingly put her in danger. He trusted Joni, so she would have to trust her, too. She had no other option.

"Joni, this is Madison Rose," Eddie said, placing his hand on Madison's back by way of encouragement. "Madison, this is Joni Langevoort. She has amazing things to teach you, so pay attention."

Joni held out her hand to Madison, and Madison, after a slight hesitation, took it in her own and shook it politely.

Introductions made, Eddie stepped into the entryway and retrieved his jacket. "My job here is done, so I'll be off."

Joni went to the front door to say goodbye to him. "One day, Eddie," she said, her eyes full of mischief, "let's double date. I'll bring my favorite recipe, you bring yours."

With a hearty laugh and a wave to Madison, Eddie Gonzales disappeared into the rainy night, leaving Madison alone with Joni Langevoort.

"Don't worry, Madison," Joni said with a grin. "I only dine on the blood of males, both animal and human. So unless you're in drag, you'll be safe with me."

TWENTY-ONE

Your room is the second one from the top of the stairs," Joni told Madison, pointing to one of the closed doors off of the upstairs balcony.

"I don't believe I'm staying long."

"No, you're not, but you'll still need to catch some sleep at some point and might want a shower. The bathroom is to the right at the top of the stairs. Why don't you take a few minutes to freshen up, then join me in the kitchen. It's right through that large door." Joni pointed to the wide door just beyond the dining table. "And bring down those photos and sketches. We'll get to work right away."

Madison's room was quaint and inviting, with pine furniture and an iron bed painted white and covered with a thick quilt. She stashed her bag and headed to the bathroom, which was modern and sparkling and decorated in a country theme to match the rest of the house. It was going to be a long working night, but Madison was used to those with Samuel. After washing her face, she felt more rested and went downstairs to see what Joni had up her sleeve. Tucked under her arm was a file containing Doug's sketches, and in her pocket was a flash drive with digital versions of the same, along with the photos she'd taken of Duff.

Just before she'd boarded the plane, she'd sent a text message to Colin and Samuel, telling them she'd learned the dead vampire's name was Duff. She didn't tell them how she'd found out, but at least she could save Colin the trouble of hunting through all the tattoo parlors in LA or prevent them from pressing Keleta. Colin had immediately sent her a message back asking how she knew, but she ignored it.

Joni looked up from her work when Madison came into the kitchen. She had just started chopping what looked like carrots. A few whole, peeled potatoes were piled nearby. Next to the potatoes was a large bowl filled with chopped celery and onions. Something was sizzling in a cast-iron Dutch oven on the stove. It smelled delicious, and Madison's mouth began to water.

"Here," Joni said, handing the knife to Madison. "Why don't you finish the chopping while I tend the stove."

"You got all this done in the few minutes I was upstairs?"

Joni winked. "The gift of speed isn't just handy for getting somewhere in a hurry. I can also clean this place top to bottom in the time it takes a paid housekeeper to make the bed and scrub the shower."

Picking up the chopping knife, Madison finished the carrots, chopping them into the same size pieces Joni had been producing. Finished with the carrots, she moved on to the potatoes. "How big do you want the potatoes cut?"

Joni turned from the stove, a pair of tongs in her hand. Caught in the tongs was a chunk of browned meat, juicy, with a crisp outside. "Small chunks. They're going into a stew."

Madison brought the knife down on the first spud, halving it deftly. "You don't have to go to so much trouble for me. I'll eat anything."

"You're a special guest. Samuel will skin me alive if I don't take proper care of you." She moved the meat around in the pan, making sure all the pieces were browning evenly. "And it's nice to have someone to cook for."

"Dodie Dedham says that, too."

Joni glanced over at Madison. "I'll just bet Dodie's cooking up a storm these days with you living there." She gazed up at the ceiling, her eyes closed in memory. "I used to love walking into that house and smelling the aroma of fresh-baked chocolate chip cookies. It was almost orgasmic."

"Samuel told me you used to be on the council."

Joni nodded. Opening her eyes, she tended her cooking. "Yes, until a few years ago. I was replaced by Kate Thornton. Samuel wanted me to stay on, but I hated the travel south. I prefer to stay right here in Marin. What I do for the council now, I can do here without all the bells and whistles of the council meetings." She turned to Madison. "I hope you like rabbit stew."

"Rabbit?" Madison stared at the pot with worry, trying not to picture a cuddly bunny dredged in flour and sizzling for her enjoyment. "I've never had it before." She tried to infuse her voice with enthusiasm.

"This recipe was a favorite of mine before I turned." Joni stopped fussing with the frying rabbit. "Where are my manners?" She turned to Madison. "Would you like something to drink? Some wine perhaps, or maybe a beer? I always have beer in the fridge for Chuck."

"I don't drink," Madison told her.

Joni turned to her with concern. "Is there a physical reason for that? Because the stew calls for red wine. I could leave it out and adjust the recipe a bit, if you'd prefer."

"Cooking with it is fine. I just choose not to drink, that's all."

"Smart girl," Joni told her with a shake of the tongs in her direction. "You need to be on your toes at all times working with us vampires."

"Tell me about it."

Joni looked over at Madison, studying her closely. "You're not one of Samuel's ladies either, are you?"

The sound of chopping stopped with a skid, then resumed. Inside, Madison fumed, wondering if there was anyone who didn't believe she was sleeping with vampires. "No, I'm not."

"But the question bothered you. Why?"

For the first time, Madison met Joni's eyes dead-on. "Look, I've been with the vamps long enough to know Samuel would never have sent me up here for sensitive and confidential training without giving you my full dossier. So let's not play games, Joni. It takes too much time and energy." She delivered the words not with hostility but with a plainspoken truth.

"You're just as Samuel said," Joni told her with a sly smile. "Smart and ballsy." Joni turned away from the stove. Placing both of her hands palms down on the counter where Madison was working, she faced her. "I think I'm going to like you, Madison Rose."

Madison wasn't convinced Joni's words were genuine, and she wasn't ready to take a BFF pledge on her end, so she remained silent, looking at the vampire, searching for any signs of sincerity. Her awkward moment was saved when a loud noise sounded on the service porch, followed by a large animal barging into the kitchen.

Madison nearly fainted but got a grip on herself in time to back away, the kitchen knife grasped firmly in her hand and pointed at the animal. "That's a wolf." Her voice was hoarse with fright.

"A wolfdog, actually. Though some would call it a wolf hybrid."

The huge dog took a few steps toward Madison on his long, spindly legs. His head was large, coming to a sharp point at its snout; his coat was an explosion of silver, black, and white. The animal kept his head lowered, but his narrow eyes looked up at Madison with wariness. Slowly she backed up until her spine connected with a wall.

"Boo, stop that," ordered Joni. "You're scaring our guest."

Slowly, the animal lifted his head, turning his attention toward his mistress. His thick tail switched in affection. Joni left the stove and crouched next to the animal. Burying her hands in his thick ruff, she playfully rubbed his neck. "This is Madison, Boo. She's a friend." Boo swiped his big tongue over Joni's face and let out a happy whine.

"Boo?" Madison asked, still not sure she wanted to lower the knife. "As in *Boo, I'm scared shitless*?"

"No, silly." Joni continued petting the animal. "Boo as in Boo Radley." When Madison gave her a blank stare, Joni added, "Haven't you ever read *To Kill a Mockingbird*? It's one of the great American novels. A classic." Joni stood up and put her hands on her hips like a schoolteacher demanding to know why homework hadn't been completed on time.

"I've heard of it, just never read it." Madison kept her eyes on Boo while she spoke. "The only wolf I've ever read about is White Fang."

"Boo Radley wasn't a wolf." Joni smiled. "But we'll discuss your serious lack of culture later. Right now, I want you to put down the knife and kneel down slowly."

Madison wasn't sure about the suggested course of action. "I'm fine right here."

"Kneel down," Joni ordered, her voice even and gentle. "Boo needs to see for himself that you're a friend."

Madison lowered the knife and slowly crouched until her knees touched the floor. It put her face dangerously close to Boo's muzzle.

"Okay," Joni said with encouragement. "Now hold out your hand and let him sniff it."

Keeping the knife in her right hand, Madison held out her left, thinking if the animal bit it off, at least she wasn't left-handed. Boo sniffed, running his wet nose over it. His tongue darted out and tasted her skin. It tickled. His tail thumped.

"There," Joni pronounced. "Now reach out slowly and touch his neck, right where my hand is, and gently rub it. It will seal the bond."

Madison's fingers disappeared into the fur of the animal next to Joni's hand. Once she felt the animal's neck under the hair, she gently started rubbing. Joni removed her hand, and Boo leaned into Madison's touch. Both the dog and Madison relaxed.

Joni stood up, leaving the two to get acquainted. She went back to her cooking. Keeping a close eye on Madison and Boo, she tossed several ingredients into the Dutch oven, including the chopped celery and onion, water, wine, rosemary, and some other seasonings. The pan sizzled, and the room filled with aromatic comfort.

"There," she announced. After giving everything a good stir, she put a heavy lid on the pot and lowered the flame till it was almost non-existent. "That needs to simmer for close to two hours. In the meantime, we can get to work."

"I'm sorry," Madison said, getting up from the floor. "I didn't finish the potatoes."

"Not to worry." Joni held out her hand for Madison's knife. As soon as she had it, she attacked the potatoes and a small pile of mushrooms with lightning speed, making Madison do a double take. "Told you my speed had many uses."

Watching her, Madison realized Joni could gut her like a trout before she could blink. Her right hand played with the bracelet on her left wrist. She'd left the bloodroot upstairs and for a moment wished she hadn't, wondering if Dodie had given it to her because she was concerned about Joni.

"I think I'd like that drink now," Madison said. "Anything you have that's nonalcoholic." Boo nudged the hand that hung by her side, demanding more petting.

With her chin, Joni indicated the dog. "Now you're in for it. He really likes you. That means he's going to be begging for constant attention." She went to the fridge. "I have orange juice, cold water, and a several cans of Coke."

"I'll take the Coke. I'm going to need the caffeine."

Joni handed her the cold can. "You a glass or a can girl?"

"The can's fine." Madison wiped the top with a nearby kitchen towel and popped the top.

Joni stuck her head into a large pantry and emerged with a big scoop of dog food. She dumped it into a bowl on the floor by the back door. Boo left Madison's side and eagerly attacked the kibble. With the dog occupied, Joni started out of the roomy kitchen and indicated for Madison to follow.

Between the front door to the cabin and the staircase was a closed door. When she'd first come into the house, Madison had assumed it was a coat closet. Taking a key from her pocket, Joni unlocked the door. Reaching in, she snapped on a light.

It wasn't a closet at all, but an office. As rustic as the rest of the cabin was, this room gleamed with the latest in sophisticated computers and office equipment.

"Welcome to vampire command central." With a sweep of her arm, Joni invited Madison to enter.

Madison stepped into the room and looked around as if she'd stepped down a rabbit hole. The room was long and narrow, running alongside the length of the house, but instead of tightly fitted and stained logs, the inside walls were regular flat walls painted a neutral color. The floor was a pale tile.

"Was this room added on?" Madison peered at one of the computer screens. Across it, colorful shapes danced a choreographed ensemble piece in silence.

"No, it was a storage room," Joni explained. "As much as I hated to do it, I covered the log walls with extra insulation and Sheetrock to maintain the temperature at an even level no matter what time of the year. This is the only room in the whole place outfitted with AC."

"This is what Samuel wanted me to see?"

"What's on these computers is what he wanted you to see." Joni went over to one of the computer stations. Pulling a fob from her pocket, she consulted it, then punched a series of numbers out on the keyboard. "And learn." Joni took a seat in one of the rolling desk chairs and scooted up to the computer. She indicated for Madison to take another nearby chair and do the same.

"How much do you know about vampire politics?" Joni asked.

Madison shifted in her seat as she dug through her brain for what little information she'd been given to date. "I've been told that Samuel came to California and took it over; that before he did, it was out of control."

"Samuel La Croix didn't just come in, he was invited." Joni paused, then added, "A hired gun would be closer to the truth."

"I was also told his cleanup was very bloody."

Joni turned her eyes to Madison. "You heard correctly. A lot of vampires died in the struggle between those who wanted change and those who wanted it to remain as it was. It was a civil war. And after, those who prevailed put on trial those who opposed them."

"You mean, they were executed." Madison's voice was flat, as if reading a grocery list. She didn't relish how often the word *execute* or some variation of it was popping up in her vocabulary lately.

"Some were. Some were not. Some were banished from California. A few were given the choice to stay and change their ways or leave. Punishment was determined on the extent of their crimes."

Madison pushed the information around in her head, trying to store and organize it. "How long ago was this?"

Joni leaned back in her chair and gave it some thought. "Forty-five years ago, maybe a few years less."

"Last night, Stacie said she'd been a vampire forty-three years. Any correlation?"

"Yes. Stacie turned vampire to assist Samuel in bringing about the change. Before that, she worked with some of them on legal matters."

Joni scrutinized Madison. It gave Madison the willies. The more she was around Joni, the more wary she became. She wondered if Joni had the same gift as Samuel, but a look of disappointment in Joni's eyes told Madison her thoughts were safe.

"Samuel said," Joni continued, "that I'm to explain anything you ask about. That's pretty high clearance for a beater. In fact, it's unprecedented. But I trust Samuel implicitly, so I trust his judgment about you."

Madison scoffed. "Truthfully, I'm not sure I want to know all this stuff. What I know now is enough to make me think I'm going crazy."

Joni turned back to the computer screen. A small smile, no more than a fine line of lip, crossed her face. "Well, buckle up, because you're about to learn a hell of a lot more."

As Joni's fingers flew over the keyboard, several different screens flew by. "I'll be giving you access to this information after I show you how to use it. It's stored on a secured site and uses a special rotating password. Before we're done, I'll give you a fob like mine."

Boo wandered into the computer room. He nudged Madison's hand. After she petted him a few times, he curled up on the floor like a big ball of variegated black, silver, and white yarn. Madison glanced at the bracelet on her wrist. She knew it would protect her from Joni, but would it protect her if Joni gave Boo a command to attack? When she returned to LA, she was going to ask Samuel the extent of the protection. She wouldn't be able to protect herself if she didn't know the bracelet's limits, and she doubted if the bloodroot would work on a dog.

"This," Joni explained to Madison, "is a database of information I've been gathering for years, even before I was a vampire. At first I kept it in a journal all by hand. Now I just input it here. I've also transferred all the old information to this database."

Madison squinted at the screen. It looked like nothing more than a long list of names displayed on a plain background in a ho-hum font. "What is it?"

"It's a vampire database."

"You track the world's vampires?" Madison couldn't keep the wonder out of her voice.

"Only those the council knows or learns about, so the list is far from complete." Joni glanced over at Madison. "There are far fewer vampires in the world than you might think. Only about a hundred thousand to one hundred fifty thousand, tops. And those numbers include a generous allowance for those vampires we don't know about. There are just shy of fifty thousand names on this list, and some of those we know have died."

Madison felt her eyebrows arch in surprise at the number but wasn't sure if it was because she expected the number of vampires in the world to be less or more. "Fifty thousand names is very impressive," she said instead, and meant it.

Joni laughed. "Not if you consider we've been working on this list for nearly two hundred years. Samuel got an idea in his head to track vampires." She glanced at Madison, one corner of her mouth tilted upward. "And I'm sure you know how he can be when he's determined to do something."

Madison gave Joni a small, knowing smile. "How do you gather the names?"

With a shrug of her shoulders, Joni answered, "They come in from here and there. Isabella provides a lot from her travels. This database isn't public, by the way." She shot Madison a pointed look. "Samuel and I started it before he came to California, and we kept it a secret. Except for myself, I'm not sure anyone outside of the present council even knows about it. And you're the only mortal I know of who knows of its existence."

"Don't worry, I know how to keep my mouth shut."

Joni gave her a tight smile. "If you didn't, Samuel would never have sent you here."

Joni pointed at the screen. "See this? That's Doug Dedham's name." She clicked on Doug's name and a new page popped open, complete with a small photo and a list of personal information. Joni stabbed at the screen with an index finger. "This tells me everything we know about Doug Dedham—information such as where he lives, what names he's used, who turned him and when."

"He was turned by Ann Hayes."

"That's right." Joni highlighted a name on Doug's page next to the term *Upline—Annabelle Fogle aka Ann Hayes*. "This link will take us to Ann's information. I just updated her name this week."

Under the line with Ann's name was the heading *Downline*. Under that were listed three names: Sebastian Worth, Mary Ellen Cox, and Dodie Dedham. Only Dodie's name was known to Madison.

"The downline," Madison asked. "Are those vampires Doug has personally turned?"

"Yes."

"There aren't many names there."

"Contrary to some popular beliefs, vampires don't roam the world creating other vampires willy-nilly." Joni swiveled to face Madison. "Most of us only make a few. Some go through eternity turning no one. Most vampires only turn someone when there's a need or purpose to it."

"Why is that?"

The corner of Joni's mouth turned up. "It's about power, Madison. Generally, a vampire can control a mortal easily, but it's much more difficult to control another vampire. Turning someone doesn't mean they become your servant. It's like children. Eventually, they want to leave the nest and create their own home and life. A smart vampire thirsting for both blood and power will keep a group of dedicated beaters around him—controlling them through money, excitement, and even sex—not a pack of unruly vampires."

The comment turned Madison's thoughts to Lady. Was she creating new vampires only to kill them if she couldn't control them? She hadn't been able to control Duff, but Madison couldn't imagine Keleta being difficult. And was Parker killed because he was stepping out of line? Keleta had said there were about seven or eight vampires at the castle. With Keleta, Duff, and Parker gone, that would leave four to five, unless Lady already had their replacements lined up. Try as she might, Madison couldn't fathom what Lady was doing with so many male vampires, especially newbies. Was it just for the sex?

Madison screwed up her face in contemplation. "I get the blood thing. That's food to you. But what's all the sex about? Seems every vampire I've met is sex crazy."

Joni laughed out loud before answering. "That's actually a very good question. I'm surprised you haven't asked Samuel that, considering his penchant for small harems." She shot Madison a sly look and received a scowl in return.

"Sex," Joni continued, "is one of the few human pleasures we are allowed. What's more, for us the enjoyment is intensified. In return, we can give our partners a more satisfying experience. Some even call it intoxicating."

Madison thought of Miriam and the other women who flocked around vampires. She thought of Chuck, Joni's lover, bouncing down the stairs with hyped-up energy. Then she remembered how Colin had made her feel, even though their lovemaking had not been consummated. She shivered but not with cold. She gripped the arms of her chair and looked down at the floor, trying to clear her mind. When she looked up, Joni was watching her like a hungry hawk eyeing a sparrow.

"If it wasn't Samuel who popped your vampire cherry, I'm guessing it was the delicious Colin Reddy. Or is there some new vampire hunk on the scene I'm not aware of? You're far too appealing not to be claimed by someone."

Madison tossed her hair back over her left shoulder, careful not to expose her right ear. The cut had been small and was already nearly healed, but she didn't want to give Joni's speculation any satisfaction. "I belong to no one, vampire or otherwise."

Returning her attention to the computer, Madison was surprised to see her own name under a column on Doug's page marked *Associates*. It was just below the name *Pauline Speakes*. She pointed to it. "Why am I listed there?"

Joni clicked on the link and brought up a page featuring Madison, including a photo of her taken during her welcome reception at Samuel's villa. "To the extent possible, we also keep information on everyone working closely with vampires. You are listed as living with the Dedhams and working with the council."

The detail of the information was impressive and took Madison's mind away from Colin and Joni's prying.

"Are V-girls or consorts listed?"

"Sometimes they are, especially if they've been with a vampire for a long time. The consorts that move around frequently are difficult to track."

With a few keystrokes, Joni brought the screen back to the list of names. "This is how you conduct a search." A small search menu popped up, and Joni inserted *Samuel La Croix* in the box. "You can put in a whole name or a partial, depending on what you're searching for. You can also put in a geographical location."

In a flash, up popped Samuel's page. Joni pointed to the column listing *Associates*. "I believe these are Samuel's three current ladies." She glanced at Madison. "Am I correct?"

"Yes."

Several names below the women, Madison spotted her own name, Michael Notchey's, and Hyun's. Just above Hyun's name was Gordon, Samuel's former driver and bodyguard. Next to his name was AD.

"What does *ad* mean?"

"It's not *ad* but *AD*. Whenever you see that, it means that associate is deceased. A lone *D* signifies a deceased vampire. If you see a *BL* next to a name, that means a human with a bloodline. We like to track those as best we can, but it's difficult unless they are associates."

Joni switched to another screen. "This is a listing of only the names and jobs of humans in the service industry," Joni explained. "It's almost like an online Yellow Pages. You're also listed there as the council's assistant."

"How do you get photos of the vampires?" Madison asked. "They don't come through very well in pictures. I know Samuel doesn't come out at all."

Joni returned to Samuel's page. "Newer vampires do come out. For the others, we take what photos we can, then enhance them using descriptions or drawings like those you brought with you. For the very old vampires like Samuel, we take a photo of someone who looks like him, then Photoshop it to resemble him better."

Madison studied Samuel's profile photo. It looked like him, but then again it didn't. "Is that how vampires get driver's licenses and passports? Do you fake those, too?"

Joni turned and smiled at Madison. "Yes, you are quite the smart cookie." Her tone was one of appreciation edged with suspicion. She turned back to the computer. "We can generate fairly good photos to submit for things like passport applications. The driver's license is tricky because the DMV wants to take their own photos. Younger vampires can do that, but when it comes to the older ones, we simply buy them very good fake licenses using our enhanced photos."

"You guys have thought of everything." Madison shook her head in wonder.

"Our survival depends on it."

TWENTY-TWO

"Samuel suggested we start with Ann Hayes," Madison told Joni after Joni showed her a few more ways to navigate the database.

"Sounds sensible to me." Joni pulled up the page for Ann Hayes. "Although we don't have much on her. Samuel asked me to consult the database as soon as her name came up a few days ago. Seems she keeps herself under the radar."

The profile for Ann Hayes was pretty bare. There wasn't even a photo of her, just a description and a note that she used to go by Annabelle Fogle. Even her downline was skimpy, with only Doug and Colin listed.

"All we ever knew about Annabelle Fogle was that she turned Doug and Colin and branded new vampires," explained Joni. "Just yesterday I updated this to add her new name. I'm hoping to get a photo of Ann before too long."

"May I?" Madison indicated to Joni that she wanted to use the mouse.

"Better yet, why don't you take the helm." Joni got up from her chair and switched places with Madison. "It's the best way to learn."

What Colin had said about his time with Ann came back to Madison. He'd been her companion for a long time before striking out on his own.

"According to Colin," Madison said, "Ann creates new companions as she needs them—changing out men every few decades like other women change hairstyles."

"Hopefully, we can expand the list while she's around."

Returning to the search feature, Madison inserted the name Parker. Several names popped up, both as first names and last, and included both beaters and vampires. Using the advanced search feature, Madison narrowed the list down to only vampires with the United States as a geographical location. The editing left only a half-dozen possibilities.

"You're catching on fast," Joni commented.

"I like working with computers. Unlike people … or vampires … they make sense."

She clicked on the link for the first Parker on the pared-down list. His name was Jonathan Parker. Up popped a profile of a young-looking vampire with long red hair and steely blue eyes. Quickly, she closed the page and moved on to the next name.

Madison stopped her search long enough to pull Doug's sketch out of her file and hand it to Joni. "This is what we're looking for."

The next two links also brought up misses, but the fourth held a lot of promise. The profile was that of a vampire named Parker Young. The photo wasn't an exact match for the second dead vampire, but it was close enough to be a possibility. He was described as being tall, with rugged features, usually with long blond hair. It was noted there was a long scar across the left side of his rib cage. Madison read his bio, noting that Parker had been an officer in the Confederate Army when he was turned—a Southerner. He had no upline, and his downline contained only two names, both men, neither recognizable to either Madison or Joni.

"Looks like we found the right guy," said Madison. Still, she checked out the remaining two names, but neither came close.

After returning to Parker Young's profile, Madison tapped the computer screen. "We can mark this guy with a D. I'm almost positive this is the same guy who was found dead in Doug and Dodie's pool. The scar and the Southern connection fit, too."

Joni looked from the sketch to the photo. "Certainly fits the description."

"The thing is, when asked, Ann Hayes claimed she didn't know who he was. But she was still branding her new vampires at the time he became a vampire." She turned to Joni. "Could there have been other vampires using the same brand? You know, like a secret or private club within the vampire community?"

"Highly doubtful. One of us would have heard something about it unless it was way, way, way underground. And that's the sort of stuff Isabella is very good at finding and reporting back about."

Madison clicked back to the short bio of Ann Hayes and scrutinized it as if the meager words might come together to reveal a clue not yet seen. "If Parker Young was one of Ann's, it makes you wonder what she's hiding."

"Certainly would make her a suspect in the killings, wouldn't it?" Joni got to her feet. "You dig around and get comfortable with the database. I'm going to check on the stew."

After Joni left, Madison went back to Samuel's profile, more out of curiosity. For a vampire who'd been around since the Roman Empire, he'd created surprisingly few vampires. Mostly they were women, but there were several men in the mix. Three names on his list caught her eye—Isabella Claussen, Stacie Neroni, and Joni Langevoort. It looked to Madison like Samuel had built his council from scratch, with his own fangs.

Next she moved on to Colin. He had under a dozen vampires in his downline, so it was quick and easy to check them out. Madison only recognized one name on the list—Julie Argudo. According to Pauline, Julie had been the cause of the friction between Colin and Stacie. Whenever Julie's name was mentioned, everyone on the council stiffened and the air took on an awkward chill.

Madison clicked on Julie's link. Her profile brought up a very pretty woman in her twenties with short, dark blond hair. Large blue eyes looked at the camera with frank defiance and a hint of familiarity. She read the physical description—tall and slender, an appendectomy scar, and a large birthmark just above her waist on her left side.

"That's odd," Madison said out loud.

"What's odd?"

Madison jumped in her seat. She hadn't heard Joni return. After catching her breath, she pointed at the screen. "There isn't a D by Julie Argudo's name. Isn't she dead?"

"Not that I know of." Joni took her seat again. "Dinner will be ready in about twenty to thirty minutes."

Madison stabbed a finger at the computer screen again, this time with emphasis. "I was told by Pauline Speakes that this vampire was dead."

For the first time since they'd met, Joni seemed uncomfortable.

"You knew Julie, didn't you?" asked Madison.

Joni nodded. "Yes, I knew her. She used to live in Southern California when I was on the council."

"And she was good friends with Colin and Stacie, wasn't she? It says here Colin even turned her."

"The three of them were inseparable." Joni looked at the photo on the screen, then back at Madison.

Madison leaned toward Joni. "What's the big deal with Julie? Why are Colin and Stacie at each other's throats whenever her name is mentioned?"

"Julie Argudo isn't dead, Madison." Joni's voice was stiff and harsh like a boar bristle brush. "She was banished, though some thought she should have been executed for what she did. I was one who voted for execution. Both Stacie and Colin campaigned hard for the banishment."

"What in the hell did she do?"

"She betrayed the council." Joni spit out the words like sour milk. "It was a few years after Samuel and the newly formed council had brought peace to California."

"But if Colin and Stacie were both arguing for Julie's life, why do they hate each other now?"

"Julie was a bloodline holder and close friend of Stacie's, who she introduced to Colin. They became lovers, and eventually Colin, at her request, turned her. Soon after she became a vampire, Julie started sowing some wild oats and fell in with a bunch of bad news vampires. Colin and Stacie tried to intervene, but Julie was hard-headed and wouldn't listen. In time it was discovered that the crew she'd become a part of was plotting to overturn Samuel and the council. They'd even murdered one early council member who'd discovered their plans and tried to warn Samuel. Four vampires were put on trial, including Julie. All were found guilty of murder and conspiracy. Three were executed. Stacie and Colin begged the council to spare Julie, saying that while she was associated with the murderers, she didn't actually commit the crime. In the end, she was banished rather than put to death. The council didn't want to appear soft on traitors, so the banishment was done quietly. Most everyone thinks Julie was executed with the others." Joni paused to take a deep breath.

"But that doesn't explain why Colin and Stacie hate each other."

"Colin introduced Julie to the gang she hooked up with—not intentionally, but she was with him when he attended one of their parties. Stacie blames him for Julie's defection and ultimate banishment."

"Do you think Colin is to blame?"

Joni shook her head. "Julie would have found trouble on her own. She loved the dark side of being a vampire." She looked at the photo on the computer. "There was something in her eyes, a wildness just waiting for the cage door to open. Samuel saw it, too. He wasn't pleased when Colin turned her, but if Colin hadn't, Stacie would have, I'm sure. Julie was very persuasive."

Madison looked at the computer screen for Julie's address. "It says here she's in Bulgaria."

"Probably hanging out at or near King Leopold's court. That's the vampire orgy and entertainment center of the world. A lot of vampires banished from more orderly communities end up there. And good riddance."

"King Leopold?" Madison didn't let on that she'd heard the name before.

"He's not a real king. Vampires don't have that kind of structure. Basically, a powerful vampire can stake out a territory and call himself a king or lord or pretty much any damn thing he or she wants. Leopold is a very old Bacchanalian-style vampire who believes vampires should not be reined in by conventional ethics or morals. He thinks vampires like Samuel, who try to bring order and peace, are fools."

Madison folded this new information into what she already knew, mixing it carefully like delicate egg whites. Hyun and Libby had been employed at Leopold's court. Ann had been a guest there. Madison didn't know if or how Julie Argudo fit in, but the Leopold connection with the others jarred her senses and put her on alert.

She studied the photo of Julie Argudo again. There was something disquieting about it, making her wonder if Julie was back and looking for revenge.

She scanned Julie Argudo's list of associates. There weren't many, and all were women. One name on the list grabbed her attention—Olivia Himmel. She switched back to Parker Young's profile. Under the associates heading was listed Olivia Himmel. Madison clicked on the link. In a flash, she was staring into the face of Notchey's sister. Somewhere along her journey, Libby had taken Gus Himmel's last name.

The brief description on the profile listed Libby as a consort. Prior employers noted were King Leopold and Gus Himmel. Her address was listed simply as Bulgaria.

Madison pointed out the name connection. "Why would someone hire a family member as a consort?" she asked Joni. "Seems incestuous, or would they have been married?"

"Consorts sometimes take the last names of their employer, especially if they are breaking off all contact with their families."

Madison had wondered if Hyun knew Libby was Notchey's sister. Now she realized he probably didn't know. The connection between Julie Argudo and Libby pointed to Julie as being Lady, unless Libby had moved on to another employer after Julie. Also, Parker might have hired her away from Julie to work for Lady. The database gave no indication of when she worked for either of them or if she did currently.

Madison leaned back away from the computer screen for a moment. She hadn't realized she'd been hunched over, staring with rapt attention at the screen, until her shoulders began to ache. She rolled her shoulders to loosen them, feeling Joni's eyes on her every moment, watching and waiting for her to drop a hint or piece of information like a scrap of food tossed to Boo. But Madison didn't say anything to Joni about her suspicions. If Joni pieced together anything from Madison's search patterns, fine, but if Madison was going to chat with anyone about this, it was going to be Samuel.

Madison wanted to take the mouse back in hand and click on Hyun's name to search for more dots to connect, but with Joni watching her so closely, she decided against it. She wasn't sure how much to trust Joni and didn't want any of her search trails leading back to Samuel. Instead, she turned to her hostess.

"What's a runner?"

Joni nearly choked with surprise. "Where in the hell did you hear that term? Certainly not from anyone on the council."

"Why not?" Madison showed Joni a mask of innocence. "It's just another beater job title, isn't it?"

Joni got out of her chair and walked to the end of the small room, her arms crossed in front of her. The question had shocked her, alerting Madison that the simple term had an important meaning. Joni turned, leaned her behind against a small table, and stared at Madison several moments before throwing her hands up in the air.

"Samuel did say to explain anything you asked about."

Boo had wandered over to Madison's side and begged for attention. Madison petted the animal and waited on Joni.

TWENTY-THREE

Leopold's," Joni began, "is a lot like Vegas. You know," Joni tossed Madison a sly grin, "*whatever happens at Leopold's, stays at Leopold's.*"

The confusion on Madison's face caused Joni to elaborate.

"Leopold's estate in Bulgaria is really a sort of vacation resort for vampires. He provides any kind of amusement a vampire could want, free from the prying eyes and laws of humans. Anything from sexual adventures to feeding orgies to the actual hunting and torture of mortals."

Madison stopped petting Boo and sat at attention. "You mean beaters are hunted and killed?"

"Just like big game in Africa, although most vampires these days are pretty mundane in their appetites. Most go for the non-stop, no-holds-barred sex and gaming."

"So gambling, too?"

"Yes, but not like in Vegas. At Leopold's there is a very popular sport called running. A vampire picks a human, called a runner, and pits himself against him out in the wild on Leopold's estate. Other vampires bet on the outcome. The vampire hunts the runner against the clock. No weapons for either, just brain and brawn. If the vampire catches him in the allotted time, he wins a substantial purse and can do anything he wishes to the runner, just short of killing him, although some runners have been killed in the process. If the runner wins, either by outlasting the clock or by dominating the vampire, he wins the purse. The most successful runners become quite famous, like an NFL or NBA player here in the States, and are given celebrity status and other perks such as luxury living quarters, additional financing, even access to Leopold's pool of consorts. When a runner reaches that level, vampires from all over the world flock to Leopold's to challenge him, and Leopold becomes all that much richer. So do the star runners."

Madison pictured Hyun running for his life, trying to outwit a bloodthirsty vampire who thought of it as sport. "Hardly seems fair," she said. "Vampires have enhanced powers and senses that a mortal doesn't have."

"Runners aren't run-of-the-mill people, Madison. Mostly they are well trained in survival, with professional backgrounds in military special forces. Many have been mercenaries. They are thrill seekers, and this is the ultimate thrill."

"Any women runners?"

"I've heard of a few, but generally it's men against men."

So, thought Madison, *Hyun had been a runner*. Probably an excellent one who had gained the right to Leopold's V-girls and to Libby.

Joni pushed off from the table and stood. "Let's go eat. I'm starving, and I'm sure you are, too. The stew should be ready in a few minutes."

"I'll be with you in a minute, Joni. I need to check in with Samuel."

Joni hesitated, obviously wanting to hear the conversation. She stared at Madison, pitting her will against Madison's in a bid to force an invitation to join in on the call. When the intimidation didn't work, Joni chuckled and started for the door. "No wonder the council's in love with you."

Boo followed his mistress out of the room.

The text to Samuel read simply FOUND BOTH LADY AND LIBBY. Before she sent it, she added MAYBE.

A few seconds later, her phone rang. "That was quite a bombshell," Samuel announced. "Why didn't you call?"

"I didn't know if Joni had that super hearing or not, and I wasn't sure you wanted this information broadcast."

"Joni's hearing is not intensified. She has speed, and I believe that's it. Even so, you're correct: I don't want this information out. Not just yet. Are you in the computer room at her house?"

"Yes."

"If the door is closed, it's nearly soundproof."

Madison got up and closed the door. "Okay, the door is shut."

"How are you learning all this, from the database?"

"No, from what I do best: eavesdropping. The database is just providing confirmation. I know where Lady is holed up. Libby is one of the consorts hired to keep Lady's male vampires happy."

"Are you sure it's Mike Notchey's sister?"

"Pretty sure. At least she matched the information in the database. I haven't told Notchey anything yet."

"Good thinking. What about Lady? Have you learned why she's doing this?"

"Not exactly, but I have my suspicions. I also think I have her identity. And Samuel, if it's true, you're not going to like it."

"I already don't like it." When Madison hesitated, Samuel added, "I'm waiting." His voice was low, almost a growl.

"It may be Julie Argudo." Madison gave him the name with no frills—just laid it out there for him to decide how he was going to react.

"Can't be."

"I'm afraid it is, or at least could be."

"Did Colin tell you about Julie?"

"No, I'd heard her name at council meetings. When her name came up in the database, I asked Joni. You told her to tell me anything I asked."

"That I did." He took a deep breath. "Well, it was just a matter of time before you did learn about her." He paused. Madison kept still, knowing his silence usually meant he was formulating a plan.

"Let's not discuss this now. I'll be in the car when Hyun picks you up tomorrow.

"No," she said, a bit too quickly. She slowed her mouth down. "I've asked Notchey to pick me up. I also had him take me to the airport. I wanted to clear the air between us."

"I figured as much when Hyun told me you'd cancelled with him. However, this time, you cancel Mike, and we'll pick you up."

"That's not the best idea."

Another long pause. "Is there some reason you do not want Hyun with us?"

"Yes, but I'll tell you when I see you."

Another pause on Samuel's end. This time Madison jumped into the middle of it. "And don't go imagining the worst," she told him. "Wait until we talk."

Madison thought about Hyun's plans to meet Libby the next day to make sure she was well. "In fact, give him the afternoon off tomorrow."

"A day off isn't exactly what I had in mind."

"I'm sure it's not, Samuel, but please trust me on this."

Another growl, then, "All right, you win. But I'm still picking you up at the airport, so call off Mike. Text me when you board your plane so I'll know it's on time."

When Madison left the computer room about twenty minutes later, she found Joni setting the large pine dining room table in the great room for supper. Places were set for three at the table. At two of the place settings, large white bowls rested on woven place mats. At the third was a large thick, blue-green glass.

"You having company?" Madison asked.

"Yes, I called Chuck and asked him to come by. He loves rabbit stew." Joni hesitated, two soup spoons in her hand. "Something tells me," she added, placing a spoon by one bowl, "you found what you're looking for in the database."

"Connections, Joni, and possibilities, that's all. I still want to do some more searching after dinner. That database may not be complete, but it's a lot of help."

"Chuck will be taking you to the airport tomorrow morning, so he might as well spend the night." Joni finished setting the table. "And since you now know how to use the database, you won't need my help, so I intend to amuse myself while you work." She winked at Madison. "You don't mind, do you?"

"Not at all, but, um, didn't you already feed off of Chuck today?"

For a moment, Joni looked bewildered, then understanding brightened her face. "You mean that young stud you met earlier?" Joni laughed. "That wasn't Chuck. That was Brian. He lives at the end of the dirt road just past my driveway. He's a former New York stockbroker who now farms pot. Good stuff, too, I'm told. At least it gives his blood a certain delicious earthiness. He's the one who brought me the rabbit for your dinner and the rabbit blood for mine."

Joni adjusted a napkin before turning to Madison with a sly smile and a wink. "Chuck's my boyfriend, but Brian's my V-boy. If you're interested, I'm sure Brian would be happy to attend to you when you're through playing with the computer. He takes care of my female guests whenever I ask, both vampire and mortal. You can think of him as dessert."

Madison tried not to appear provincial, as if proposals like that were commonplace in her life. "Ah, no, I'm good—but thanks for the offer."

TWENTY-FOUR

The parking lot of the motel on Agoura contained only three cars when Madison pulled into the lot in the nondescript rental car. In the back seat were Doug and Dodie Dedham. In the front was Samuel. It was two hours before Hyun was supposed to meet Libby.

She backed the car into a spot by the targeted room, then walked to the motel office while the others waited, each with a hat on to shield them as much as possible from the midday sun.

"Hi," she said to the pudgy, middle-aged woman at the front desk. "I'd like a room."

"Just for yourself?" The woman pushed a stray lock of graying hair out of her eyes and put on the eyeglasses hanging around her neck by a beaded chain.

"No, there are four of us. My husband and I and my grandparents."

"Two rooms or one?"

"Depends on whether room 107 has two beds or one." Madison leaned forward and lowered her voice. "My grandmother is very superstitious and insists on room 107 whenever we stop somewhere." She rolled her eyes to emphasize the nuttiness of the request.

The woman suppressed a small smile and checked her room register. "I'm sorry, but room 107 is taken. How about room 106? It's right next door and has two queen-size beds. Room 107 only has a king."

Madison shrugged. "Sounds great to me. It's only for one night anyway. Maybe she'll get room 107 tomorrow night when we stop in Phoenix."

Madison took out the fake driver's license given to her in the last hour by Samuel. It stated that her name was Nancy Dodd and she lived in Henderson, Nevada.

"I'll just need to see your credit card," the woman told her.

"I prefer to pay cash. Is that all right?" Madison looked at the women with wide eyes. "My husband and I are trying to pay them off. You know how that is."

"Absolutely; however, you won't be able to make outside calls or order in-room movies unless we have a credit card or a cash deposit toward expenses."

"No need. We have our cell phones, and regular TV is fine."

The Dedhams and Samuel were relieved to get inside the room and out of the sun. The first thing Dodie did was close the drapes.

"Oh, look, dear," she said to Doug. "They have room-darkening drapes. How thoughtful. We'll have to remember that."

Madison stared at Dodie like her brain had done a wheelie. "Like when, *Grandma*, are you ever going to come back here again?"

"You never know, *Nancy*," the old woman answered. "Didn't ever think I'd be here now, but here I am."

———————————

The plan Madison and Samuel had put together on the way home from the airport was in motion.

When Madison emerged from the terminal at LAX, she didn't have to wait long before Samuel pulled up to the curb in his beloved Mercedes sports car and hopped out. He was driving and alone. A baseball cap was pulled down low over his forehead, and his sunglasses were in place. He wore faded jeans and a gray sweater. He looked like a celebrity trying to escape notice but too vain to give up the flashy car for the purpose. Madison looked around. No one was paying a bit of attention to them. It would be different if they knew that the man with the wide smile and casual elegance was a thousand-plus-year-old bloodsucker. Bet showing fangs would get the TSA folks to move the security line a little faster.

Samuel grabbed her bag from the curb and flung it into the area behind the passenger's seat. When Madison started to get into the car, he stopped her.

"No, you drive."

"Me?" Madison looked the hundred-thousand-dollar car over with concern.

"The sun is making me weak, and I want to reserve my concentration for what you have to say."

"Okay." Once in the car, she asked, "Are we going to your place or to the Dedhams'?"

"The Dedhams.'"

They rode in silence until they got away from the airport. After a couple of miles, Madison forgot about the expensive machine she was driving and began to enjoy the muscle beneath her.

"You can begin any time," Samuel finally told her. It was an order, not a request.

Keeping her eyes on the road ahead, Madison started at the beginning, explaining how she'd called a realtor about properties resembling a castle.

"Very resourceful of you," Samuel commented, with obvious pride on her behalf.

She ended her long narrative with the various connections she'd followed in the vampire database. The entire time Samuel remained silent, staring straight ahead, not giving away the slightest hint of what he was thinking or feeling, not even when Madison mentioned Hyun.

"So you don't know for sure Lady is Julie Argudo?"

"Not a hundred percent, no. But I am sure that Olivia Himmel is Libby Notchey. I'm also sure the only reason Hyun didn't say anything about the castle and Lady to you is because he was trying to extricate Libby before something nasty erupted."

She glanced over at Samuel. He seemed relaxed. He continued to stare straight ahead, his left arm stretched out, with the hand against the back of her seat. But Madison knew his brain was as honed and humming as the engine in the powerful car. He was considering all the information from different angles.

"Did you know Hyun was a runner at Leopold's?"

"Yes, I did. He was among the best. It's one of the many reasons I hired him. A successful runner has the highest dedication to survival. His instincts are sharp, his mind always on alert. He's never sloppy in his actions. In this case, Hyun was willing to put his own life on the line and risk angering me to save his woman."

"That doesn't say much about his instinct to keep himself alive."

"Maybe not, but it does say a lot about his selfless loyalties."

"Are you going to kill him for not being upfront with you?"

"I don't know. He's worked with vampires a long time. He knew the risk going in."

It was a brutally honest answer and not the one Madison had hoped to hear, but she had expected it.

"I also think," Madison said, moving the conversation along, "that it's possible Ann Hayes knew Parker Young. She might even have been the one to turn him."

"What makes you think that?"

"Joni said it's highly unlikely that there's a group of vampires branding potential newbies without the council hearing at least a rumor about it."

"She's right."

"We know Lady is branding, and we know Ann used to brand. If Parker is older than Lady, then it could be that Ann branded and turned him, and he eventually hooked up with Lady. He might even have been the one to give her the idea about branding."

"Nicely thought out. Though didn't you say Ann Hayes was also in Bulgaria? Maybe she mentored Lady at one time, and that's how Lady got the idea to brand."

Madison considered that angle. "It could be that we're dealing with two angry vampire bitches. If Lady is Julie, then she could have returned to the States to seek revenge on the council. Ann, on the other hand, wants revenge on Doug and Dodie."

She turned toward Samuel. "Do you believe for one minute that Ann Hayes is over Doug Dedham?"

Samuel laughed. "I've met my share of grudge-holding women in all my years, so no, I do not."

"Speaking of which, were Joni, Isabella, and Stacie once your mistresses?"

"Stacie, no, though I turned her. The others, yes. In fact, Joni and Isabella were with me around the same time." Samuel's mouth opened in a shit-eating grin. "Joni always refers to it as my blond period."

"But Joni is much older than Isabella."

"Joni wasn't turned right away. She wanted to marry and experience a human life first. When her husband died, she came to me to be turned."

"She's a hoot. At first, I wasn't sure I liked and trusted her, but by the time I left, I liked her quite a bit."

Samuel pulled down his sunglasses and looked at Madison. "And did you change your mind about trusting her?"

Madison took a deep breath before answering. "No, and I'm not sure why. It's not that I think she's malicious or would betray you or anything, but she's sort of like that half-wolf pet of hers. Tame enough face to face, but I wouldn't turn my back on it."

"You are very intuitive, Madison. Another of your qualities the council and I value." Samuel stared out the window before asking, "So what do your instincts say I should do about Hyun?"

"Wow, that's a tough one. Not sure I want to be a part of that decision."

"You're not, but I'd like your gut feeling."

"Okay." Madison weighed the options before speaking. "First, I think we need to make sure Hyun is not involved in the murders of the two vampires. If he's only trying to protect Libby, then we need to help him do it." She cut her eyes to the passenger's side. "And I'm saying that partially out of friendship to Notchey."

They were almost at the turnoff from Pacific Coast Highway to Topanga. To the left of them was the Pacific Ocean. Samuel looked across Madison to take it in through her window.

"Did you know that sometimes, right before I retire, I sit out by my pool and watch the sun rise?"

Madison remained quiet, understanding he wasn't looking for a response.

"A few times I've stayed so long that Foster and Enid have had to help me back into the house and put me to bed." He lowered his window and stuck his arm out, letting it feel the heat of the sun on his skin, but only for a moment. "After all these years as a vampire, I still miss the glorious feeling of the sun on my face every day."

TWENTY-FIVE

The three of them—Doug, Dodie, and Madison—waited for any sign of Hyun and Libby with impatience. Only Samuel seemed cool and collected. He was stretched out on one of the beds without his sunglasses, watching CNN.

Soon after entering their room, they had discovered a connecting door to room 107.

"This is going to help us hear better," commented Dodie. "The door will be much thinner than the wall." She pulled a stethoscope from her large handbag and wrapped it around her neck. "This will help, too. We want to hear everything."

It was Samuel's idea to get the Dedhams involved. Both of them had sensitive hearing. The first part of the plan was to try to overhear any conversation between Hyun and Libby to determine what might be going on in Lady's household, including the identity of Lady. The second half involved breaking in on the couple and taking Libby by force.

"I still don't understand, Samuel," Doug said after peeking out into the parking lot from behind the drapes, "why we don't just grab the girl and take her back to your place. We can question her better there."

Samuel never took his eyes off the TV. "Because she's more likely to give up information to Hyun when she feels safe. I want to hear as much out of her as possible before she feels threatened or trapped." From the bed, he looked up at Doug. "Who knows, depending on what we hear, maybe I'll change my mind about taking her at all. Maybe I'll let Libby return to the castle so as not to disrupt whatever Lady has in mind. It might bring it to a head faster."

Madison checked the lock on the connecting door, then went to her bag. Digging out a long, thin metal nail file, she went back to the door and began working the lock. The three vampires watched her with interest but said nothing, choosing instead to shoot silent looks between themselves.

It took Madison a full five minutes of concentration, but finally she heard the lock click. Turning the door handle, she pulled the connecting door open, revealing a room on the other side much like their own but with only one large bed instead of two.

Samuel got off the bed and looked through the door into room 107. "Well, Madison, there's another talent we didn't know you possessed."

"What can I say? Every useful skill I have, I learned in foster care, this one at the hands of Orly Thomas, a master thief by the time he was fourteen."

Samuel closed the connecting door, then opened it again, making sure the lock didn't reengage upon closure. "That could come in very handy."

Doug agreed. "Certainly less noticeable than pounding on the front door."

When he wasn't keeping watch out the window, Doug studied the room. While not an expensive motel room, it also wasn't a dive. It was clean and comfortable, with matching furnishings and dark floral comforters on the bed that matched the drapes. Even the carpet was clean and freshly vacuumed. On the table was a vinyl portfolio containing brochures of various Los Angeles area attractions and menus from nearby restaurants.

"There's something about being in a motel," Doug observed. "They always make me randy."

"Douglas!" Dodie snapped.

"Oh, come on, Dodie. You and I have had some wild times in rented rooms. Even before you became a vampire." In spite of herself, Dodie giggled.

"Ugh," Madison said in disgust. "What is wrong with you people? You're supposed to be my grandparents."

"Doug's right. There's something wicked and fun about motel rooms, especially during the day." Samuel playfully grabbed Madison around the waist and buried his head into her neck, making wet, noisy kissing sounds. "Maybe we should have gotten two rooms. After all, I am your husband."

Madison pushed him away, straining to keep a straight face. "Don't make me pull out the bloodroot."

"Shh," Dodie cautioned them. They all froze. "I just heard a car pull up outside."

Doug peeked out the window. "She's right. It's Hyun."

In two strides, Samuel was next to Doug. "And the girl?"

"No sign of her. Hyun's heading for the office. Probably going to check in."

A short time later, Doug reported, "A woman just drove up—dark hair, silver Honda."

"That's her," Madison confirmed.

"Hyun's returning, and she's getting out of the car to greet him." He paused. "She looks very upset."

Samuel gave a signal for everyone to be quiet. Dodie got into position by the connecting door, her stethoscope ready to be pressed into service.

Even without special hearing, they could all hear Libby saying something to Hyun in a high, rushed voice while he opened the door to the room.

"She just told him something bad is going on at the castle," Doug reported in a whisper. "He pushed her inside and shut the door."

Dodie applied the stethoscope to the flat surface of the connecting door. "She is very upset," she whispered. Doug, Samuel, and Madison gathered close to Dodie. "He's trying to calm her down."

"Is it about Lady?" asked Samuel.

Dodie held up a hand, telling him to wait a minute. "Yes, something about new vampires at the castle ... several new vampires showing up last night." She listened in again. "Libby told Hyun he was right, something bad is about to happen, but she doesn't know what. She also told him she's sure Lady killed Parker and Duff."

Samuel straightened with interest.

Dodie listened several moments more before reporting again. "Oh, that poor child."

"What?" asked Madison in a frantic whisper.

"Hyun is very angry because Libby has several bad bite marks on her neck. She said last night the new vampires got out of control when there weren't enough consorts for them all." She listened again.

Madison grabbed Samuel's arm. "We can't let her go back there."

"I quite agree with Madison," added Doug. "Mike's our friend. We have to protect Libby."

Samuel indicated to Dodie to get out of the way. Putting one hand on the doorknob, he quickly pushed open the connecting door and rushed into the next room, fangs bared and ready. Behind him were Dodie and Doug, also in attack mode. With catlike reflexes, Hyun jumped over the bed where Libby lay crying, to get between her and the threat. In his hands was a large handgun trained on Samuel's heart.

"No!" yelled Madison. She rushed into the room on Samuel's heels.

"Do what you want with me," Hyun said, his voice even and under control. "But leave her be."

Samuel put away his fangs, but his eyes never left Hyun's face. "We'll discuss you later. Right now, I want to know everything about Lady and her plans."

Dodie and Madison helped Libby get up and sit in the chair by the table. She was weak and pale, and one of the bite marks was oozing. Dodie went into the bathroom and returned with a warm, wet facecloth and soap. "Let me see them, dear." She shot a stern look at Samuel. "In spite of Mr. La Croix's bluster, we are here to help you."

Libby looked up at Samuel, focusing on him for the first time. "You—you're Samuel La Croix?"

"That I am."

"I ... I overheard your name last night. I was going to tell Hyun."

Dodie tugged gently at Libby's V-neck sweater. "You'll need to remove your top, Libby, if I'm to clean your wounds properly."

Hyun moved over to Libby. "Why don't you let Mrs. Dedham take you into the bathroom and fix you up. Then you can answer questions."

"No," said Samuel. "She'll remain here and do both at the same time."

Hyun straightened and faced Samuel, his face hard with defiance. "I'll not have you all ogling Libby like a piece of meat. She's had enough of that."

"No, Hyun, it's okay. I'll stay." Libby lifted her sweater and, with some effort and help from Madison, managed to pull it over her head.

When she did, everyone, vampire and beater alike, gasped. Unlike her neck, which had two large, nasty bites, Libby's chest, including her full, round breasts, was covered with small pairs of fang bites like multiple nicks made by a small, sharp knives held parallel. The cups of her pink bra were dotted with bloodstains.

"Libby," Dodie asked gently. "Are there bites in other places, too?"

Her eyes cast downward, Libby nodded.

Hyun's jaw tightened and his eyes blazed. He pointed the gun back at Samuel. "I should kill you all for this."

"No, Hyun." Madison wedged herself between Samuel and the gun. "They really want to help. Libby is Mike Notchey's sister."

Keeping his gun on Madison and Samuel, Hyun asked, "Is it true, Libby? Is Mike Notchey, the LA cop, your brother?"

"He was," she answered, dissolving into more tears. "But he's dead."

Dodie stopped dabbing at Libby's wounds. "No, dear, he's not. And he's a very good friend of ours."

"But Gus said he was killed—shot because of me."

"He was shot," explained Doug. "But he lived through it. After he got out of the hospital, my wife here nursed him back to health."

Libby looked up into Dodie's face for confirmation. The older woman nodded, her face full of kindness. "He's fine, Libby. And he's been looking for you all these years. Even Samuel here has tried to help him."

Ignoring Hyun's gun, Samuel moved from behind Madison and knelt in front of Libby. He took her hands gently in his own. "We're going to take you to Mike, but first we need to know what Lady has planned."

Madison left and went back into the other room, where she retrieved a piece of folded paper from her bag. It was a printout of Julie Argudo's photo. After dinner with Chuck and Joni, she'd done more research on the vampire database and had printed out the profile to show it to Samuel. She'd brought the photo today to show Libby.

"Is this Lady?" Madison unfolded the paper and showed it to Libby.

Libby studied it a long while before answering. "It looks sort of like her, but it's not. That's Julie."

Samuel squeezed Libby's hands. "How do you know Julie Argudo?"

"I . . . I worked for her for a short time, right after Gus died. Not as a consort but as a maid. When she died, King Leopold hired me as a consort for his court. The pay was much better."

"Are you sure Julie's dead?" Doug asked.

"Yes," Libby answered, looking from Samuel to Doug. "I saw it happen."

Hyun put a hand on Libby's shoulder. "You never told me this."

"It was before we met and something I wanted to forget."

"How did Julie die?" urged Doug.

Everyone could tell Libby didn't want to talk about it. Samuel stared into her eyes for several beats of her heart, then said, "It's okay, Libby. We don't need to know. She's dead, and that's it. It's Lady we're interested in now. Tell us, please, what name does she go by?"

"We're not allowed to speak it. She insists we call her Lady. She's told us all if we ever tell people about her, she'll kill our families." Libby looked over at Hyun. "Or anyone we care about."

"Is that why Keleta won't say anything?" Madison asked. "Because he's afraid for his family?"

"Yes. Lady tracked his family down and showed him photos to prove she knew where they were. I know because he once told me when we were together. She does that to all the new vampires and consorts to bind them to silence. But that's no different than other vampires. You all hold our tongues with death threats of one kind or another."

It was true. As Madison stood in the motel room listening to Libby, she remembered being threatened with death if she betrayed the vampires. Threats from the very creatures she lived with, worked for, and almost made love to.

Samuel asked, "Does Lady know about you and Hyun?"

She shrugged, then winced from the bites. "I don't know. He and I have been very careful about our relationship, both here and at Leopold's, even before I was employed by Lady. But she could have spies. She's never said anything to me about it, but I think she's aware Hyun is your bodyguard."

Samuel scrunched his brows and kept his eyes on Libby. "How do you know that?"

"Because of what I heard last night. It sounds like she's been following you. If she has, she knows who your driver is."

"What else did you hear last night, Libby?" asked Samuel with intensity. "I know you heard something. Let's start with what you heard about me."

Libby swallowed. "I was outside Lady's room on my way to my assignment for the evening. I overheard her joking with Adam, one of her new favorites. She told Adam she was close to exposing you—that it would happen soon and that she'd be killing two birds with one stone. That's exactly how she put it. She also said she was going to draw names to see which of the new vampires would die next." She paused. "They both laughed. Adam's as crazy as she is. He's the one who did this to me." She started sobbing. "He and a new guy named Coby."

The muscles in Hyun's neck nearly popped from anger. He tried to intervene, but Samuel stopped him.

"It's okay, Libby, tell us."

Libby's nose was running. Dodie dashed into the bathroom and returned with a wad of tissue. Libby blew her nose.

"This morning," Libby continued, "when most of the vampires were asleep, Adam came into my room and did this." She indicated the hundreds of tiny bites. "He said it was like snacking on peanuts—once you started, it was hard to stop. Then he called in Coby and he joined in."

"Why didn't you go to Lady?" Dodie asked. "Good vampires protect their mistresses and consorts."

Libby started choking on mucous. She coughed into the tissue, then said, "Lady watched."

Hyun stalked over to the common wall between the rooms and swung his fist, leaving a good-sized hole in the plaster. "Goddammit, Libby! You said Lady would never hurt her consorts. That's the only reason I let you go back there yesterday."

Libby stared at Hyun with red, swollen eyes. They stood out from her pale face like the bloodstains on her bra. "I'm sorry, Hyun. But she's never done anything like this before, I swear."

"Samuel," interjected Dodie. "If this Lady person is following you or has spies on her consorts, then we need to get this girl out of here immediately. Plus, I need to attend to all of her injuries. I can't do that here."

Samuel remained kneeling in front of Libby. "One last question—and the right answer will buy your safety, so think about it carefully before you respond."

Everyone in the room waited. Hyun once again went to Libby's side. Placing a hand on her head, he bent and kissed the top of it. "Do the right thing, Lib. For all of us."

Samuel fixed his milky eyes on Libby's once more. In a deep, clear voice, he asked, "What name does Lady go by?"

Keeping her eyes fastened onto Samuel's, Libby filled her lungs with air, then released it with a long, slow sigh of surrender and relief.

"Julianne Jaz."

TWENTY-SIX

That's impossible." Madison's voice was shrill with doubt.

Every face turned to Madison in surprise.

"Do you know this Julianne, Madison?" It was Doug who asked.

"Yes, and she does have red hair—light red hair. I met her on the trail where I run in the morning."

"Lady took up running about a month ago," Libby told them. "Not sure why, because vampires don't need to exercise to stay in shape. Sometimes she goes alone, and sometimes she takes one of the newer vampires with her. She claims it relaxes her."

"Very early in the morning?" asked Madison.

"Yes, right about dawn. When she returns, she showers, sometimes feeds, then retires for the day. What happened with her and Adam happened right after they returned from a run this morning."

Madison smacked her forehead with a hand. "*That's* where I know Duff from." Everyone looked at her. "That last dead vampire," she explained. "I thought he looked familiar, but I couldn't place him. Usually Julianne and her running partner wear baseball caps pulled down low." She turned to Libby. "Did Duff sometimes run with Julianne?"

"Yes, right up until a few days ago when he disappeared."

"Yeah," Madison added, still annoyed that she hadn't made the connection with Duff sooner. "She had a new guy with her on Friday morning."

Libby looked like she was ready to cry again. "That would have been Adam."

Madison looked at the vampires. "I sometimes run with Notchey. You think Julianne knows Libby is his sister?"

Samuel stood up and ran a hand over his bald head. "Madison, she's not monitoring Notchey, she's monitoring you, and I think you realize that."

Madison did, but she didn't want to believe it. She'd thought she'd finally made a friend, only to find out it was probably a setup. She fought the urge to vomit, remembering the morning Julianne had offered her a ride.

"Makes sense," added Doug. "If she's watching any of us, she'll know who you are. Sounds like she's been watching us all. She certainly knew when to dump the bodies into our pool and when Stacie wasn't home."

Samuel pulled out his cell phone and punched at the keys. "And she might even know where we've stashed Keleta and is looking to finish what she started." As soon as the call was answered, Samuel left Byron and Ricky a voice mail telling them to take Keleta someplace safe as soon as possible and stay there until they heard from him.

His concern gave Madison an idea. She moved over to Libby. "Did you ever meet a vampire by the name of Ann Hayes or Annabelle Fogle?"

"I've seen Ms. Hayes a few times at Leopold's. She was a close friend of his and visited often, but I've never officially met her. Lady spoke of her often, though."

The news sparked Samuel's interest further. "So they're friends?"

"Hardly. They hate each other."

Doug, Dodie, and Madison shared a look of raised eyebrows.

"Any idea why?" Madison probed.

"Not firsthand. But the rumor is that Parker was with Ann Hayes before he took up with Lady, and that he'd been with Ann for a very long time."

Dodie crossed her arms in front of her chest. "And we all know how Ann feels about losing a man to another woman."

Samuel ignored the remark. Doug winked at his wife.

"But what about these new vampires Lady has been creating?" Samuel asked Libby. "Do you know what they're for?"

She shook her head. "No, but they are all fairly new, and she's not training them properly, except to fight. I have noticed that the newer ones seem rougher and more violent than those she's turned before."

"Samuel," said Dodie, "that doesn't necessarily mean she's sending them after us."

"No, it doesn't, Dodie. But whatever their purpose, it can't be good."

Samuel let his eyes rest on Libby again. "Libby, do you have a cell phone with you?"

She nodded.

"Good," Samuel told her. "I want you to call Lady or someone at the castle and tell them you're not coming back. Tell them after what happened this morning, you're quitting, and you never want to see them again."

"I don't!"

"Then say that and let the tears flow. Tell them you're leaving town, getting as far away from them as possible. If you don't, they might come looking for you. I want you off their radar."

"But they might look for her anyway," Hyun observed.

"True, but then again, they may not, especially if Lady has stopped caring about her consorts and is about to kick into action a much bigger plan."

"But what about the other girls?" Libby asked. "I just can't abandon them."

This time it was Hyun who knelt in front of Libby. "Sweetheart, you may have to."

Libby held out her arm toward her bag, which was on the table. Dodie dug through it, found the cell phone, and handed it to her. She hit a button and placed the call.

"Heather?" she said into the phone. She looked down into her lap as she spoke. "It's me, Libby." Libby didn't have to force the tears; they came naturally. "I need you to give Lady a message for me. Tell her I quit. After last night and this morning, I can't work for her anymore. I'm done. After what she let Adam do to me…," she sobbed. "I just can't." Libby wiped her nose with a tissue. "No, I'm not coming back, not even for my things. I'm on my way out of town. I'm starting over." She paused again. "Heather, you should leave, too. You and the other girls. Get out before she lets them kill you. Remember Mary, that young girl from Oklahoma who disappeared? She didn't run away from us like Lady claimed.

Mary was murdered by Duff—*that's* what happened to her. Get out now, Heather."

Samuel took the phone from Libby and snapped it shut. He smiled down at her. "Well done."

———

They left the motel, each with their marching orders direct from Samuel. Dodie had wanted to take Libby back to their home, but Samuel nixed that immediately. "If our homes are being watched, we'd be better off all together at my place. I have all the first-aid supplies you'll need there. Plus, my estate has the fewest neighbors."

Samuel pulled back the drapes and looked out at the parking lot. "Thankfully, it will be dark soon, and the other council members will be getting up." He took out his phone and started making calls. His first call was to Colin, telling him to not pick up Keleta but to meet at the villa before the party. He also told Colin to call him the minute he received the message.

The message surprised Madison. "You're not still thinking about us going to that party, are you?"

"Where better to face Ann than in her lair, when she's playing hostess and off-guard?" Besides, I need to go, and I want you with me at all times." Samuel chucked Madison under her chin. "We'll find you something special for tonight."

Doug was concerned. "You don't think Julianne will be at that party, do you?"

"On the contrary, I hope she is." He turned again to Madison. "You'd recognize her, wouldn't you?"

Madison nodded, then tried to reason with Samuel. "But I know where the castle is. Why can't we just raid it right now while they're asleep?"

"Because we're exhausted, and you and Hyun can't do it on your own. I don't want any more innocent people hurt. Let's find out more about this Julianne and her plans, then forge a plan of our own." He caught Hyun's eye. "Do you agree, Hyun?"

"Yes, Mr. La Croix. We need to find out exactly how many are there and what their intent is, so we can strike efficiently."

Samuel turned to the Dedhams. "Is Pauline at your house?"

"No," Dodie answered. "She has both today and tomorrow off."

"Call her and tell her to take Monday off as well, just to be safe." He hesitated, then added, "Call Stacie and Kate. Tell them all to get to my house immediately and to give any household help they might have off until Tuesday. I don't want any of our associates in the way. Foster and Enid will stay with me. They have nowhere else to go."

"Kate and Jerry are touring museums in Europe right now," Dodie told him. "They left yesterday."

"Even better." Samuel stopped to think, then called Kai and left a message telling her with regret that their date for Sunday night had to be postponed and that he'd call her soon.

"Give Eddie a call and alert him as well," he said to Doug. "He should call Joni. I don't think they're in danger, but we can't be too careful, especially with all that computer information Joni keeps. Isabella is out of the country."

When they left the motel, Hyun drove Libby's car, and Madison followed in Hyun's. They were to hide Libby's car, then drive together to Samuel's house. Dodie and Libby rode in the back seat of the rental. Doug drove, with Samuel riding shotgun. They were going first to the Dedham house to pick up a few days' worth of clothing for themselves and Madison, then head to Samuel's villa.

Before they took off, Madison pulled Samuel aside. "What about Notchey? Shouldn't we tell him about his sister?"

"Call him and ask if he'll drop by my home. Don't tell him why, just convince him it's important. I'd rather he be told there, with us around, than on the phone."

Madison made the call as soon as Libby's car was safely out of the way and she and Hyun were on their way to Samuel's, with Hyun driving.

"Hey, Notchey, it's me. I need a favor."

"Have you noticed that every time you call lately, you need something? A dead body in the pool. A ride to the airport. A ride from the airport. 'Oh, wait, Notchey,'" he said, mimicking a ditzy, high-pitched woman's voice, "'I've changed my mind about the ride home. My bad.'" His voice returned to normal. "What do you think I am, some fucking taxi service with a wide-open schedule?"

"Okay, I'm sorry I changed my mind about the ride back from the airport, but it was very important. And so is this."

"I'm listening. Make it good or I'm hanging up."

"Samuel needs you at his house as soon as possible."

"I'm a fucking LAPD cop, Madison, not some dead man's errand boy."

"Please, Notchey. Just trust me on this. It's a matter of life or death."

"Well, it must be your life, because they're all dead."

"Seriously, Mike, it's extremely important."

"Aw, shit. There you go calling me Mike again. Where are you?"

"I'm with Hyun. We're heading to Samuel's."

"Must be important if the big guy's covering you with his own bodyguard." His tone was snide.

"Quit being such a wise ass." Madison felt tears start to swell. She took a deep breath, but her voice cracked. "We need you, Notchey. All of us."

"Did I just hear tears, or are they just as fake as the pot roast a few days ago?"

Madison made one more effort. "When you find out what this is about, Notchey, you're going to hate yourself."

"Too late for that, Madison. I already do."

TWENTY-SEVEN

As soon as they reached Samuel's house, Madison made a beeline for the office and the computer.

Dodie was attending to Libby, immersing her in a warm, soothing bath in one of the guest room whirlpool tubs to which she'd added soothing herbal essences. Shortly after examining Libby, Dodie had reported that the bites didn't appear as bad as they looked but were excessive in number and obviously meant to torture the recipient. Enid was thrilled to pitch in and prepared something light and nourishing for Libby. The two older women fussed like a couple of old hens over the emotionally exhausted and abused woman.

"While I admire your work ethic, Madison, I think you should relax a bit before we go out tonight." It was Samuel. He'd come into the office, sitting down heavily on the leather sofa near the desk. He looked drained, his handsome brown face ashy. "Doug and I are going to grab a few hours of rest. Dodie will, too, as soon as she's done with Libby. Vampire or not, I suggest you do the same."

Madison kept plugging away at the keyboard, her frustration growing with each error message. In front of her was the security fob Joni had given her. "I want to check the database for something," she told Samuel without a glance. "Joni showed me how to gain access to it remotely with this thingamajig." Another error message beeped from the screen in front of her.

"Damn! The problem is, I only have about a minute before the password on the fob changes or I have to start all over."

"Slow down," Samuel advised in a tired voice. "Take your hands off the keyboard, then close your eyes and go over the steps in your head."

She shot him a goofy look. "That's lame."

"Do it and you'll see. You're too wound up and it's affecting your memory. Take a deep breath, go through the instructions in your mind, then tackle it. Don't rush the process."

"Well," she conceded, "it couldn't hurt."

Following Samuel's advice, Madison closed her eyes and mentally went over the instructions Joni had given her for accessing the database. She'd written them down but had left them on her desk at home. Before leaving Marin, she'd gone through the exercise several times, until Joni was satisfied she knew the procedure by heart.

It was at least a full minute before she opened her eyes. When she did, she placed her hands on the keyboard and went through the access steps, one after the other, with a calm mind and steady fingers, in plenty of time before the fob changed passwords. Up popped the opening page to the database.

"We're in!" Madison beamed at Samuel like she'd won a goldfish at a school fair.

Samuel chuckled. "Slow and steady wins the race, Madison, nearly every time." He got up and leaned over Madison's shoulder to look at the screen. "So what are you looking for?"

"A profile for Julianne Jaz."

Going through the search procedure, she found the profile for Julianne Jaz. There was a photo, and it looked a lot like the woman Madison had met on the trail in Topanga. With Samuel watching, she flipped over to Julie Argudo's profile.

"Wow, they really do look alike, don't they?"

"At least in the photos." Samuel leaned forward to examine the photo on the computer. "This touched-up photo doesn't do Julie justice. She was much prettier in person, with more delicate features. That's one of the problems with vampire photos—they're usually just a resemblance rather than accurate."

Madison turned her head toward Samuel. Still looking over her shoulder, he was so close her nose nearly touched his face. "You knew Julie Argudo was already dead, didn't you?"

Samuel didn't look at her. "Yes, I did."

"And you know how she died. That's why you didn't push Libby to say anything more about it."

Samuel finally turned his head toward her, his lips nearly touching hers. "Yes, I know what happened."

"You took her out, didn't you?"

He didn't confirm her suspicions, nor did he give any further explanation. Madison knew none would be coming.

They both returned their attention to the computer screen. Madison switched back to Julianne's profile. There were no names listed under associates or downlines. The upline and bio were another story. "Look at this," Madison pointed to the screen, first to the upline listing, then to the bio. "It says here Julianne was turned by Julie Argudo. Before that, she was a consort to King Leopold."

It didn't take Samuel long to cover the considerable distance from the office, through the main part of the house, and down the long corridor of the guest wing. He entered the room now occupied by Libby without knocking, a concerned Madison half-jogging behind him.

Libby was in bed. Hyun sat in a chair next to the bed. They were both surprised by the intrusion. Hyun leapt to his feet as soon as he saw the scowl on his boss's face.

"Libby," Samuel said, jumping to his purpose. "Did you know Julianne Jaz before you became one of her consorts?"

Libby looked frightened. She reached out to Hyun, who took her hand. "Yes, I did. Did I do something wrong, Mr. La Croix?"

"Tell me everything you know about Julianne," he ordered. "Right now."

Libby fumbled like a drunk to dig through her memory and get the words out in an orderly fashion. "She was a consort at court before she was turned vampire. When she became wealthy and powerful, she hired consorts for her own household and asked me if I'd consider managing them for her."

"Who turned her into a vampire and when?"

"I … um …," Libby faltered.

"Spit it out, girl," Samuel boomed, flashing his fangs.

Hyun stiffened, ready to defend Libby. "There is no need for that, Mr. La Croix."

"He's right, Samuel," Madison added. She rested a hand on Samuel's upper arm. "Slow and steady, remember?"

Samuel jerked his arm away but retracted his fangs.

"Well?" he demanded.

Libby sat up straight. "Julianne was a popular consort at Leopold's court," she began. "Both Julie and I met her when she attended a party Julie gave. They found it amusing that they looked alike and even had similar first names. Almost immediately, they became close friends, and Julie received permission from Leopold to turn Julianne. After that, they were inseparable—they even referred to each other as sister."

She looked to Samuel to see if he was satisfied. He gestured for her to continue. After taking a deep breath, Libby did. "After Julie was killed, it was Julianne who helped me get the consort job with Leopold. The rest is as I told you—she later hired me herself, shortly before she moved to California."

Samuel walked to the French doors that opened onto the pool area, a feature of all of the guest rooms. He stared out at the pool that sparkled in the night, the submerged lights making it look like a cauldron of crystals.

"Did either you or Julianne know who killed Julie Argudo?"

When Libby didn't answer right away, Samuel turned around and fixed her with one of his famous glares.

"No, sir. At least I didn't know the vampire who killed Julie. I had never seen him until that night." After a short hesitation, Libby added with emphasis, "Nor since. Nor have I ever told anyone what I saw … until today."

Samuel approached the bed. "Not even Julianne?"

"No. Julie and I were alone that night. If Julianne knows, it's not from me. She's never mentioned it in all these years." She met Samuel's stare with one of her own. "Whoever killed Julie did me a favor, Mr. La Croix. She was almost as bad as Gus Himmel."

When Samuel was finished giving Libby the third degree, he and Madison left Libby's room and walked down the hall.

Samuel stopped outside the door to the guest room Madison usually occupied when she stayed overnight. He opened the door. "Like I told you, I want you to get some rest. We have a very long night ahead of us. I'm going to turn in myself. Later we'll find something for you to wear. I'm sure there's a party dress around here somewhere."

"We're still going to the party?"

"Yes, of course. I want to find out how Ann Hayes fits into all this. Could be dumping branded vampires, especially Parker, is simply Julianne's way of tweaking Ann's nose while carrying out her bigger plan. I'm hoping Ann will cooperate and tell us something. At the very least, she lied to us about knowing Parker, and I want to know why."

Madison grabbed Samuel's arm and dragged him into the room, shutting the door behind them. "Do you think Julianne is coming after you because you killed Julie Argudo?"

"Who said I killed Julie?"

"That's the point, no one said it, but the suggestion is hanging in the air like bullshit at a county fair."

"Another colorful phrase. You seem to have an endless supply of them." When Madison said nothing, he added, "It could be she's after the council because we banished Julie."

Madison shook her right index finger at him. "I don't buy that. How long ago was that banishment—thirty-five, forty years ago?"

Samuel offered up a casual shrug. "About that. So what's your point?"

"My point is, Libby disappeared about seven years ago. Since she worked for Julie sometime after that, and if you account for Libby spending a year in Julianne's employment and maybe a couple at Leopold's court, it would put Julie's death somewhere in the neighborhood of three to seven years ago." Madison put her hands on her hips. "Why would anyone connected with the council wait over thirty years to carry out an overturned execution like some vigilante?" Madison squinted at Samuel. "And I know you would never kill someone without a good reason."

"Again, who said I killed Julie?"

Madison plopped down on the bed and pounded the mattress with her fist. "I want to know, Samuel. I know I'm just a teeny-weeny speck in your lifespan, but I want to know why Julie Argudo died, especially if it had anything to do with you or the council. I work for you. I put my life on the line for you. I deserve to know what's going on before I walk out that door tonight with a target on my back."

Samuel leaned against the closed door and studied Madison, his face dark and unreadable. Madison fidgeted, knowing that one day she might go too far and he'd take her head off.

"A little less than five years ago," Samuel finally began, "Julie Argudo killed a former mistress of mine, a bloodline holder who I turned, much as I turned Isabella and Joni after our time together. Her name was Rebecca. She'd been a vampire only a few years and was in Bulgaria on holiday with some friends. Julie did it out of cold-hearted revenge against me."

With sadness, Madison looked down, almost wishing she hadn't made him tell her.

Samuel pushed off from the door and approached her. Roughly grabbing her chin with one hand, he squeezed her cheeks together and forced her head up to look at him. His opaque eyes blazed like white-hot coals.

"I kill those who kill mine." He let loose of her face with enough force to push her backwards on the bed. "If you haven't learned that by now, Madison, you haven't been paying attention."

TWENTY-EIGHT

Notchey didn't show up at Samuel's house until close to eleven at night, just as they were getting ready to leave for Ann's party. Hyun greeted him at the front door and showed him into the living room, where Colin, Doug, Samuel, and Madison were gathered. Dodie was with Libby. Stacie had called. After Samuel filled her in, she said she'd meet them at the party. Doug and Dodie would stay behind.

When Notchey's eyes caught on Madison dressed in a short, strapless sheath in midnight blue, her long hair done in a French braid, he jeered, "The big emergency you called me about can't be too big of a problem if you're dressed to go out on the town."

Samuel approached him, his hand offered in greeting. "Nice of you to come, Mike. We have a situation. Several, actually."

Notchey didn't take his hand. "I'm not here because you or Madison summoned me. I'm here on police business."

"Sit down, Mike." Samuel gestured to the large sofa.

"I need to speak to you alone, Samuel."

Samuel studied Notchey, digging deep into the cop's mind for the true purpose of his visit. What he saw caused him to stagger slightly, but he composed himself and quickly showed Notchey toward the left wing of the house and to his office. Everyone else stared at each other in silence, wondering what could have caused such a reaction in the usually rocklike Samuel.

A few minutes later, a wail came from the left wing that sent chills up and down Madison's spine and rocked her balance. It was unlike anything she'd ever heard, primal and beastly in both its volume and complaint. Hyun was the first to react. Grabbing a gun stashed at the small of his back, he ran for the office to protect his employer, but Doug and Colin passed him with their speed. In strappy high heels, Madison ran in last place.

They found Samuel on the leather sofa, his head buried in his hands. Notchey was standing on the other side of the room, his face dark and brooding. Samuel lifted his head. His fangs were drawn, his eyes glowing. He screamed again, rocking the windows on the French doors. The sound hurt Madison's ears, but she made no move to cover them.

They heard footsteps, and soon Dodie was at the door. "What on earth is going on? Are we under attack?"

Notchey turned to the others. "Kai is dead."

"What?" Madison started to go to Samuel, but Colin stopped her, holding her tight.

"You can't," he whispered, "it's too dangerous."

Madison started to protest, then Samuel tilted his head and opened his terrifying mouth. He let out another roar, longer and more deadly than before. The air in the room went almost wet with the depth of his fury. He lashed out, his arm smashing a hole in the wall next to him.

Dodie threw herself on the sofa and wrapped her steel-strong arms around Samuel. He struggled against her grasp, but she hung on.

"Everyone out," Dodie ordered. "Doug and I will stay with Samuel." She looked at the bodyguard. "You, too, Hyun. This isn't something you can help with."

Everyone, including Notchey, left the room, leaving the Dedhams to deal with the distraught ancient vampire.

Keeping a tight hold on Madison lest she bolt back to Samuel, Colin directed her to the large sectional sofa in the living room and sat her down. Her entire body trembled as she sobbed. He took the seat next to her and pulled her into his chest, holding her tight while she cried. Notchey watched them both, weighing and measuring their reactions to the news and their relationship to each other.

"What happened, Notchey?" Colin asked.

Notchey took a seat across from them. "Kai's body was found in the hills by the Hollywood sign a few hours ago." He looked at Madison, unsure if he should continue.

Madison looked at the cop. Smudged mascara ran down her face like tiny black snakes. "How?"

"Looks like someone grabbed her, took her there, and killed her. We won't know more until the body's examined."

"A sex crime?" Colin asked.

"Could be, except …," Notchey's voice trailed off. He cast another look at Madison.

Madison wiped her face with her hand. "I want to know."

"Kai's body was badly mutilated." He saw Madison flinch. He paused before continuing, to let her absorb the shock before handing her another. "It looked like a pack of animals tore her apart. She was wearing workout clothes at the time, and they were in shreds."

"She worked out on Saturday afternoons at a yoga studio in West Hollywood," Madison told Notchey in a broken voice. "A place on Melrose. I went with her a few times."

Notchey pulled out a notepad and jotted the information down. "You got a name?"

Madison thought a moment, but it didn't come to her. "No, but it had a New Age sound to it. *Spiritual* or *spirit* or something like that."

"We'll check it out. Someone there might remember her. It could tell us the time she was taken, whether it was before or after the class."

"I have to go to Samuel." Madison tried to stand, but Colin held her in place.

"No," Colin told her. "Didn't you see how he was? He might not recognize you. He might try to hurt you and not even realize it."

Madison held out her wrist to show the bracelet. "But I have this."

"Voodoo or not," Notchey snapped, "listen to Colin. He's right about this."

Colin put his face near hers, trying to comfort her while still confining her movements. "The bracelet will protect you. But if Samuel does try to harm you and can't, it could frustrate him more, increasing his agitation. What he needs is to collect himself. Doug and Dodie will know how to help him."

With new worry, Madison looked up into the face of the vampire she'd nearly bedded. "Do you all get like this, or just him?"

"Samuel lost control of his human side, Madison," Colin explained, his words thick with warning. "Potentially, it could happen to any of us if we allow ourselves to be engulfed by anger. It's not all that different from human rage, just intensified."

Madison shivered, but she'd stopped crying. She'd seen Samuel angry many times, but this was beyond her imagination.

"Speaking of which," Notchey said, "the other cops on the case are looking for a sexual deviant for this murder. I think it was done by vampires—angry vampires with a grudge against Samuel. You think this is connected to those dead vampires?"

"Very likely," Colin answered.

"Yeah, I thought so, too."

Hyun remained silent, standing off in the background, never taking his eyes off of Mike Notchey.

"Wait a minute," said Notchey, leaning forward. "Didn't Kai have one of those anti-vampire bracelets like Madison's?"

Colin straightened in understanding. "Yes, of course she did. So it might not have been vampires who killed her."

Madison shook her head. "Kai didn't wear hers all the time, especially when she wasn't around vampires. She hated it and thought it was ugly. I remember Samuel scolding her about it many times."

Notchey sat back. "Well, that theory's tanked. You have no idea how much I don't want this to be a vampire killing."

Colin agreed. "You and me both, pal."

Madison struggled to get free of Colin, but he was latched on tight. "Let go of me, asshole. I promise I won't go near Samuel."

Colin released her while Notchey looked on with interest. Madison headed in the direction of the kitchen. When she returned, she had a box of tissues in her hands and was wiping her face.

"We have Julianne's address," she told the men. "Why can't the cops just go and arrest her?"

"Who's Julianne?" asked Notchey.

Madison stood by the doors leading to the patio and pool area. She looked out at the lights of the city. They twinkled below like fallen stars. "Julianne Jaz. She's the vampire who's been leaving dead vampires as calling cards."

"So you're sure it's not Ann Hayes?"

She nodded. "Seems Julianne may have a score to settle with Samuel, and possibly another with Ann. At least we know the two women despise each other. She might have been setting up Ann and getting back at Samuel at the same time."

Colin left the sofa and went to Madison. "This score with Samuel, you know what it is?"

Madison turned away from him.

"Now who's being the asshole?" Colin grabbed her upper arm and spun her around. "Is Julianne connected to Julie Argudo somehow?"

When she didn't answer, he shook her.

"Careful there, Reddy," Notchey cautioned, getting to his feet.

"Yes," she admitted. "Seems they were besties back in Bulgaria." She looked up into Colin's face, trying to read it, wishing some of Samuel's talents had rubbed off onto her. "You know about that?"

"Samuel asked my permission to terminate her. I gave it."

"He asked your permission?" Madison was incredulous. "He needed your permission?"

"I turned Julie. He asked out of respect for me."

Madison shook off Colin's grip. "Like I said, Notchey, go and arrest her dead ass. I'll even drive."

Notchey swung his head slowly back and forth. "You can't do that with vampires, Madison. I guarantee there will be no evidence, no DNA, no fingerprints—nothing to connect them to Kai. Not to mention the long-term ramifications if this Julianne decides to go public with what she is if we bring her up on charges."

"But what about Kai?" Madison walked up to Notchey and stood in front of him, hands balled into fists, demanding an answer.

"Like it or not," Notchey said, "in the end, Kai's death will be deemed an unsolved crime. I can't take a vampire in. I can't tell my superiors a vampire did this heinous thing. It would open a can of worms no one is ready to face. That is, if they believed me at all."

Madison turned to Colin. "Then we will just have to do something."

Colin gave her a slow, sad grin. "I'm way ahead of you. All except for the *we* part."

She went up to Colin, poking him in the chest. "You know damn well Samuel is not going to let Julianne or any of her minions live after this."

"True."

"Then we need to help him. And I mean *we*."

Notchey dropped back down and leaned his head against the back of the chair. He stared up at the ceiling. "What a fucking nightmare."

"Is everything all right?"

Everyone turned, including Notchey, toward the soft, hesitant voice. It was Libby. She stood in the archway leading out of the living room dressed in a floor-length cotton nightgown, her long hair loose. Hyun went to her immediately.

"There's been a problem, sweetheart," Hyun told her. "Seems Julianne may have slaughtered Samuel's favorite mistress."

Upon hearing the news, Libby staggered much as Samuel had. A hand went to her mouth to stifle a cry. Notchey got to his feet and stared at her like she was a ghost. Libby noticed him and stared back. A cry escaped her lips, and this time she didn't try to hide it.

Going over to Notchey, Madison placed a hand on his back, her outrage for Kai momentarily replaced with warmth for the living. "This is the emergency I called you about," she whispered to him. "We found Libby."

She gave him a push, sending him toward his sister.

Notchey covered the distance to Libby in a few long strides, then stopped short in front of her. Without a word, he held out a hand and stroked her cheek. When Hyun backed away, Libby fell into Notchey's waiting arms.

When Libby and Notchey retired to the library to talk in private, Hyun stayed behind. He approached Colin. "How are we going to handle this Jaz woman?"

Colin sat on the arm of the chair Notchey had just vacated. "Killing Kai was a declaration of war. The only outcome is her elimination. If we don't kill her and her followers, she won't rest until she gets Samuel or even the whole council."

Hyun stood like a soldier awaiting orders. "Are we going in tonight, Mr. Reddy?"

"Samuel filled me in on the information Libby passed along, such as how many vampires and consorts are living there. Sounds like every night's an orgy, so we might be able to surprise them if we treated it like a clandestine operation." Colin looked at the bodyguard with respect. "That's where you come in, Hyun. I was trained to take on my opponents face to face on an open battle-field. If I get more blokes to go in with us, could you get us into the castle for a surprise attack?"

"It's very possible. Libby can give us an idea of the layout of the grounds and building—where everyone sleeps or spends their time." Hyun gave it more thought. "Though it might be best to go in around daybreak. Seems Julianne likes to run at dawn. If she keeps to her schedule, we could go in while she's gone. Libby said the others in her entourage went to bed before then. We wouldn't have the cover of darkness going in, but we would meet with less resistance, if any."

"If it was right at daybreak," noted Colin, "our vampires might still be strong enough to fight. Much later, and we'd start weakening. It would be best if Julianne was out of the way when we attack. Fighting men without their leader are far easier to conquer."

Madison stepped forward. "I can help with that."

TWENTY-NINE

When Samuel returned to the living room, he was more like his old self, but it was clear something had snapped inside him like a branch broken from a strong tree.

Colin approached him first. The two embraced. Taller than Samuel, Colin clasped a hand behind Samuel's head and bent his own until their foreheads touched. "We are going to get the bastards who did this. I promise you."

Colin mapped out his plan like a captain to his general. Samuel listened, making the occasional comment and suggestion. When Colin was finished, Samuel stood straighter and a single-mindedness of purpose emanated from him like a strong cologne. His jaw was set, his mouth thin and tight with bloodlust. More importantly, he was back in control of himself.

Because it was so late and Madison was not supposed to know Julianne was a vampire, she texted Julianne rather than called her. She left a simple message: *SORRY ABOUT LAST MINUTE. WANT TO RUN SUNDAY 6 AM?*

About twenty minutes later, she received a message back: SURE. 6 GREAT.

"I'm going with you," Notchey insisted, not at all pleased. He and Libby had emerged from the library with wide but sad smiles about the time Samuel had rejoined the group and in time to hear the plan for attacking the castle. Brother and sister were sitting next to each other on the sofa.

"No, you're not," Madison said, putting her foot down. "She'll be suspicious if you show up."

"She doesn't know who I am."

"This is supposed to be a girls' run."

Notchey would not be put off. "So you're going off in the woods at dawn with a killer. Smart, Madison. Very smart. And just because you're going alone doesn't mean she will be."

"I'll be wearing my bracelet, Notchey. She won't be able to hurt me."

Notchey's eyes swept the gathering in Samuel's living room. "Is that bullshit really true?"

All the vampires nodded in various degrees of speed.

"Quite true," answered Colin. Samuel remained silent, turning instead to stare out the window, his hands clasped behind his back.

"No." Notchey stood up, ready to push home his point. "Leave Madison out of it. This isn't her fight."

Madison approached him. "I want to do this."

He grabbed her arm. This time it was Colin who stiffened. "They're using you as bait again." Notchey's voice rose, and his face flushed in anger. "Can't you see that?"

"I offered, Notchey." Madison put her hands on her hips. "And I'm going to do it. I'll have my cell phone and a bottle of bloodroot with me."

"What in the hell is bloodroot?"

It was Dodie who fielded the question. "It's the only thing that will knock out a vampire. And it's herbal," she added with a smile.

Notchey addressed the group again. "Are one of you going with her?"

"We'll all be at the castle," Colin explained. "And we'll need every hand if we're to succeed."

"I still don't understand why she needs to go. She's already baited the trap. Julianne will be there and out of the way for your attack."

Madison spelled it out to him. "And if I don't show, she might smell the setup and return to the castle before it's taken by our guys."

Samuel finally turned around. "It's Madison's decision, Mike."

Notchey walked up to Samuel, going almost nose to nose with the vampire. "You just suffered a great loss, Samuel; I respect that and am sorry for it. But, considering what happened to Kai, are you willing to put another young woman you care about at risk?"

Samuel studied Notchey with such intensity that everyone expected his fangs to pop out. Finally, he said, "Kai wasn't Madison. She wasn't prepared for what happened. Madison is."

"But—" Notchey continued to argue.

Samuel stopped him. "I appreciate everything you've done for us and for Kai, Mike, but I think it's time you left. Feel free to come back tomorrow and visit Libby, but for now we need to discuss matters you cannot be involved with."

"Just like that, I'm being dismissed?"

"Not dismissed, Mike, protected." Samuel turned back to stare out the window. No one else spoke.

Notchey spun on his heel to leave, but Libby hopped to her feet and stopped him. "Mike, please don't be angry. They really are trying to do what's best for all of us."

Notchey kissed his sister on her cheek and held her tight for a few moments. "I'll be back tomorrow. Count on it."

After Notchey left, Samuel took Madison aside. "You need to go to bed if you're going to be sharp in the morning."

"No," she told him. "It's only a few hours away, and I'm too keyed up to sleep."

Some of the iridescent spark had gone from Samuel's eyes, but it didn't affect his insight. "You're a natural leader, Madison—courageous, smart, and dedicated—and, I'm afraid, a bit of an adventurer. Are you sure it wasn't the thrill seeker in you speaking earlier? If so, you can change your mind. We won't hold it against you."

"Kai was my friend. I will see this through. Notchey will just have to live with that. He only sees a helpless girl when he looks at me."

Samuel smiled. "No, he sees a woman he wants to love but doesn't know how."

They all gathered around Samuel's massive dining table and went over the morning's plans. Libby helped them learn the various entrances and corridors of the mansion, including some passages that were hidden. They were almost done when the front doorbell rang.

Colin looked up from the plans Doug had drawn from Libby's descriptions. "That would be Stacie. I asked her to bring a little something by after the party."

Hyun disappeared to the front of the house to get the door. Shortly after, he returned, leading Keleta, with Byron and Ricky, behind him.

"As soon as Colin called us with the news," Byron explained, "Keleta insisted we come here."

Approaching Samuel, Keleta dropped to one knee in front of him and said something in a foreign language. No one else knew what he was saying, but everyone understood the passion in his voice. Samuel clapped Keleta on his shoulder and replied, his voice more somber than the young vampire's. Keleta said a few more things, this time with more fire. Samuel studied his young, strong face a moment, then answered, giving a slight nod. Keleta beamed and stood.

Samuel turned to Colin. "Keleta insists on joining us."

"I can help," Keleta told the gathering. "Lady, she trained me for fighting, but I told her I would not. I think that is why she tried to kill me."

Doug stood up from the table. "We are not asking you to fight, Keleta. We will have plenty without you."

"No," Keleta said with determination. "She ruined my life. She threatened to kill my family, so I remained silent. Now she has murdered Mr. Samuel's consort. I cannot remain silent any longer. She must die."

It was then Keleta's eyes caught on Libby. "Libby!" He gave her a wide smile, obviously quite fond of her. "How did you get to this place?" He rushed to her, but Hyun moved to stand between them. Keleta was confused.

"She's no longer a consort," Hyun said, spitting out the words.

"No, Hyun," interrupted Libby.

"You are Libby's Hyun?" He smiled at the man ready to accost him. "She told me much about you."

Libby pulled on Hyun's arm. "Keleta and I were friends. He would never hurt me."

Hyun looked to Libby for confirmation. She nodded and smiled. He turned back to Keleta and offered him his hand. "Glad to have you aboard."

"Absolutely," confirmed Colin. "With Keleta with us, we won't have to rely on remembering Libby's instructions."

They were bringing Keleta up to speed on the plan of attack on the castle when the doorbell rang again. Colin looked up. "I hope that's Stacie."

Hyun, his gun drawn, went again to the door. This time he brought back Stacie. With her was Ann Hayes, her hands and legs trussed tight, her mouth gagged, her magnificent red hair wild in its disarray. Ann shuffled along in baby steps like a lame duck. When they reached the dining table, Stacie deposited her hard into a chair and removed the gag.

"How dare you," Ann spat at Stacie.

"Yeah, yeah, yeah," Stacie said with disgust. "I've heard it all before. Save it." She stuffed the gag back into Ann's mouth.

Colin moved to stand over Ann. Looking at Stacie, he asked, "Have much trouble?"

"Nah, I waited until most everyone left or were otherwise occupied in private. Then I snuck up on her in the sack with some stud vampire I paid to help. From there, it was just a matter of shutting her up and getting her to the car."

For the first time that evening, Samuel chuckled. "Money well spent, Stacie. Make sure you put in a reimbursement slip."

Stacie turned to Samuel, her usual bulldog demeanor softened. "I'm very sorry about Kai, Samuel."

"Thank you."

Stacie bent and gave her old friend a kiss on the cheek.

Though the gag, Ann Hayes whined and mumbled. Samuel indicated for Colin to remove it.

"Really, Mr. La Croix," she sputtered, "from you I expected more dignified behavior than a kidnapping, but obviously I was wrong."

"Grabbing you was *my* idea, Ann."

She looked up at Colin. "Then shame on you. I turned you. Show some respect and at least unbind me."

"You were brought here for your own good," Colin explained. "Julianne Jaz is behind the murdered vampires. Who knows what else she's going to try."

"Oh, please. I already knew that. She's just a copycat bitch. Couldn't even come up with her own original brand, had to use my old castoff, just as she picked up my discarded lovers."

"You mean Parker Young?" asked Madison.

"Yeah," added Stacie. "Why did you lie to us about knowing Parker?"

"This is a fight between Julianne and me, not something that needed to involve all of you."

"It involved us, Ann," noted Doug, "the minute the first vampire was dumped into our pool."

"I was dealing with it in my own way."

Colin leaned down, putting his face close to Ann's. "By throwing a party, hoping she would come? Well, isn't that very Gatsby of you."

"I simply wanted to confront her, but I didn't know where she was. She always did love a good party—drawn to them like a harlot to platform shoes."

"Only one problem with your half-baked plan: Julianne didn't show up, did she? Instead, she was out murdering an innocent woman." Colin jerked a thumb at Madison. "Madison here found Julianne in no time. It just took patience and brain power, something you are definitely lacking as time goes by. I didn't know vampires could become senile."

"Shut up, Colin."

"No, you shut up, bitch." Madison got to her feet and went to Ann.

"Don't you dare talk to me like that, beater bitch."

Madison wasn't the least bit phased by the rudeness. "If you had told us the truth from the beginning, we would have been able to stop Julianne before she killed again." Madison slammed her fist down on the table. "Kai would still be alive."

"Who's Kai, another beater bitch?" Ann stuck her nose up in the air and sniffed. "You're all a dime a dozen, sugar."

Without thinking, Madison reached out and slapped Ann hard across the face. When no one stopped her, she slapped her again.

Ann only sneered. "Dumb girl—like that's going to make me feel bad."

"Maybe not, but it made *me* feel a hell of a lot better." Madison leaned down, going eye-to-eye with Ann. "Though not as good as driving a stake through that cold, black heart of yours."

Ann hissed and bared her fangs like a rattlesnake. Madison was undaunted.

Turning to Doug, Ann tried a different tactic. "Are you going to let one of your servants treat me like this?"

Doug smiled with pride at Madison and put an arm around Dodie's shoulders. "She's not our servant, she's our granddaughter, and she's only saying what we're all thinking—stake and all."

THIRTY

Madison danced from foot to foot as she waited for Julianne in the cool morning dampness. Sunrise wasn't for another fifteen minutes. Overhead, the sky was the color of a porpoise, shiny and sleek with just enough shimmer to show the running path. There was a light drizzle coming down. Officially, the trail didn't open until seven o'clock, but those who liked to get out earlier paid no attention to that.

There had been no sign of other runners yet. Madison hadn't wanted to make the run quite so early, but the more time she gave Colin and his crew before sunrise, the stronger they would be. It was a delicate balance—early enough to assure they were at their peak versus late enough so that at least some of the vampires at the castle were already asleep and therefore vulnerable to attack in their deathlike suspension. The extra thirty minutes could mean the difference between success and failure.

They had calculated that it would take Julianne about twenty minutes to reach the trail from the castle. Colin and the others would already be near the castle, waiting for Julianne to leave, buying them another chunk of time to carry out their mission. By Madison's estimation, they should already be in the house and taking care of business. Although she wasn't looking forward to seeing Julianne Jaz, Madison knew the sight of her meant that so far the plan was working. Julianne not showing up could mean big trouble back at the castle.

When Dodie and Doug had stopped by their house to pick up clothes for them all, Dodie had had the insight to pack Madison's running shoes and some leggings, so it was easy to piece together a running outfit. Madison had topped it off with the tee shirt she slept in and a gray hoodie she'd borrowed from Hyun. It was a bit too large for her but was keeping her warm in the dampness. Her hands were stuck in the pockets, her left hand on her cell phone. If anything went wrong, she was to immediately call Samuel's house. Colin had asked Byron and Ricky to stay behind to keep an eye on Ann Hayes. Even gagged and tied, he didn't want to leave the manipulative Ann alone in the company of Libby, Enid, and Foster.

Madison's right hand fingered the spray vial of bloodroot. That and her bracelet were her only protection. She felt naked and exposed, and out of her mind with worry for those attacking the castle.

They didn't know if Julianne had any indication that she'd been exposed or if she thought anything out of the ordinary about Libby leaving, except for the reason she'd given—that she was frightened and disgusted by the recent violence being visited upon the consorts. They also didn't know if Heather had heeded Libby's advice and gotten herself and the other consorts out. Colin was operating under the assumption that there were mortals still in the castle.

Julianne's SUV drove up and found parking in the small lot opposite from where Madison stood. Julianne got out of the driver's side. From the passenger side emerged the young man she'd seen with her on Friday morning. Two against one—now Madison wished she'd had Notchey with her.

"New wheels," Julianne observed, noting the plain white rental car. Madison's car was still at the Dedhams'.

"Just a rental. My car's having a diva moment. I'm thinking it's time to buy another."

Madison then noticed a second man getting out of the back seat of the SUV. He was tall and slender, with high-cut cheekbones and longish dark blond hair pulled back at the nape of his neck. Now it was three against one; not good odds at all. She fingered the bloodroot in her pocket, wondering how many she could hit before things got really nasty.

"I thought it was going to be just us girls," Madison said in a joking manner.

Julianne glanced over at the men. "It was, then Adam said we ladies shouldn't be running alone in the dark, so he came to protect us." At the name Adam, Madison forced a smile at the dark-haired man she'd seen on Friday. He was the vampire who'd tortured Libby.

"The other one's Coby," Libby said by way of sloppy introduction. "He's crashing with Adam for a few days." Julianne leaned in close and whispered, "Who knows, you two might hit it off. When I told him you were cute, he slapped on his sneakers."

Coby—the other guy who had attacked Libby. Madison shuddered and pretended it was a chill. If Julianne had any idea what was happening at her rented mansion while she bantered with Madison, she gave no indication.

"I'm getting cold," said Madison to the three of them as she jogged in place. "Shall we get going?"

They started up the trail, Madison jogging alongside Julianne. Behind them were the two men. Madison wished they were up ahead, where she could keep an eye on them. "If you guys want to push it," she said over her shoulder, "don't let us hold you up."

Julianne looked back at them. "She's right. You wouldn't want to listen to our gabfest anyway."

The two men picked up their speed and passed them. They didn't take off but put some distance between themselves and the women while still remaining in sight.

"How did your business trip go?" asked Julianne.

"Boring and exhausting. Glad to be home."

"What is it you do?"

Madison looked over at Julianne. Her ponytail had been threaded through the back of her baseball cap and bounced playfully with every step she took. Madison's hair was pulled back, too, but lay like a damp, thick rope coiled in the hood of the sweatshirt.

"I'm an executive assistant for a nonprofit foundation. How about you?"

"Not sure."

Madison shot her a look. "You don't know what you do for work?"

"Guess you could call me a headhunter of sorts."

Had she not been terrified, Madison would have found the comment funny. "You find jobs for people?"

"More like I find prospects and mentor them." Julianne jogged a few more steps before elaborating. "I look for losers and give them a second chance at life."

"So you train them for new jobs?"

"Basically."

"Your job must be very rewarding."

Julianne cackled with laughter. "You have no idea."

Madison's earlier amusement turned to disgust, but she fought not to show it.

They were jogging uphill now, almost to the top, lobbing along silently at a nice pace. Madison's mind wandered to the castle. Had Colin and his band managed to get into the place and overtake Julianne's ragtag army of newly turned vampires, or was there still a heated battle going on? If the run went as planned, Julianne and Madison would part as new pals, and Julianne would return to the castle to face defeat and capture.

Up ahead, the men disappeared around a bend. Madison went on alert, giving the situation her full attention.

"Tell me, Madison," asked Julianne, without looking over. "How do you enjoy working for Samuel La Croix?"

Inside her chest, Madison's heart skipped a beat. "I'm sorry. I didn't understand that."

"Oh, come now. Don't play games." Julianne stopped on the trail. "I know damn well who you are. But it's about time *you* knew who *I* was." She roared, her fangs snapping out and filling her mouth.

Madison pretended shock. "You're a vam—a vampire?"

Julianne sneered. "More game playing? Not to mention bad acting."

Madison wasn't sure what to do. She looked up ahead and didn't see the others, and assumed they were waiting in ambush. She started walking backwards down the hill, keeping one eye on Julianne, the other on the trail.

"Let's see," Julianne said, following her but keeping her distance. "You live with vampires. Work with vampires. No doubt even fuck vampires. Not sure why you're so surprised I turned out to be one."

"What do you want with me?"

"You, my dear, are my ticket to Samuel La Croix. I'm going to destroy your boss, and you're going to help. I've already tweaked his nose. All those dead vampires left carelessly around? I did that. Samuel's dead whore?" Julianne cocked a thumb at herself. "My handiwork." She took another small step toward Madison. "But you'll bring home the prize."

"Like hell I will!"

Madison turned and lit down the hill as fast as she could, praying Julianne and her friends did not have the gift of speed.

"After her," yelled Julianne.

Without looking back, Madison knew the vampires were on her heels even without extra speed. She dug deep, looking for a burst of extra energy. Samuel had been right, she should have gotten at least a little sleep. She looked up at the sky. The sun was coming up. Between the rising sun and it being their bedtime, the vampires should also be exhausted. And unless the rain didn't keep them away, other people might be on the trail down below.

Madison thought about Hyun running for his life for a living and found more speed. She was about one third of the way down the trail when her sneaker hit a patch of loose gravel. She stumbled but didn't lose her balance. After a few awkward steps, she found her groove again. A hundred yards more, she stumbled again. This time she fought to remain upright. Someone crashed into her from behind. The force sent her sprawling into the brush alongside the trail. Her face and arms stung from scratches. She started to get to her knees when someone grabbed her from behind by her hair and pulled her up. It was Coby.

Once on her feet, Coby dragged her up the trail several yards to where Adam and Julianne waited with self-satisfied grins.

"Now listen up and listen good," Julianne warned, getting in Madison's face. "You will go back down the trail with us, and you will behave. You try to warn anyone we meet along the way, I'll kill you as entertainment for anyone willing to watch."

"You can't hurt me." Madison concentrated on keeping the fear in her voice to a minimum. She held up the arm with the bracelet.

"So," laughed Julianne. "I see you're not as stupid as Samuel's bimbo." She gave Madison a wide, ugly smile and licked her fangs. "I saw that on you before and brought backup just in case you had a habit of wearing it."

Coby jerked Madison's hair. She let out a short cry of pain. They laughed.

"Coby isn't a vampire—at least not yet." Julianne blew him a sloppy kiss. "So I'm afraid he can do whatever he wants with you and no one can stop him ... or will."

To prove the point, Coby took out a small knife and nicked Madison on the neck, just below the ear Colin had nipped. Keeping a tight hold on her, Coby bent down and ran his tongue over the blood that trickled out of the incision. It made her shiver, but not in the same way as Colin's actions had.

"Tasty," he told the others.

Adam showed his fangs and eyed the slow-dripping blood with barely contained lust.

"In time," Julianne told Adam, patting him on the back.

Coby put his mouth on Madison's neck and gave the wound several loud, noisy sucks. She wanted to vomit.

"Come now, Coby," Julianne warned. "It's not nice to tease us like that." She looked up at the sky, alight now with the promise of the day to come. "We have to get back and get her secured before we turn in. Tonight, we'll bring down La Croix, and she'll be our victory feast."

"But the bracelet?" reminded Adam.

Putting her hands on her hips, Julianne looked at him and sighed. "It's a good thing you're good in the sack, Adam, because you sure aren't very bright." She glanced over at Madison. "Coby will kill her and drain the blood for us," she spelled out to the dull-witted vampire.

As Adam's light went on, he snarled at Madison in anticipation.

The four of them started down the trail, walking at an even pace. Still maintaining a tight grip on her hair, Coby walked along Madison's left side. The two of them led the way, with the two vampires several yards behind them. Madison put one foot in front of the other like a robot, her hands in her pockets. To anyone passing them coming up the hill, they looked like two couples returning from a leisurely morning walk. Because of the danger, Madison now hoped other people wouldn't be on the trail. She didn't want to chance Julianne deciding to have a snack on the way back to the car. It didn't seem to be on her agenda, but Madison was learning that Julianne was unpredictable and her hatred for Samuel might only fuel her instability.

With her fingers playing with the spray bottle of bloodroot, Madison tried to devise a plan. She didn't have long, ten minutes at the most, until they reached the parking area. The bloodroot wouldn't take out Coby, but a spray of the red liquid to his face might loosen his grip on her and render him temporarily off-balance. The vampires could chase her all they wanted, but until Coby was back in action, they couldn't do anything to her. Madison saw it as her only chance.

With her hand still in her pocket, Madison tested the sprayer by depressing it a little. It was stiff, but went down. She tried again. This time it lowered easily and her fingers grew wet with the sticky liquid. The juice was probably staining the pocket of the hoodie but with the vampires behind her, she doubted they could see it. With the tip of her index finger, she felt for the direction of the spray opening and positioned her grip so that it went in the right direction when pulled it out of her pocket.

"Let her go," an unseen voice called from the side of the trail.

The party of four stopped in their tracks.

"Let her go, or I'll shoot." From behind a tree stepped Notchey. He moved toward them slowly, his gun aimed directly at Julianne.

Julianne laughed. "I'm a vampire, you fool. You can't kill me."

"I can if the bullet hits you directly in the heart."

"You're not that good of a shot."

"You willing to take that chance?"

"Shoot this guy, Notchey," Madison called to him. "He's not a vampire."

Realizing his vulnerability, Coby stepped behind Madison, using her as a shield. He crouched slightly until his head was almost resting on her left shoulder. It was her moment of opportunity.

Whipping out the bloodroot, she hit the plunger, shooting the bright red liquid over her shoulder and directly into Coby's eyes. He yowled and let go of her.

Madison rushed to Notchey's side. "They're the ones who killed Kai."

Coby was on his knees on the ground. "I can't see."

"Quit whining, you crybaby," snapped Julianne. With her chin, she indicated for Adam to move to Notchey and Madison's flank. "He can't shoot us both that accurately."

Adam followed her instructions and moved to cover their left.

"Unlikely," admitted Notchey, never taking his eyes off of her. "But you're the one I'm aiming for, not him."

Madison held the bloodroot out, aiming it at Adam.

Julianne raised her face and sniffed the air like a dog sensing danger. "She's got bloodroot, Adam. Don't let it near your mouth and nose or you'll go down like a sack of stones."

Keeping his eyes on Madison, he nodded his understanding.

"The sun's getting higher," Madison whispered to Notchey. "They're going to be getting weaker. Wait them out."

Adam continued to move in, but still Notchey didn't take his gun off of Julianne.

It was Adam who made the first move. He rushed Madison and Notchey. Madison ran forward, spraying him with the bloodroot, but the vampire shielded his nose and mouth with his arm and charged her. The two of them went down in a pile, the force of the strike sending them both into the dirt not far from Notchey.

The stronger of the two, Adam untangled himself from Madison and straddled her, pinning her to the ground. Notchey's eyes flashed between them and Julianne, but he kept his gun on Julianne.

"Don't worry, Notchey," Madison called to him. "This creep can't hurt me. Take out Julianne."

Adam jumped off of Madison and dove for Notchey's legs. The blow tumbled the cop to the ground, his head striking a tree trunk as he fell. Julianne and Adam both pounced on Notchey. Before the gun was knocked from his hand, he managed to get off two shots. Both of them hit Julianne, wounding but not killing her. She rolled off of Notchey, whimpering like a hurt animal, and retreated to collect herself.

Madison looked around for the bloodroot, which had been knocked from her hand, but couldn't find it. Adam sunk his fangs deep into Notchey and began tearing the flesh. Notchey screamed in pain, then went silent. Grabbing a large rock, Madison raised it up and brought it down on Adam's head. Over and over, she hit the vampire devouring Notchey. Each blow filled the air with a loud cracking noise. When Adam finally rolled off of Notchey and onto his back, Madison grabbed the fallen gun and stood over him. She fired once, surprised by the kick of the pistol. It hit the vampire in the chest but not directly in the heart. Weakened but not dead, Adam snarled and slowly began to rise. She kicked him hard in his jaw and he fell back. Before he could get up again, Madison placed the gun directly over his heart and pulled the trigger. Adam went limp. His eye sockets emptied.

"Get her, you useless piece of shit," Julianne yelled at Coby. Coby had gotten to his feet and was shaking off the bloodroot's effect on his eyes. The juice had stained his face red. One look at Adam's corpse and he took off down the trail.

Julianne let out a scream of anger. The earlier bullets had entered her left arm. It hung by her side limp and useless for the moment. Soon it would be sound again, but Madison didn't know how long it would take.

Julianne looked at Madison, then at Notchey. "I may not be able to kill you," she said to Madison, "but I can kill him." She flashed Madison a sick grin. "And I'm going to make you watch." She started slowly for Notchey, keeping one eye on Madison and the gun.

Madison moved toward the injured Notchey herself. He was badly hurt and out cold. She fired at Julianne, hitting her in the gut. The vampire yelped and clutched the wound. It didn't kill her but stopped her long enough for Madison to remove her protective bracelet and slip it onto Notchey's wrist.

"You're crazy," Julianne told her, licking her fangs.

Madison pointed the gun at Julianne. "You want me, bitch? Come get me."

Julianne slowly started for Madison. "I am going to drain you and use your skin for a flag."

Madison kept the gun trained on the vampire. Moving off to the side, she drew Julianne deeper into the brush. She wanted them away from Notchey just in case some of her shots went wild. A few more steps back, Madison shifted directions. Julianne followed like a lioness circling her prey.

Once sure Notchey was behind her and the gun, Madison decided it was time to make her move. She knew she'd never hit Julianne directly in the heart unless it was dumb luck. She needed to get close, close like Adam, and make the shot count.

Madison stopped and pointed the gun. She pretended to fire it, but nothing happened. She looked up at Julianne, fright filling her eyes. She didn't have to fake the fright, it was real even if the gun jamming wasn't.

Julianne gave off a sinister laugh and moved in closer. Madison pretended to fire again. Nothing. She backed up. Julianne jumped forward, pinning Madison against the tree behind her. She drove her fangs into Madison's neck. Madison screamed in pain. Julianne pulled back, her lips and teeth covered with Madison's warm blood. She laughed and took another bite, this one deep.

Latched on to Madison's neck, sucking her blood hard and fast, Julianne never noticed the gun pressed against her chest or felt the bullet that pierced her heart like a high-speed mini stake.

THIRTY-ONE

otchey's injuries weren't as bad as Madison had first feared. The amount of blood made it look worse. There was also a knot on his skull from smashing into the tree headfirst.

As soon as she made sure Julianne was dead and Notchey okay, Madison called Samuel's house and told Byron what had happened. He said he'd get the knacker up there right away.

Jesús arrived in twenty minutes and found Madison and Notchey, weak and exhausted, sitting on the ground against a large tree. With Jesús were two helpers, shovels hoisted over their shoulders. Jesús introduced them as his sons. They looked like regular trail maintenance workers.

"Colin warned me it was going to be a busy day," the little man told them as he examined the dead vampires. "He asked me to come to the area and wait for a call." He motioned to his sons, and they started digging in the soft earth under a thick canopy of branches.

"You're not taking the bodies with you?" Madison asked.

"No need. Their bodies will be gone within two days, even the young vampire's. We'll just strip them and bury them deep."

Madison bent next to Julianne's body and dug through the pockets of her running pants. She pulled out a set of car keys and took them to Jesús. "There's a black SUV in the parking lot that these go to. If the other guy hasn't taken it by now, it will have to disappear. Can you do that for us?"

"Happy to, but there wasn't any SUV down below. Just two cars, a plain white one and Detective Notchey's."

Madison and Notchey exchanged looks. There was no telling where Coby went, but it was Madison's guess he was heading back to the castle to either gather help or warn the others. She placed a call to Colin, hoping he was able to answer. When he didn't, she called Dodie's phone. Again, no answer. Madison feared the worst.

Madison and Notchey stayed until Jesús and his sons were through disposing of the vampires. They were heading for the castle next. Just as they were finishing up, Jesús received a call from Colin.

Relieved, Madison motioned for Jesús to let her have the phone. Having already spoken with Byron, Colin knew what had happened on the trail.

"Colin, be on the lookout for a black SUV driven by a guy named Coby with a red-stained face. He's a beater, but he's one of Julianne's followers. He may be heading your way."

"He's already here," Colin told her. "Drove right up to the front door and into our waiting arms."

As soon as Jesús left, Madison and Notchey, their arms wrapped around each other for support, slowly made their way down the rest of the trail.

"Where is everyone?" Madison asked, noticing no others on the trail. She'd been too occupied to think about it earlier.

Notchey squeezed the arm he had around her shoulders. "I closed the trail."

"You what?"

"I didn't want civilians up here any more than you did."

When they reached the parking lot, she saw what he meant. Using his vehicle, he'd blocked the entrance and put up a large sign with big handwritten letters: TRAIL CLOSED DUE TO SLIDE.

"If anyone passed by that, they were on their own."

Notchey walked Madison to her car. "You feel okay to drive?"

She nodded.

"Then you head straight back to Samuel's," he ordered, pointing a finger at her. "No going to the castle."

"Don't worry, I got the same lecture from Colin. I'm to return to the villa. If I don't, I'm sure they'll be calling the knacker for me, and not because of this bite."

"Did Colin tell you anything about what happened?"

"No. He told me Coby was there and that I was to stay away. That's it. Then he hung up."

Notchey shuffled from foot to foot. He seemed reluctant to leave. "Thanks for saving my life," he finally said. "And for finding Libby."

"It was purely by accident, Notchey, but I'm very glad she's back."

He pulled the council's bracelet off his wrist and slipped it onto hers. "You must never take that off again, no matter what."

"I'd do it again if I had to."

"I know." With his fingertips, he lightly touched the scratches on her face. She flinched slightly but didn't pull back. "I'm just telling you don't."

His hand moved to the collar on her blood-soaked hoodie. He pulled it back and checked the damage done by Julianne. "Does it hurt much?"

"A bit. How about yours? It looks worse than mine."

"It hurts like a bitch."

"You should come back to Samuel's so Dodie can take a look at that."

"I should do a lot of things."

After a short, awkward hesitation, Notchey grabbed the back of Madison's neck with one hand and pressed his mouth to hers, kissing her with longing. When the kiss ended, he looked into her eyes. "You're really something, you know."

"Does that mean something good or something … um … questionable?"

"Jury's still out."

———————————

By the time they both drove back to Samuel's, everyone who'd gone to the castle was waiting for them except for Colin, Doug, and Keleta. The council's army had been victorious, managing to capture the castle and destroy all the vampires in Julianne's household. There were only a couple of consorts still on the premises, and they took off as soon as Colin and his small band of troops showed up.

Colin and Doug had remained behind to coordinate the disposal of the vampire bodies with Jesús. Stacie had received a bad injury and was convalescing in one of Samuel's guest rooms.

Dodie happily reported that Stacie would be her old self in a day or so.

When asked about Coby, Samuel informed them that shortly after arriving back at the castle, Coby had managed to escape. All attempts to find him had failed. As he gave the news, the head vampire looked directly at Notchey, expecting a challenge of some kind. He received none. Instead, the detective met his gaze head on. Madison watched the two men exchanging silent information and instantly understood that Coby had been executed by the vampires, though it would never be acknowledged openly. She also understood that Notchey knew it, too.

"What about Keleta?" Madison asked.

Dodie was attending the bites on both Madison and Notchey while Samuel gave them a full report about the castle. He'd already been briefed on the situation with Julianne by Madison.

"Ouch," Notchey said as Dodie took another stitch to close up the ragged bite he'd received from Adam.

Samuel went to Madison's side. "Keleta didn't make it, Madison. He was killed by one of the other vampires."

Madison was seated at the kitchen table, drinking hot tea Enid had made her. The bites from Julianne had already been cleaned and dressed. Samuel stroked her arm as he gave her the news of Keleta's death. Across the table, Dodie had stopped working on Notchey to watch Madison.

Madison remembered how it had been just one short week since she'd found Keleta floating in the Dedhams' pool. One short week—seven very long days.

"He died a hero," Dodie told her.

Samuel agreed. "Without Keleta, we might not have been able to take the castle so quickly or with so few injuries or fatalities on our side."

"But he was so young and doing so well." Tears welled in Madison's eyes.

"In a couple of days, we will have a memorial service for him," Dodie told Madison in a comforting voice. "As soon as Jesús has his ashes ready."

"I was thinking," added Samuel, "that his ashes should be scattered in the rose garden here at the villa. What do you think?"

Madison shook her head, unable to speak for a moment as emotion engulfed her. "No, Samuel. It's a lovely gesture and all, but I think his ashes should be scattered in the flower beds surrounding the Dedhams' pool. That's where we first met him."

THIRTY-TWO

Madison parked her car in the circular drive in front of Samuel's house and grabbed her overnight bag as she got out. It had been four weeks since the battle at the castle, and life had nearly returned to normal. She was juggling work for the council with her school assignments and splitting her social time between both Notchey and Colin.

"Hey, Madison," called Libby as she and Hyun came down the stairs from their apartment. "We're heading out for a late dinner, want to join us?"

Libby and Hyun were going to be married in three weeks. The ceremony would take place shortly after dark under a flower-covered gazebo in Samuel's back yard in front of their friends, vampire and mortal alike. Dodie had offered to act as the wedding planner, and little else occupied her mind these days. It worried Madison that Dodie would be looking to marry her off next just to have another wedding to plan, even though Madison had told the hovering vampiress not to get any ideas.

Madison and Libby were growing close, almost like sisters. Often she and Notchey spent time with Hyun and Libby. Still at times gruff and infuriating, Notchey had shown evidence of softening since Libby's reappearance. He was also not treating Madison like a leper, though they still had a long way to go in sorting out their relationship, as did Madison and Colin.

"Thanks," she said to Libby, "but Samuel and I have a lot of work to do tonight." When the couple got close, she added in a quiet voice, "How's he doing?"

Hyun shrugged. "Seems okay, but he hardly goes out anymore. Most of my evenings are free." He shot a sly look at Libby. "Though I'm hardly complaining."

Libby blushed, then her face took on worry. "I do think Samuel's giving us time together, Madison, but it's not just that. Enid's worried, too. She told us he's hardly eating. And when he does, it's takeout from Scarlet's."

"Going to pick it up is about the only driving I'm doing for him anymore," added Hyun.

"He's not seeing his other mistresses?"

"Not that we can tell."

Madison was concerned. She'd expected Samuel to be low-key for a while but not remain quite this secluded. In the past few weeks, he had given her work she could do from home or during the day at the villa while he slept. She'd only spent the night at his place twice, and that was when he had gathered the council for meetings. Outside of those meetings, she'd seldom seen him. When she did, it was difficult to gauge how he was feeling. The closeness they had been building seemed to be walled off, and Madison wasn't sure if the wall was made of paper or concrete.

She found Samuel at his desk in the library, writing out checks to pay the council's bills. Two days ago, she had left a file containing the statements for him to review and to go over with Eddie, the council's treasurer. He looked up when she came in, gave her a slight smile, then went back to his work. She settled in at the computer desk.

"I have several letters I'd like to get out tonight, Madison," he said to her without looking up. "And I left you some notes about updating the vampire database."

While Joni still maintained the database, in the past few weeks it had fallen on Madison to update the profiles as information came in. It made sense, since most of the updates came to Samuel first, often through Isabella. Needs for new profiles and photo enhancements were shuttled off to Joni.

Madison tapped in her password and starting going through the e-mails that had accrued in the council's e-mailbox. Many she could answer; those she couldn't, she printed out for review by Samuel or forwarded to the council member whose job covered the topic.

"There's an e-mail here from Isabella," she told him. "Seems Ann Hayes was banished from Switzerland recently."

Samuel shook his head. "Banished by us. Banished by the Swiss. Pretty soon her shenanigans will only be welcome at Leopold's."

"Oh, and I received an e-mail today from Nina Weinberg." Madison kept her eyes on the computer screen. "You know, that realtor I hoodwinked into searching for castles."

Shortly after the incident at Julianne's castle, Madison had called Nina personally to tell her that while her boss appreciated her efforts, none of the properties suited his needs, and he was going to shelve his plans for the time being. The disappointment in the realtor's voice was obvious even though she put on a professional front.

Samuel glanced up with faint interest. "And what did she have to say?"

"She said a property that fit my employer's requirements perfectly has just come on the market." Madison turned to look at him. "It's a mini castle located at the intersection of Timpangos and Wonder View. Says the seller is very motivated."

For the first time in weeks, Samuel laughed. It wasn't his usual deep and hearty laugh, but it was a start. "I have half a mind to buy the property personally and raze that monstrosity to the ground." He got up from behind his desk. "But I have better things to do with my money."

Walking over to Madison, he handed her the file folder. "All the checks are ready to go, and those paid online have been approved. There's a special check on the top."

She took the folder and opened it. The special check was made out to her and was for a substantial amount of money. "What's this?"

"It's from the council. A little bird told us you were thinking about a hybrid for your next car. That should cover the cost of one, plus any bells and whistles you'd like to get with it."

"Wow! Thanks!" Madison hopped up and down in her seat. She'd never had a new car.

"Why don't you go car shopping this weekend. Take Mike Notchey. No car dealer should screw with you with a cop along."

Madison's excitement waned. "I don't know about that. He wasn't too keen on you guys giving me a car."

Once again, Samuel flashed a small smile. "Who do you think told us about the hybrid?"

Samuel leaned against Madison's desk and dug into the pocket of his khaki trousers. He pulled out a piece of paper and handed it to her. "And this is for you from me."

Madison opened the slip of paper. It was another check, this one drawn on Samuel's personal bank account. The amount matched that of the car check. She looked up at Samuel, her mouth resembling a open mine shaft. "I . . . I don't understand. Is this a severance check?"

Samuel tilted his head back and laughed. Still not his old self, but closer. "Not at all, you silly girl. It's a personal thank you for everything you did for me and the council recently."

He took a seat on the sofa near the desk and leaned forward. "Remember what I said about you saving against the time when we might all need to disappear?"

She nodded and cast her eyes down. Losing the vampires was something she didn't want to think about. It would be like losing her mother and great aunt all over again.

"Well, that almost happened a few weeks ago. If Julianne Jaz had succeeded in outing all of us, we would have left, leaving you and Hyun and even Foster and Enid behind, with no jobs or means of support."

"Doug and Dodie told me if that ever happens, I should stay in their house. It's paid for, and they've even put my name on the deed, just in case. They've done something similar for Pauline."

"I would expect nothing less from the Dedhams." He tapped the check in Madison's hands. "You put most of this away in case that happens, but some of it should go for fun, and that's an order. Take a vacation. Buy something frivolous. I don't care. But

I want you to spend a nice piece of it on something just for you." He gave her a wide smile. "Take Notchey on a cruise. Let him see how good being kept feels, even if it's just for a week. Maybe that'll get the stick out of his backside once and for all."

They both laughed, but tears were running down Madison's cheeks.

"What's the matter, Madison? I thought this would make you happy. It would make most people delirious with joy."

She looked into Samuel's blue-white eyes. "I would give it all back, both checks, to make things as they were before Julianne Jaz came on the scene."

Samuel sat back and studied her, his own face clouded over. "And I know you don't just mean about Kai, do you?"

Madison shook her head. "I keep having nightmares about … about, you know."

"Being bitten?"

"Yes. The other night at a party, Colin flashed his fangs at someone. He was just joking around, but I almost went into hysterics."

Samuel leaned forward and held out his hands to her. She put down the folder and checks and placed her hands in his. They were cool against her warm skin.

"I would give anything for you not to have been savaged on your first biting experience. Anything." He squeezed her hands. "A mortal's first vampire bite should be like first sex, done with someone you care about and trust. But, as with your first horrible sexual experience, what's done is done. The bites are gone on the outside. Give yourself time to heal on the inside."

With one last squeeze of her hands, Samuel let go. "Now let's both bury our cares in our work. There is a lot to do tonight."

The sound of a splash woke Madison. She went to the French doors in her bedroom and pulled back the drapes just enough to look out onto the back patio and pool area of the villa. The moon was low in the sky. Soon it would be morning. In the long, rectangular pool a figure was swimming laps, cutting through the water smoothly and with the purpose and speed of a sleek torpedo.

Opening the door, Madison stepped out and headed for the pool. Los Angeles was currently experiencing a small heat wave, and even in the predawn of late March the air was balmy. She sat on the edge of one of the double-wide chaises and watched. Back and forth, back and forth, Samuel swam until Madison lost count of the laps. Finally, he stopped at the end of the pool facing the house and easily pulled himself up and out of the water. He was naked.

"I'm sorry if I woke you," he told her. He grabbed a huge pool towel from a stack on a table, roughly ran it over his body, then wrapped it around his waist.

"It's okay." She stood up. "I just wanted to make sure you were all right."

"Like you, I will be." He turned and looked at the pool. "We used to swim together, Kai and I, after we made love. She was an excellent swimmer."

"You loved her, didn't you?"

"Yes, I did." He turned to look at Madison. "I've had hundreds of mistresses, consorts, and lovers over the years, but I've only truly loved a handful of them. Kai was like a wife to me."

He chucked Madison under her chin with tenderness. "You go back to bed. I'm going to stay out here a bit." When she looked concerned, he added with a smile, "Don't worry, I'll make sure I go in before the sun comes up."

Madison was halfway through the doors to her bedroom when she turned around and returned to the pool with purpose. Samuel was stretched out on his back on the double chaise, fully exposed to the night air. When she stood in front of him, he didn't say anything, nor did he make a move to cover himself. He simply looked into her face.

"When I first had sex," she began, "and I don't mean when I was raped as a kid, but when I first decided to have grown-up sex, I told myself it didn't matter what had happened to me before. When it came to making love, I was still a virgin. I somehow understood that by separating the two, I would be able to make love to my boyfriend and enjoy it."

"And?"

"It worked. It was a bit rocky at the beginning, but it did work."

Madison stripped off the tee shirt she'd worn to bed and dropped it to the ground. Then she stepped out of her panties. "I want you to bite me, Samuel. Show me how it's supposed to be. Make love to me, and bite me. Let's heal together."

Samuel didn't have to ask if it was really what she wanted. He could see it in her eyes and read it in her mind. She wanted him, and she wanted it all. He wanted it just as much.

Without a word, Madison straddled him. As soon as their bodies joined, both let out a soft cry of release and arched their backs in excitement. She leaned forward, her breasts grazing the soft curly hair on his chest, and kissed him. Samuel clutched her head in his hands and mashed his mouth against hers.

When the kisses ended, he clutched her to him and rolled over, putting her on the bottom. The lovemaking was at times tender and at times rough, but always exciting. His hands traveled her body, and his mouth found every nerve. Just when she thought she couldn't stand any more, he'd pull back, letting her catch her breath, then he'd take her to the brink of total abandonment again.

Close to climax, Samuel unleashed his fangs and looked at her. "Are you sure?"

She arched her neck back in final invitation.

Samuel thrust his body into hers just as his fangs pierced the soft tissue above her right breast. She cried out both in pain and in orgasm.

When it was over, they lay together like nesting dolls. Her butt was tucked into his lap, his arm draped around her torso. One of his large hands cupped her breasts. A sharp stinging sensation shot through her skin at the location of Samuel's bite, but Madison didn't care. She moaned in delight.

"Does this mean you want to become my mistress?" He kissed her ear.

"No, Samuel, it doesn't. When the sun comes up, it will be as if it never happened."

He turned her toward him and began suckling her left breast, playing his tongue over the erect nipple. She moaned again. He covered her body with his own.

"Then we must hurry," he whispered as he began to make love to her again. "Because I am still very hungry."

THE END

Dedication

For my nephew Derek.
He'd make a great vampire.

Acknowledgments

Year after year, my agent, Whitney Lee, and my manager,
Diana James, have stuck by my side, keeping me on track as
I slash through the weeds of publishing. Thanks, ladies;
I couldn't do it without you. And, as always, thanks to all
the good folks at Llewellyn Worldwide/Midnight Ink
who continue to produce fabulous books.

A spirited new series from award-winning,
critically acclaimed Odelia Grey mystery author
Sue Ann Jaffarian

A GHOST OF GRANNY APPLES MYSTERY

*Along with a sprinkling of history, this ghostly new
mystery series features the amateur sleuth team of
Emma Whitecastle and the spirit of her pie-baking
great-great-great-grandmother, Granny Apples.
Together, they solve mysteries of the past—starting
with Granny's own unjust murder rap
from more than a century ago.*

Ghost
à la
Mode

Granny was famous for her award-winning apple pies—
and notorious for murdering her husband, Jacob, at their
homestead in Julian, California. The only trouble is,
Granny was framed, then murdered. For more than one hundred years, Granny's spirit has been searching for someone to
help her see that justice is served—and she hits pay dirt when
she pops into a séance attended by her great-great-great-
granddaughter, modern-day divorced mom Emma Whitecastle. Together, Emma and Granny Apples solve mysteries of the
past—starting with Granny's own unjust murder rap in the
final days of the California Gold Rush.

Ghost in the Polka Dot Bikini

Imagine spending eternity with your backside hanging out —that's what Emma Whitecastle and Granny Apples can't help but think when they meet the ghost of Tessa North frolicking in the surf off Catalina Island. Tessa, a young starlet who died on the island in the 1960s wearing nothing but a polka dot bikini, won't cross over until Curtis comes for her. To help the winsome bikini-clad spirit, Emma and Granny must find out who Curtis is and how Tessa died. Their investigation takes them from the grit and glamor of Hollywood to Kennedy-era political intrigue before hitting dangerously close to home.

The hugely popular mystery series that features unforgettable amateur sleuth Odelia Grey

You'll love Odelia Grey, a middle-aged, plus-sized paralegal with a crazy boss, insatiable nosiness, and a knack for being in close proximity to dead people. This snappy, humorous series is the first from award-winning, critically acclaimed mystery author Sue Ann Jaffarian.

AN ODELIA GREY MYSTERY

Too Big to Miss

Book One

Too big to miss—that's Odelia Grey. A never-married, middle-aged, plus-sized woman who makes no excuses for her weight, she's not Superwoman—she's just a mere mortal standing on the precipice of menopause, trying to cruise in an ill-fitting bra. She struggles with her relationships, her crazy family, and her crazier boss. And then there's her knack for being in close proximity to dead people…

When her close friend Sophie London commits suicide in front of an online web-cam by putting a gun in her mouth and pulling the trigger, Odelia's life is changed forever. Sophie, a plus-sized activist and inspiration to imperfect women, is the last person anyone would ever have expected to end her own life. Suspecting foul play, Odelia is determined to get to the bottom of her friend's death. Odelia's search for the truth takes her from Southern California strip malls to the world of live web-cam porn to the ritzy enclave of Corona del Mar.

The Curse
of the
Holy Pail

Book Two

I s the "Holy Pail" cursed? Every owner of the vintage Chappy Wheeler lunchbox—a prototype based on a 1940s TV Western—has died. And now Sterling Price, a business tycoon and client of Odelia Grey's law firm, has been fatally poisoned. Is it a coincidence that Price's one-of-a-kind lunch pail—worth over thirty grand—has disappeared at the same time?

Treading cautiously since her recent run-in with a bullet, Odelia takes small bites of this juicy, calorie-free mystery—and is soon ravenous for more! Her research reveals a sixty-year-old unsolved murder and Price's gold-digging ex-fiancée with two married men wrapped around her breasts—uh, finger. Mix in a surprise marriage proposal that sends an uncertain Odelia into chocolate sedation and you've got an unruly recipe for delicious disaster.

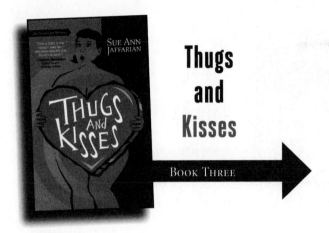

Thugs and Kisses

BOOK THREE

W ith the class bully murdered at her thirtieth high-school reunion and her boss, the annoying Michael Steele, missing, Odelia doesn't know which hole to poke her big nose into first. This decision is made for her as she's again swept into the action involving contract killers, tangled relationships, and fatal buyer's remorse. Throughout this adventure, Odelia deals with her on-again, off-again relationship with Greg and her attraction to detective Devin Frye.

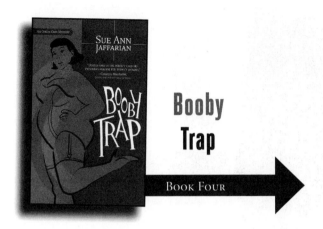

**Booby
Trap**

BOOK FOUR

ould the Blond Bomber serial killer possibly be Dr. Brian Eddy, plastic surgeon to the rich and famous? Odelia never would have suspected the prominent doctor of killing the bevy of buxom blonds if she hadn't heard it directly from her friend Lillian—Dr. Eddy's own mother!—over lunch one day. This mystery gets even messier than Odelia's chicken parmigiana sandwich as Odelia discovers just how difficult—and dangerous—it will be to bust this killer.

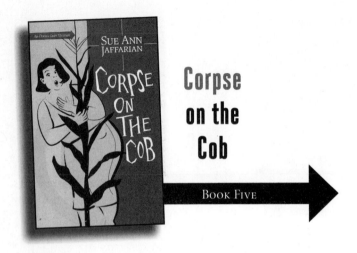

Corpse on the Cob

Book Five

What do you have to lose when you go searching for the mother who walked out of your life thirty-four years ago—besides your pride, your nerves, and your sanity?

Odelia finds herself up to her ears in trouble when she reunites with her mom in a corn maze at the Autumn Fair in Holmsbury, Massachusetts. For starters, there's finding the dead body in the cornfield—and seeing her long-lost mom crouched beside the corpse, with blood on her hands…